JAMES Y. BARTLETT

P.G.A. Spells Death

A HACKER GOLF MYSTERY

For Susan

*I keep six honest serving men (they taught me all
i knew); Their names are What and Why and When
And How And Where and Who.*
— Rudyard Kipling

Author's Note:

THE WORLD OF television technology and production is one
that's mostly foreign to an old print guy. Luckily, however, I
have an expert in the family, and one with excellent blood-
lines. My father-in-law, Robert Alshouse, was one of the
pioneers of TV news in south Florida.

I married one of his daughters; the other, my sister-
in-law Janet Alshouse, was hired by Roger Ailes to become
the first news director for a fledgling little network he was
starting up called Fox News. Her advice, expertise and
general cheerleading have been invaluable in the creation of
this novel and are much appreciated.

1

The meeting was held in a windowless room on the 34th floor of the IBS Building in Manhattan. Way up there, without a window to let in any sunshine, or views, or air, we couldn't hear the constant noise from the street far below. No honking car horns, no screaming NYPD sirens, no hydraulic bus brakes *pfsshing* as the bus pulled away from the curb, ground through the gears and exhaled clouds of diesel exhaust. Up here, we were wrapped, captured maybe, in our silent and sterile environment.

It was early March and the Golf Sports Group of the International Broadcasting System was gathering to discuss the plans for the upcoming slate of PGA Tour tournaments we would be broadcasting to a grateful nation, including the biggie here on IBS, the PGA Championship, one of golf's four majors, scheduled for mid-May. In the interest of generating the most revenue possible, the various golfing bodies and institutions had doled out broadcasting rights to the four major championships to four different networks: CBS, of course, owned the Masters; NBC got the British Open, Fox Sports the U.S. Open and IBS the PGA. The Golf Channel suckled on the hind teat of all of them by broadcasting the

Thursday/Friday rounds of all the majors except the Masters, which worked with ESPN.

People were slowly drifting in to the long rectangular room, painted in navy and decorated with an array of flat screen monitors covering the far wall. Half of the screens were dark, but some showed the live feed from what was being broadcast at the moment (a soap opera—it was just after lunch) and others had silent camera feeds from various news studios in the building and elsewhere from IBS' extensive worldwide network of stations.

I knew a few of the people who filed in, took a seat and nodded at one another. But most of them were complete strangers to me. I found a seat midway down the length of the table. I had officially joined IBS at the beginning of the year, after my longtime job as the golf writer for the Boston *Journal* had been eliminated the year before. I had spent the intervening time writing a book for the U.S. Golf Association, helped uncover a financial scam at Pebble Beach during the U.S. Open and welcomed my son, DJ, into the world. Rather an eventful year, all told. And then the Pebble Beach-based movie star and director Jack Harwood had put me in touch with Bill Pulte, head of IBS Sports, and we had talked and here I was. My title was "correspondent" and my job was to feed colorful, interesting and historic pieces of golfiana into the IBS golf broadcasts to make the "talent"—the announcers—sound like they knew what they were talking about.

None of the talent was expected to join this high-altitude meeting today. That group, a mix of experienced broadcasters and former Tour players grown long of tooth and sent off to the booth, didn't need to bother their pretty heads with schedules, logistics and technology updates. Their job was just to show up, clear their throats, climb the ladders to the aeries above the various putting greens and wax poetic about the action unfolding down below.

So the attendees at this meeting were the executives in charge of technology—the RF cameras and the satellite uplinks and the flyboard units—logistics—the 18-wheeler trucks and the cable layers and the tower scaffold builders and the mess hall staffers—and marketing and promotions. I wasn't exactly sure what purpose my attendance served, but I had been told to show up and meet some of my co-workers, so I had, despite my lifelong aversion to meetings. As the golf writer for the *Journal*, I had pretty much kept my own hours, traveled almost every week, rarely worked in the office, and the only meetings I ever had were over the phone with my obese executive editor, who was a blithering idiot. Which had kept our meetings short. And profane.

This one had been scheduled to begin at one thirty. At one forty-five, most of the tall-backed chairs around the long mahogany table were filled, along with about half of the row of chairs set against the walls, and the conference table itself was covered with notebooks, laptops, Coke cans and coffee cups. There was a dull hum in the room as people chatted with each other.

And then the door opened and Ben Oswald walked in. The room fell instantly silent, as if an invisible hand had flipped the talk and chatter switch to OFF.

To say the executive producer and director of IBS Golf had a presence would be like saying George Washington was once the head of something. Ben Oswald exuded command and control. He was a small man, size-wise, with a head of curly gray hair, a long, sloped forehead and amber-lensed avi-ator-like glasses. But he walked with a body in tension and looked like every sinew was wound as tightly as possible and on the verge of snapping. His mouth was pursed in a constant frown, one of his signatures, and his eyes danced around the room without expression, taking everything in, nodding here and there at some of the gathered. He wore black corduroys, a white open-collared dress shirt with wide collar points, and an expensive-looking multi-hued sweater.

He was followed into the conference room by a young man who looked to be in his mid-twenties, wearing a pin-striped suit, exquisitely tailored right down to the pocket square and vest, and a pair of ankle-high black shiny boots that probably cost a grand at Barney's. He was carrying a leather binder in cordovan red. He took a seat against the wall, zipped open his notebook and began making notations with a huge Cross pen he extracted from his inside coat pocket. I noticed that most of the people in the room avoided looking directly at him. Everyone was focused on Oswald, the alpha male.

Oswald plopped himself down at the head of the table, back to the wall of monitors, and surveyed the room. Naturally, his gaze stopped on me.

"Who the hell are you?" he snapped.

"Hacker," I said. "Correspondent."

Oswald turned and raised one eyebrow at the young man in the expensive suit.

"New hire," the young man said primly. "History and color. Bill recommended him."

"Fuckin' Bill," Oswald said, shaking his head. He turned to glare at me again. Everyone else in the room was looking at me too. I thought about bursting into song—for some reason "It's a Hard Knock Life" from *Annie* came to mind —but I managed to keep myself under control.

"Whaddya you know about television?" Oswald spat at me.

"Ummm," I said, "If it bleeds, it leads?"

There was a deathly silence in the room for a few beats. Then I heard someone snort and someone else giggled. Maybe not the gales of laughter I had hoped for, but I'd take it.

Oswald didn't say anything. His face was impassive, unreadable. His fingers twitched on the table. His eyes stayed locked on mine.

"Fuckin' wise guy, huh?" he said.

His eyes left mine and moved around the table.

"Chuck," he said, barking out that unfortunate's name. "What's up with that new mini cam? I heard CBS got one."

"Right, Ben," said a man sitting across the table from me. He was large, bald and looked worried. "Got one right here." He held out his hand and showed us all a small black box maybe three inches square with a round lens on one end. "HDR, 60 fps, 4K output, but weighs just 128 grams. You can bury it in the wall of a bunker, or stick it on a pole and wide-angle the tee box. Shoots in 4K and downconverts automatically. Pretty cool shit."

"Good," Oswald said. "Order six of them and let's get them into the mix."

"Budget!" The voice came from a woman three seats down from me. She had a large spreadsheet unfolded in front of her. "Those things cost fifteen thousand each. We budgeted for three."

Oswald's face turned red. He glanced over at the three-piece suit kid, who shrugged and nodded.

"Okay, get me four, then," Oswald said. "And if we miss a good shot because we don't have enough cameras, Camilla, I'll come find you and eliminate your life and your little dog's too."

Oswald pointed at another unfortunate sitting two chairs away from me.

"Billy Bob," he said. "What's happening with the drones? If we're gonna put the Goodyear blimp out of business, those fuckin' things gotta work. I want to be able to dive bomb one of those things so I can see every pimple on Phil Mickelson's ass."

"R-r-right Ben," Billy Bob quavered. "AirShot has a fourth generation machine out. Noise level is less than twenty decibels and it can go as high as two thousand feet. And they're supposed to be strong enough to carry the AB-75 HD camera with a directional mic. I'm going out to Palm Springs next week for a demo."

"I don't want 'supposed to be,' you moron," Oswald said. "If it works, buy it. Better still, just lease a half dozen. Then Camilla won't have a coronary. Right darlin'?"

"Whatever you say, Ben," the woman from accounting said, her head buried in her spreadsheet.

Oswald went around the table and the room in a similar vein. He'd bark out a question, wait for the stumbling answer, and then respond with some kind of acerbic insult or comment. It reminded me of his nickname in the industry—"The Assassin." It had been applied to Oswald permanently, according to the story I'd been told, at a production meeting years ago when one of the former PGA Tour players who had transitioned into the broadcast booth had endured about 30 minutes of nonstop insults for challenging something about the "IBS way" of doing things. After being called every name in the book, and asked if his IQ was possibly higher than that of a garden slug, the player-turned-broadcaster had looked at Ben and asked "Say, Oswald, are you related to Lee Harvey, by any chance?"

After that, they called him The Assassin. Mostly behind his back, but those close to Oswald had said that he was secretly pleased with his nickname. He thought it gave him power, for some reason.

The door to the conference room opened and an older man walked in. He was dressed in a well-tailored suit, but not nearly as pristine as the one worn by Oswald's assistant. He had a head of curly, graying hair, a pencil-thin mustache and a look on his face like he was suffering from some kind of severe gastrointestinal distress.

"Listen up people," Oswald said when he saw the man. "For those who don't know, this is Frank Corso, our senior veep for golf production. He might have something interesting to say. Frank?"

Corso stood at the head of the table opposite Oswald, and nodded towards the group.

"Won't take up much of your time, Ben," he said. "Just wanted to say on behalf of the network that this is an important year for our golf telecasts. You've all probably heard that the network is in merger talks, right? There's nothing definitive I can tell you at this moment, and probably nothing will happen before the end of the year. But I just want to remind you that we expect you to continue producing the best golf broadcasts in the business this year. Whatever happens on the corporate level, this team just needs to keep doing the job you have demonstrated you know how to do. You take care of your business, and we'll do the rest. Okay? Thanks, Ben."

Corso nodded again, then turned and walked out. The room was silent for a moment after he left. I could almost feel Ben Oswald swelling up with snark at the head of the table, and I had only known him for about thirty minutes.

"Well that was a word sandwich full of baloney," Oswald said finally. "I think what he meant was do your fucking jobs or I'll fire each and every one of your sorry asses. Of course, that's nothing new. I've said that at the beginning of every year I've been doing this job, which is … how many, Arnie?"

"Twenty-one, Ben," said the young man in the suit.

"Twenty fucking one years," Oswald said. "Old enough to drink, drive and screw, so I oughta know how to do a golf broadcast. And so should you. So screw what the suits say … just do your job or I'll find someone who can. We all straight?"

There were murmurs of agreement around the room.

"Good," Oswald said. "Now get out of here and get back to work. We've got Savannah coming up in three weeks and we're gonna be ready or I'll be kicking some ass. Go!"

The meeting broke up as everyone stood up, gathered whatever material they had brought in, and began to leave.

"Digby!" Oswald's voice was like a whip crack. Everyone in the room flinched. "And Hacker! Stay."

I sat back down. Across the table from me, so did the person named Digby. He was a youngish man, maybe late twenties, dressed in a white dress shirt and blue jeans. He was round in shape, maybe not quite pudgy but far from ripped. His cheeks were puffy and his stringy hair on the wild and unmanageable side. His complexion was spotted. And his eyes were wild, white, darting, nervous.

The room cleared fairly quickly, as people seemed anxious to get away from Oswald. You could almost hear the exhalations of relief when they made it to the hallway outside without any further metaphorical daggers protruding from their backs.

Oswald kept his seat, his fingers drumming on the surface of the conference table again. The three-piece suited fellow also stayed in his chair against the wall. His notebook was still open and he was looking at Digby and me with a small smile playing at the corners of his mouth. He seemed to be anticipating, with some pleasure, what was to come.

"OK, Digby," Oswald said when the room had finally emptied out and the door swung shut. "You know why you're here, right?"

"I-It wasn't my fault, Ben," Digby said. His voice was on the high side. Tremulous. And it sounded nervous.

"It's never your fucking fault, is it Digs?" Oswald said, his voice dripping with venom. "Every single last time you screw something up, it's somebody else's fault. Why is that, you fat faultless fuck?"

I had to give Oswald high marks for alliteration, but Digby looked like he wanted to cry.

"The control synthesizer was connected to the out-ward-bound router on the server," he said, voice wavering but not breaking. "Something went wrong on the upload to control. We don't know what it was yet. We're still running tests …"

"Tests." Oswald repeated the word as if it were a synonym for excrement. "I got a live broadcast going out over the air and I cannot see the replay graphics because you put Wire A into some goddam incorrect Connector B and you're fucking giving me *tests*!"

He turned and looked at the notebook guy, who I now understood to be his aide-de-camp, major domo or personal assistant. Whatever they called them these days. "How many times has this piece of hardware failed in the last six months?" he asked.

Notebook guy flipped through some pages. "Six," he said finally.

"Six!" Oswald's whipcrack voice repeated the number. Loudly. Both Digby and I flinched.

"Now you listen to me, fat boy, and you listen good," Oswald said. "If by any chance we manage to get to the number seven …" He stopped. "Why don't *you* tell *me* what will happen."

"Uh, my ass is grass?" Digby said.

"Oh, Digs, we are way beyond grass," Oswald said, shaking his head sadly. "We are past grass, into a whole other dimension of plant life. Another mother-fucking *universe* of grass, my jowly little friend. I will have you drawn and quartered. I will have you de-pantsed. I will cut off your balls and jam them down your throat. I will pull the toe nails off your feet with a pair of pliers. I will take that outward-bound router and send it inward bound into your small intestines. Have I made myself clear?"

"Y-yes, Ben," Digby said, head down, face red, eyes hidden.

"Go forth and sin no more," Oswald said, and Digby left the room as if shot from a cannon.

When he was gone, Oswald smiled at the Notebook Guy.

"Tell me again why I can't fire his fat ass?"

"He's our most talented tech engineer," Notebook said. "A little messy, a bit sloppy in performance. But very smart. Thinks outside the box. Good brain."

"Needs too much babysitting," Oswald said. "And I'm getting tired of changing his nappies. Let's start looking for a replacement. But we'll keep him around until we find one."

Notebook made a note. Oswald turned and leveled his eyes at me.

"If it bleeds, it leads,'" he said. I smiled winningly back at him. "Funny."

"Thanks," I said.

"I don't do funny," he said, eyes narrowed and glaring. "I don't do wise guy, smart ass, hail fellow well met or yuckety yuck. I do television. Serious television. You got that?"

"Right," I said. "No jokes. Super duper serious at all times. So, like if Woody Austin is trying to hit a shot from the edge of a pond and falls into the water after making his swing, you don't want anyone giving him a snorkel and mask set the next day when he plays that hole?"

"That was hilarious," Oswald said, smiling at the memory. Then he stopped smiling. "Wait…was that you?"

I shrugged. Tried to look modest. It actually *wasn't* me, but I had been there.

"OK," he said. "There are times when funny works. But not often, and never in my meetings. You got that?"

"Sure, Mr. Oswald," I said.

"Mister Oswald is my father," he said. "And he's dead. I'm Ben or Boss, either one."

"Right, Boss," I said. "And I'm sorry for your loss."

He stared at me. I could feel the screws inside this strange little man get ever tighter.

"Are you fuckin' with me, Hacker?" he said. "Because if you're fuckin' with Ben Oswald …"

"I can expect something to be shoved up my colon," I said. "I know, I heard."

Notebook Guy began to laugh, breaking the tension in the room which had begun to make the walls bow. I was surprised that none of the monitors on the wall behind Oswald's head shattered spontaneously.

"Oh, my God," Notebook said. "This is going to be such a fun season. I can't wait."

Oswald and I just stared at each other.

2

Oswald dismissed me, and once outside of the meeting room torture chamber, I headed down the hall towards the bank of elevators at the far end of the building. About halfway down, I passed a brightly lit lunchroom. It had four wooden tables and folding chairs, a bank of vending machines against the wall, and a counter with some coffee making stuff, a microwave and a small sink. There was a small white refrigerator over in the corner.

Digby Allen was sitting at one of the tables. He was alone in the room and he looked like he might be alone in all the world. He was just sitting there, staring at the wall. His face was red. Hands were clasped in his lap, and I noticed they were clasped so tightly his fingers were white.

Don't ask me why, because I couldn't give you a cogent answer, but I went in. I walked over to the coffee counter, inserted one of those plastic pod cup things, pushed the button, waited for my cup of joe to stream out and took it over to the table where Digby was sitting.

"Mind if I join you?" I said and pulled out a chair and sat down.

He didn't respond.

"That was my first meeting with The Assassin," I said. "They all go like that?"

He didn't respond. Didn't even look at me. I sipped some coffee.

"Dunno," I said, "Based on that meeting, I'd call him The Ass, not the Assassin."

Digby smiled at that. Well, I saw the corners of his mouth twitch a little in what seemed to me like an upward arc. Could have been a smile.

"He wants to fire me," Digby said. His voice was a hollow whisper. It came from a place of despair somewhere deep inside. "He thinks I'm a fucking idiot."

"Yeah, well, Hacker's first rule is you don't care what they think," I said. "You just do the best you can. If he doesn't like that, well, that's on him, not you."

"Who's Hacker?" he said.

I stuck out my hand. "That'd be me," I said.

"Oh," he said and this time he did smile. Sheepishly. "I'm Digby Allen." He shook my hand. His hand felt moist.

"Yeah, I got that," I said. "I also got that you need to do something about that router thingy."

"The w-what?"

"Whatever it is that keeps breaking down," I said. "Oswald and that well-dressed dandy—what is that guy's name, anyway?"

Digby chuckled. "That's Arnie Wasserman," he said. "Ben's shadow. His assistant. Title is associate producer."

"Yeah, well, Arnie says that this is the sixth time that equipment has failed," I said. "How come?"

Digby shrugged. "AirWaves provides all that gear," he said. "They're in charge of uplinking the bird to our control room. Every time it's failed, I tell them they need to fix it, and they haven't. And I get the blame."

"Who is AirWaves?"

He looked at me and smiled a bit more.

"You're that new guy, right?" he said, nodding to himself as if saying *that's why he's such a dummy.* "We contract with outside companies for almost everything on the production side these days," he explained. "One company trucks in all the gear and sets up the infrastructure around the course. Cables and relays and signal intensifiers and all that stuff. Another company sets up the flybox…er…the control room. Somebody else provides and sets up the cameras and sound. They put microphones all over the course. IBS owns nothing. Everything is leased or contracted out. Ben and about twenty network guys come in and produce the show. And the talent belongs to IBS. But most of the gear belongs to someone else, even though me and the other people in the Tech department have to keep it running during the show."

"Ah," I said. "Outsourcing. It's great unless it doesn't work."

Digby nodded. "Right," he said.

"So have you told AirWaves about the latest failure?"

He shrugged. And looked sad again.

"Yeah," he said. "Got the same old, same old."

I sipped some of my coffee and thought for a minute. The coffee was horrible and I almost spit it out, but that would have coated poor Digby and he already had enough problems.

"Can you get someone from AirWaves on the phone?" I said. "Someone high up the chain."

"Right now?" Digby asked, eyebrows raised.

"No time like the present," I said, giving him my best earnest smile. Which usually didn't work on most people. But it did with Digs.

He pulled out his phone, punched and swiped on it and finally hit the speaker button and put the phone down on the table. We listened to the metallic ringing and then someone answered.

"Hello, Digby," said the voice on the other end. "Why are you bothering me again?"

"Who the hell is this?" I said, turning my voice into a harsh rasp. Digby reared back in shock.

"This is Bill Frankel at AirWaves," the voice said. "Who the hell are you?"

"I'll tell you who this is," I barked back. "I'm the goddam Grim Reaper who's about to make your fucking life miserable, you worthless piece of shit. Now you listen up and get this straight. Your chickenshit piece of worthless crap known as a control synthesizer failed to upload correctly last week. That's the sixth time that shit has happened, and my man Digby tells me that he's complained about it all six times. So I want you to hear this loud and clear, and it's coming from the top, do you understand? The T-O-P! And this is the message…if that fucking thing goes down again…*ever*…I will cancel the fucking contract between IBS and AirWaves so fast that the ink will catch fire. You got that? I've already spent more time on this fucking bullshit than I want to think about. And I'm not gonna debate with you or reason with you or even talk with you about this again. You are going to find and fix this problem today or you can go peddle your worthless junk to some cable station in Paducah that doesn't give a crap. This is fuckin' IBS and I will not put up with your bullshit incompetence. Have I made myself as clear as a fucking bell, Bill?"

"Y-yes, Ben," the voice said. "I will personally take care of this right away."

"See that you do, you moron," I said. "And one more thing…next time Digby calls to tell you something didn't work right, you better goddam take care of it right then and there. If I ever hear that he's being ignored again …"

"Right Ben," the voice said. "Please, accept my personal apology. We'll get that thing fixed. And I'll call Digby and apologize to him."

"That's more like it," I said. I reached over and punched the call disconnect button.

Digby Allen, who had been listening to this with ever widening eyes and mouth agape, could only shake his head.

"You sounded just like him," he said, sounding amazed. "How did you do that?"

"Just one of my many talents," I said. "I think Bill bought it. Do you?"

"Oh, yeah," Digby said. "Totally."

"Good," I said. "And now he thinks that you and Ben are tight, so he'll likely spread the word that Digby Allen is one connected dude, not to be fucked with. I think you'll find that going forward AirWaves are a lot more responsive."

"Geez," Digby said. "Thanks."

"No problem," I said. I got up and tossed my cup of awful coffee in the waste bin. "You going to be down in Savannah?"

"Yeah," he nodded. "I'll be there."

"I'll see you later, then."

I left. Hacker's good deed for the day.

3

An hour later, I was waiting outside the office of somebody named Stephanie Collier. She was the senior vice president of golf operations for the Gold Organization. It said so right on the business card I had been given by someone at IBS when I was told to go meet with her. Two meetings in one day. How did I ever get so lucky?

I had strolled over from the IBS building on Sixth Avenue south of Times Square, wandering up Fifth Avenue almost to the Park and entered the magnificent golden atrium of the fabulous Gold Tower, which had become one of the main tourist attractions in a town filled with them. The five-story-high atrium was loaded with super-luxury European shops, fancy restaurants and cafes, and, of course, the Gold Museum, the monument to the life and story of Conrad Gold his own self.

I had managed to ignore all of that—I didn't find myself in need of a four hundred dollar tattersall shirt from the English house of Turnbull and Asser, and I pretty much knew the rags to riches story of Conrad Gold—and jumped on one of the high-speed elevators which had whisked me up to the forty-somethingth floor at a speed that made my ears pop.

The sign over the lobby door outside the elevator told me I had arrived at the Golf Operations Division of the Gold Organization, and a lovely young receptionist welcomed me cheerfully, offered me a cup of Jamaican Blue Mountain and told me Stephanie would be right out.

Gold's coffee was much better than the cafeteria crap I had almost spit out at IBS, and was served in a lovely Haviland china cup and saucer. I added some raw sugar and a dollop of fresh cream. There were a couple of issues of *Gold Magazine* on the coffee table in the waiting area, which I glanced at and did not read. Conrad's own gleamingly bald coconut graced all the covers. Like Oprah does in her magazine. I dunno, if I ever start *Hacker The Magazine*, I'm thinking I'll go with Taylor Swift or Scarlett Johannson on the cover.

The walls of the waiting room, painted a shade of royal hunting green, were filled with extra-large framed photos of Gold's international collection of golf resorts and real estate developments. He had them in Florida, Arizona, Texas, southern California, upstate Michigan, Cape Cod, and, overseas, in Scotland, Ireland, southern France, Corsica, Greece and Israel. The man got around. I checked off the ones I'd been to, and could only remember about five. And three of those I'd visited before Conrad Gold bought them and added them to his golden stable of resort properties.

Of course, Gold also owned several pieces of expensive New York real estate, and even more out in L.A. Despite some setbacks with some Las Vegas casino deals that had gone south, Conrad Gold was still one of the richest men in the city and country. And while he had calmed down lately, ever since he had married a French movie starlet—wife number four, I think—he had once been one of the playboys of the western world. If you wanted to find him, all you had to do was pick up a copy of the National Enquirer, or the Page Six gossip pages, and there he'd be. Usually with some buxom beauty on his arm. Fending off reports that he owed back taxes, had been caught doing lines of coke in some nightclub or was feuding with one governor or another. Conrad Gold was a public man who liked to pretend he was a man of the public.

Another lovely young thing came prancing out from the back offices and told me Stephanie was ready for me now. I followed her back past the cubicles and glass-doored offices, all filled with trendy, fresh-faced and fashionable young people looking busy as bees. I'd heard that Conrad Gold only hired good looking people…no obese, zitted or scraggly haired types for him…and based on this sample, what I'd heard seemed to be true.

The senior vice president of golf marketing operations apparently was worthy enough to be assigned a very roomy corner office, with two window walls which framed the steeples and turrets of St. Patrick's Cathedral, a block or so away.

"Mister Hacker," she said, standing up from behind her desk as I was ushered in. "Stephanie Collier. So nice to meet you."

"Thanks," I said as we shook hands. I nodded out the window. "Not a bad view."

She turned and looked out her windows as if it was something she had never done before. "Oh," she said, "yes, it is, isn't it? I confess that after the first week working here, I hardly take notice. Unless it's raining or snowing or something."

She motioned me into one of her guest chairs and I sat down. Stephanie was in her late thirties. Long blond hair, nice St. John knit dress that clung to and emphasized all her curves, which were quite nicely curving, and bright, alert blue eyes. Her pale wood desk was mostly empty, save for her lap-top and telephone. There was a gold framed photograph next to her telephone showing her with a smiling, goateed man and a young boy of about three who was trying to smile for the camera, but looked more like he was grimacing with a stom-ach pain.

"So Conrad told me a lot about you," she said, "And some of your adventures in St. Andrews a year or so ago. "Did you really crash into one of our suites with the special forces from Mi5?"

I chuckled. "Um, no," I said. "I think that story has been upgraded a bit from the truth of it. I watched the op-eration from the safety of the command vehicle outside. But those guys were quite efficient at what they do."

"I'll bet," she said. She reached into her desk drawer and pulled out a brochure.

"What do you know about the Gold Hudson Links?" she asked.

"Practically nothing," I said. Which was true. Obvi-ously I knew that Conrad Gold had managed to get the PGA of America to reward his new golf development with the up-coming PGA Championship. But even back in the halcyon days when I covered the game of golf for the Boston *Journal*, I had never spent much time or effort trying to keep track of new golf developments. That was a job for the real estate or travel editors, not the golf writer. Of course, it had been de-cades since the Journal had had either one of those on staff.

"Well, this will help then," she said and slipped the brochure across the desk toward me. I picked it up and glanced at the cover, which showed a golf hole photographed dramat-ically in late afternoon, so the shadows cast across the fairway were long. It showed a green set near the blue waters of the

Hudson River, low rolling hills in the background on the far shore and a hint of mountains in the background. The picture looked like one of the painters from the Hudson River School had executed it in fine oils.

"We consider the Hudson Links to be one of our premier properties," Stephanie continued. "It's just 55 miles from Manhattan, which is less than a 30 minute helicopter ride from the West Side Heliport."

"How long if you're riding a mule-drawn buckboard?" I asked. "Which is more my speed."

She laughed, tossing her head back.

"Conrad told me you were a wit," she said.

"Did he now?" I said.

"In fact," she continued as if my wit had not intervened, "Conrad first saw the land that is now the Gold Hudson Links riding in a helicopter flying up the Hudson River."

"Is that right?" I said.

"Yes," she said, nodding earnestly. "It was about ten years ago, and Conrad was on his way to play golf at the Paramount Country Club in New City—that club was founded in 1918 by Adolph Zukor who started Paramount Pictures. And Conrad looked out the window of the copter and saw the property—wetlands and river frontage and rocky high ground—and thought 'That would make a great site for a club.' And he asked around, began assembling the parcels and…well, here we are!"

"Yes," I said, "Here we are. But the question is…why?"

She laughed again. Tossed her head again.

"Well," she said, "If you are going to be the color correspondent for IBS at the tournament in May, we wanted to make sure you had all the color you need."

"Ah, yes," I said. "Color. I think the network is hoping I come up with golf anecdotes to add to the tournament coverage. Like a story about Tillinghast getting caught in some quicksand while walking around the property and being rescued by the local farmer. You know, stuff like that."

"Who is Tillinghast?" she asked.

I paused. I guess the thirty-something senior vice president of golf marketing operations couldn't be expected to know about the golf course architects from the Golden Age of golf. I wondered, for a moment, how many generations will pass before no one remembers who Bobby Jones was.

"He was a golf course architect," I said. "Back in the Roaring Twenties."

"Oh," she said, smiling. "Well, it's interesting to know that Conrad Gold worked very closely with Clyde Stewart, who designed the Hudson Links course. Clyde, of course, is from Aberdeen, and is just finishing up an exciting new course on the Isle of Skye. Another of Mister Gold's projects."

"Yes," I said, "That is interesting." I stopped wearing wrist watches decades ago, but if I still had one, this is where I would glance at it and then say I had another appointment and get the hell out of here.

Stephanie, however, was still going great guns. She flopped open an appointment book.

"Are you planning on joining us for Media Day?" she asked. "We're shooting for April 25th, a month before the PGA. We're hoping for good weather, but it can be iffy in April in New York. Can I put you down?"

I smiled. "I think I'm scheduled to join the broadcast crew from IBS for a preview round," I said.

"Oh," she said, a frown turning her smile upside down. "I wasn't aware of that. Some of those guys used to be tour pros. I'm not sure they'd enjoy having … you know …"

"A hacker holding them up?" I suggested. "Pun intended, of course."

Her face reddened a bit. A voice from the doorway rescued her.

"Hacker is no bloody hacker," the deep voice said. We both turned to see Conrad Gold himself standing in Stephanie's doorway. His famously cueball bald head reflected the overhead can lights beaming down. He was not a tall man, but seemed to be in good shape, and he was dressed in an impeccably tailored pinstripe suit with his trademark gold tie and a pocket square in crimson. He was smiling.

"This man played on the Tour," he told Stephanie. "It was a few years ago, but he always had game. He'll give Jimmy Williams and the rest of that crew a good run for their money. I may lay down a few bucks on him myself!"

I stood up and shook his hand.

"I played against Jimmy, both in college and in the pros," I said, referring to IBS's main color announcer. "I think the best I ever did against him was a tie for third somewhere. He was always better than me."

"Don't care," Gold said, shaking his head. "I'm still putting my money on you."

He sat down in Stephanie's other guest chair and I sat down again. Steph just looked at us with wide eyes. Her meeting had just veered off into uncharted territory with the sudden arrival of the main guy, and she was now just trying to hang on for dear life.

"How've you been?" I asked Gold. "How's the hotel in St. Andrews doing?"

"Pretty damn good," he said, nodding. "Sales have been up twelve percent since the Open. Even though I had to rebuild that suite after Mi5 got done."

"Well, I guess they figured they had to take the Russian mob by surprise," I said. "My caddie friend Johnnie was their prisoner, remember. They had to use that flashbang and come crashing in the window. No other way."

"I suppose," Gold said, smiling. "Actually, Her Majesty's government paid most of the costs to restore the room."

"Most?"

"Well, all of it," he said. "Plus a little extra for pain and suffering."

"Who's pain and suffering?"

"Mine, mostly," he said, and flashed that famous Conrad Gold grin.

I laughed. Stephanie tittered. Conrad looked at her.

"Collier here giving you everything you need?" Gold asked.

"Oh, yeah," I said. "More than enough. I really appreciate her help."

"Good." Gold nodded. He glanced at his watch. Rolex Oyster. Gold, of course. "Well, I have another meeting to get to," he said. "Good to see you again, Hacker. Thanks, Stephanie."

He vanished as quickly as he had appeared. Stephanie looked across her desk at me. The dynamic had changed and we both knew it. I was now a Friend of Conrad, and she was 'Collier here.' But I don't play those stupid office politics games.

I thanked her for her time and left.

4

At three a.m., I heard a sound that at first I thought was my cat, Mister Shit, who occasionally—usually during a full moon—prowls around the apartment in the wee small hours and mewls about something. But the cat-like sound turned into a rhythmic sobbing beat…*lala* break *lala* break *lala*.

Then Mary Jane gave me the elbow in the ribcage, and I was wide awake and in action. DJ's crib was stuck in the bedroom corner in our North End apartment, and I quickly picked him up, carried him over to the changing table, unsnapped his onesie sleeper, swapped his sopping diaper for a new dry one and brought him back to our warm bed. Mary Jane was ready lying on her side, and he quickly nestled between us on the bed, fastened on to one of her breasts, began sucking and was soon making contented little sighs.

Most of the time, I could quickly go right back to sleep, but this morning, for some reason, I stayed awake and just watched my son have his early breakfast (there would be another at six, eight and ten). One of his incredibly cute little hands rested on his forehead, the other on his mom's chest. Each hand had five perfect fingers, matching the toes hidden by the footies of his sleeper.

DJ was now six months old, and every day was just an amazing experience. I could tell by the way he followed me with his eyes, giggled when I tickled him and looked at his big sister Victoria that he was a genius child with an IQ well into the 200s. Whenever I mentioned that, Mary Jane rolled her eyes. *You'll show her,* I silently said to the back of his head, with its wispy threads of hair. Oh yeah, in addition to being a budding genius, he had been born with a good head of hair, most of which he still had. A genius *and* a good-looking one! He was obviously destined for great things,what with all my brilliant Hacker genes bubbling around inside him.

I had been back from New York for a little over a week, and was scheduled to fly down to Savannah after the upcoming weekend. While I was home, I got to watch DJ while Mary Jane and Victoria went off to school—MJ as a fourth grade teacher, Vick as a sixth grader. The kid was a good napper, so I usually was able to get in a few hours of research—I was making notes of past events for the golf tournaments we would be broadcasting, since I was now the staff historian and color info man—but when he was awake I kept him fed (Mary Jane always left a few bottles of harvested breast milk), clean and dry, and when the weather permitted, we'd go for a walk around the North End of Boston. We were already favorites among the *nonne* in our mostly Italian neighborhood, and we usually came home from one of our walks with bags of biscotti and other home-baked treats.

I'd like to think DJ and I were bonding during these days together, but I suspected that at this age, he looked on me mainly as the tall hairy guy who'd occasionally feed him, change his nappies and give him all kinds of colorful plastic things to gum so the tall hairy guy could get another fifteen minutes on the computer. I made a mental note to ask him about it when he was sixteen.

"Y'know Hacker," Mary Jane said to me one night as we took turns dandling the little guy on our knees so the other could scarf down some pasta, "It might be time to think about moving."

"Gack," I said. That being the universal male word for "OMG, *we just had a baby and now you want to disrupt our lives further by moving to a new place?*"

"I know," she said, as Mary Jane understood the male language pretty well. "But DJ is going to need his own bed before long, and that means he's gonna need his own room."

"He *cannot* move in with me," Victoria said with determination. She was twelve now and you could see the teen years gathering speed and coming rapidly down the pike. "I will *not* share my space with a male. Even if he is my brother."

Mary Jane could have reprimanded her daughter, but instead chose to ally with her.

"See?" she said. "We are going to need more rooms."

"I thought you liked the city," I said. "You guys can walk to the school from here. And I'm just a train ride away from Logan."

"I do like the city," she said. "But Victoria will be moving on to middle school in just another year, and that's a bus ride away. And you can get to the airport from anywhere. Uber *uber alles.*"

DJ was on my lap and wiggling. I held him up so we were nose to nose.

"This is all your fault," I told him. "We may have to send you back."

He giggled.

"Do you have some ideas?" I asked.

Mary Jane got up from the table, went into the bedroom and came back with a manila folder. It looked pretty full.

"I withdraw the question," I said. Mary Jane took DJ from me and went into the living room and laid him down on a blanket on the carpet there. I began leafing through the New Housing File, as it was labeled. Mary Jane had been busy. There were notes and brochures about two or three large apartment buildings in the Back Bay, one in Cambridge, and some letters and printed emails from some real estate agents in the 'burbs. Newton, Westwood and even Cohasset, down on the South Shore.

"Houses?" I said, surprised. "Aren't you supposed to have saved up a bunch of cash for the down payment before you buy a house?"

She smiled at me from the living room. DJ was on his back, kicking his legs in the air like one of those huge summer beetles, occasionally grabbing one and stuffing his toes into his mouth.

"Carmine said he could help," she said sweetly.

I thought about that for a bit. Carmine Spoleto was Victoria's bio-grandfather. He had been Mary Jane's father-in-law until her husband, Angelo, had joined the Choir Invisible in a mob hit in Charlestown when Victoria was just a few months old. Oh, yeah: Carmine Spoleto was also the *capo di tutti* in the Greater Boston area, and had been for more than forty years now. Strangely, I actually liked the man, he had been good to me, and was the most doting of grandfathers to the kids. Even though he was a vicious criminal with buckets of blood on his hands.

"Are you sure you want to borrow money from a leg breaker?" I asked.

"Well," she said, "It would probably be your leg that got broke if you didn't pay him back. Me and the kids are family." But she smiled sweetly as she said it.

"Why don't we just move into his place out in Milton?" I said. "He's got about fifty thousand square feet out there. We only need one or two."

"Now, Hacker," she said. "It wouldn't look right to do that. Plus, how would you feel as a man and a provider if you just took your family to live with your father-in-law?"

"I'd feel like security was good," I said. "Doesn't he have some staff goombahs living out there with him?"

Mary Jane leaned down and spoke into DJ's face. "Your daddy is such a joker," she cooed. DJ smiled at her.

"And if we move out of the city, we'll need another car," I said. I had been feeling pretty good about the salary I was making from IBS. But the contract was only for ten months. And there were no guarantees it would last another season. Especially given The Assassin's feelings about me. I suddenly saw the rent payments, and the car payments, and the insurance payments and the auto maintenance payments and the heating bills and God knows what else stacking up like planes over Logan at rush hour. My stomach began to hurt.

"Now honey, don't fret," Mary Jane said. "It's not like we have to move next week or anything. But it is probably time to start thinking about it."

I went into the kitchen and poured myself a couple of fingers of Bowmore, a fine single-malt Scotch whisky from the island of Islay, dark and peaty. I usually saved it for special occasions. It was my thinking whisky. Until I had three of them. Then it was my stop-thinking whisky.

There are pros and cons to everything, I thought, as the fiery malt burned its way down my gullet. While it would be better if I was fabulously wealthy and able to buy any piece of property in and around Boston, I was decidedly not. Not after my long career as a golf writer for the Boston *Journal*, a job which had never paid better than just above lousy. I suppose I should have worried about that more during all those years, but instead I was mostly enjoying my work and the people and the freedom to follow the Tour and my bliss at the same time. Piling up wads of cash had never been a major goal.

So now I had to rely on the kindness of family to provide for my own. There was part of me that protested about that: *that's not what* real *men do*, said that small inner voice. On the other hand, buying a house was a big, important step and I knew lots of men who had accepted, even welcomed, help from their families to do it. Of course, their families were not The Family. That presented even more problems to think about.

"Honey?" Mary Jane called from the living room. "Can you come watch DJ? I've got a lesson plan I need to work on for tomorrow."

I tossed back the last of my Islay malt. *Slainte*! Then I went out to play with my son. Thinking time was over, for now.

5

Ten days later, I was in Savannah, Georgia, preparing for the telecast of the Southern Plantations Open, which would be my first IBS tournament as the network's color and history correspondent. Be still, my beating heart.

Most of the broadcast prep work, so far as I could tell, involved my fellow correspondents, a.k.a. the "talent," heading out to play golf somewhere nice. On Monday, they all went up to Hilton Head and played Harbour Town at Sea Pines, that narrow, unforgiving course carved through the lagoons and pines by Pete Dye, aided and abetted with advice from a young Jack Nicklaus. Today, they were out at one of the courses out at The Landings, an exclusive, multi-course real estate development to the south of Savannah. Wednesday, they were scheduled to drive up into the South Carolina Lowcountry coast a ways and play a fancy private course called the Secession Club. Politically incorrect, but said to be a nice track.

I had not been invited to join the on-air personalities for all these golf outings. I wasn't upset about that. After all, I was the FNG—effing new guy—and although I had met and knew most of the IBS crew, it was still their party, not mine. Besides, I wanted to spend some time focusing on my job—to provide some interesting color and history to the telecast.

Because I didn't want to get yelled at by the Assassin, Ben Oswald. Nor did my colon.

I had gotten a call from Arnie Wasserman, Oswald's major domo, who told me that I had been assigned to work with Tony Sciutto, one of IBS' longtime cameramen.

"Ben wants a three-minute segment," Arnie told me.

"About what?"

He laughed. "He didn't say," he said, "But you're the color and history guy, so I'm guessing something colorful about history."

He was still laughing as he rang off. Arnie seemed to be one of those types who likes to stir the pot and watch what happens. Probably hoping for some fun colon stuffing.

I called Sciutto's cell number. He was out at Plantation Pines, the private country club on the outskirts of Savannah where the weekend's tournament was to be played.

"Oh, hi Hacker," he said, "Listen, I got some stuff to do out here today. Can we hook up in the morning, maybe? Talk about the script for the weekend?"

"Script?" I said.

There was a moment of silence. Then I heard a chuckle.

"Sorry, I forgot," he said. "You're brand new to this game, aren't you?"

"If you mean the television game, yes," I said. "Golf I know something about."

"Yeah, that's what I meant," he said. "You're a newbie. That's OK, I've worked with newbies before. Not to worry. Do you have anything in mind for the history segment?"

"Not really," I said. "Didn't know until twenty seconds ago that I had to write a script."

"That's OK," he said reassuringly. "We'll sort it out in the morning. Just be thinking of some interesting things we can shoot. We'll sort of wing it on this first one. I'll make sure Becky Ann is standing by."

"Becky Ann?"

"Becky Ann Billings," he said. "She's the best video editor we got. Fuckin' Scorsese can't cut film like she can. And don't tell him, 'cause we don't wanna lose her."

"Right," I said. "Secret's safe with me."

"Beautiful," he said. He stretched the syllables out: *bee-yoo-tee-ful.* "How about we meet for breakfast. Eight o'clock. Hotel cafe. Roger?"

"Ten-four," I said. "See you then."

So with nothing else to do except worry about writing a three-minute television script about who knows what, I headed out to wander around Savannah. Like most people who had visited Savannah casually, as a tourist, I was familiar with the city's grid-like layout, broken up every block or two by a lovely public square, all shaded by gnarled-limb liveoaks draped in Spanish moss, with brick sidewalks and lots of public benches and the occasional spurting fountain or Confederate statue. Street after street is filled with rows of Georgian and Edwardian mansions, all brick and wrought iron, brass and gas-light, containing fortunes in treasured antiques and populated by as strange a collection of American weirdos as can be found anywhere in the lower 48. The people of downtown Savannah are not normal: they all have twisted Gothic pasts, they all drink like alcoholic fish and their interest in the rest of the world does not extend very far past Forsythe Park on the city's outskirts.

Still, it's a wonderful city to wander through on foot, and eventually you get down to the waterfront, where the old cotton warehouses overlooking the steadily flowing green-gray water of the Savannah River—coming down from Augusta and flowing out past Tybee Point into the Atlantic—now contain tourist shops, shrimp restaurants, boutiques, crab cake restaurants, boozy country music bars, a hotel or two, and a long, cobblestoned boulevard where an unsuspecting or drunk tourist can easily turn an ankle.

The grid-like street design of the city was the brainchild of its founder, the British General James Edward Oglethorpe, whose concept for the colony of Georgia he founded was to provide a place for all the men stuck in debtor's prison back in London to come start a cotton farm and become fabulously wealthy. Good idea, but a bit ahead of its time, so Gen. Oglethorpe went back to Britain and helped defeat Bonnie Prince Charlie in the Rising of the '45.

A hundred years later, Savannah managed to avoid the torch from General Sherman, at the end of his long march downstate from Atlanta, who, instead of burning the place down, begged Mr. Lincoln to allow him the honor of presenting him the city as a Christmas gift back in 1864. Once that bit of unpleasantness was out of the way, Savannah slowly drifted into sleepy backwaterdom, its citizens drank, screwed and intermarried each other and the city threatened to rot away in the hot Georgia sun until an urban renovation movement took hold in the 1970s and turned the city into the tourism mecca it is today.

At mid-morning I went out to look at the Savannah Golf Club on President Street, separated from the Savannah River by acres of shipping and container facilities. They claim the club was founded back in 1792, which would make it almost a hundred years older than what the USGA claims is the country's oldest golf club (St. Andrews, Yonkers, New York, 1888). The place reeked of old money and the current golf course, which actually dates from 1899, looked flat and boring, except for all those nice liveoak trees with their gnarled limbs draped in Spanish moss.

I parked my rental car and wandered around the back of the elegant brick clubhouse. There were rows of glistening green carts set out waiting for members to come and play, overseen by an elderly gentleman with ebony skin and white hair, working at a stand shaded by an umbrella.

"Heard this place has some history to it," I said when I walked up to him.

"Oh, yassuh," he said, nodding and smiling. "Plenty o' that 'round these parts."

"Is this where Bagger Vance was a caddie?"

He chuckled, low and deep from his throat.

"Now, don't you go talkin' 'bout that piece of mess," he said. "Them movie fellers don' always tell you the truth straight up."

"So Will Smith never worked here, huh?"

The man smiled at me, his teeth bared.

"They was one part of that movie, where Massa Smith was a sittin' on the clubhouse steps sippin' hisself some nice ice tea," he said. "If'n he done that back in 19 and 31, he woulda found hisself hangin' from yonder trees." He nodded down the fairway. "True dat."

"Never thought about that," I said.

"Uh huh," the man said, shaking his head sadly.

A car pulled to a stop in the nearby bag drop area, and my friend shuffled over to help them unload their clubs. I looked around at the opening and closing holes, lying empty in the hot morning sun. I took in a big breath of air. It smelled of sulfur. Not because of the history lesson I had just received. It was the smell from one of the big paper processing plants on the outskirts of town. 'The Southern smell of money' an old friend of mine had once described the odor found throughout the Lowcountry where pine trees are turned into newsprint, paper towels and toilet paper.

"Can I help you, sir?" came a voice behind me. I turned. The voice belonged to a pleasant-looking man, about 50, who looked like a golf professional. Maybe it was the well-pressed polyester sans-a-belt trousers or the Savannah Golf Club logoed shirt or the FootJoy spikeless teaching shoes in a nice two-tone saddle style. Or maybe it was the official plastic name tag pinned over his heart, which said "Clark."

I stuck out my hand. "Hacker," I said. "I'm with IBS. Doing a little historical research for this weekend's telecast."

"Welcome to the club, Mister Hacker," Clark said. He looked behind me, toward the parking lot. "You come with a crew?"

"Nah," I said. "Just me. Scouting some locations." I wasn't sure what that meant. But it sounded official.

Clark nodded. "Got just the thing," he said. "C'mon."

He jumped into one of the golf carts and motioned for me to join him. "Clark Vickers," he said as we tooled silently away from the clubhouse and headed out onto the course. "I'm the head pro."

The course was tree-lined and mostly flat. As we circled a few of the greens, I noticed they were mostly raised and table-topped, falling away in all directions.

"Looks like Donald Ross was here," I said, referring to the famous Scottish-born architect who worked in golf's first Golden Age, around the turn of the last century.

"Good eye," the pro said. "He re-did this course around 1927. He did a lot of work here in Savannah."

"Who laid the place out in 1792?"

He laughed. "I like to think it was General Oglethorpe himself," he said. "But nobody remembers. Probably just some of the members filled with grog knocking their balls around a field."

He pulled the cart into a woodsy copse between two holes. I could hear the traffic from busy President's Street nearby.

He pointed. "You see that raised hump over there? How it extends a bit towards the south? " I looked, and could make out the shape he was talking about, covered with some shrubs and a few medium size trees. "That was a Confederate earthworks line," he said. "Just north of us was Fort Boggs, which had a pretty big artillery battery to guard the river approach from the east. The earthworks line extended down through here, hooked up at another fort to the south of us, and then circled back around to protect the southern flank of the city."

"Guess it didn't stop Sherman," I said.

"Naw," Clark said. "He came in from the southwest. He captured Fort McAllister down on the Ogeechee River in about fifteen minutes and that was about that. The Union navy was anchored offshore, waiting to sail in and start bombarding, and the Confederate generals decided to take their troops up into the Carolinas and live to fight another day. When the Union troops marched in, we offered everyone a Planter's punch, it being Christmas and all. Sherman thought that was nice, so he decided not to burn the place to the ground, like he did in Atlanta. There are some very wealthy real estate agents in these parts who are very glad our city fathers rolled over. Saved 'em a helluva lot of excellent downtown inventory."

I laughed.

"I was talking with your cart man about Bagger Vance," I said. "He didn't seem to have too high of an opinion about the movie."

"Oh, that film was interesting in its own way," Clark said. "But historically speaking, total crap. It was a retelling of an ancient Hindu myth, and they actually did most of the filming up on Hilton Head."

We got back in the cart and headed to the clubhouse.

"Now if you want some real historical figures, there's Gene Sauers and Hollis Stacy," he said. "Both from Savannah and both played their junior golf here at this club. Did fairly well on their respective tours."

I jotted down the names. "I remember Gene," I said. "I think he played before me in college."

"Hollis won the women's Open three times, which is pretty damn good, you ask me," he said. "Came from a big family, ten kids. Her younger sister Martha won the Mid-Amateur, played in it for years and years. Pretty strong golfing family."

He was silent for a moment as we zipped along the cart path.

"True story," he said. "Back in those days, the club wouldn't let kids out on the course on their own, except for certain times. So Hollis, Gene and the other kids would chip and putt a lot instead. When Hollis was inducted into the World Golf Hall of Fame, she thanked the members of the club for giving her a great short game!"

I laughed. "Funny," I said. "And good material."

Vickers dropped me off at the clubhouse. We shook hands and I drove back into town. It was just after noon, but I took a chance on getting in to Mrs. Wilkes Boarding House on West Jones. People start lining up in the morning to have lunch at this place, where the seating and the service is all family style: you sit down at a large table with lots of other strangers and everyone passes around the food: barbecue pork, fried chicken, meatloaf, plus dishes of mac n' cheese, candied yams, collard greens, butter beans, rice and gravy, pickled beets, cole slaw and more, all washed down by huge icy glasses of sweet tea.

I was lucky enough to get in with the last bunch of lunchers, and stuffed myself silly. The people who have lived in this town for generations now may be crazy as hell, but they do know how to eat well.

Once I was loaded up with Southern comfort food, I staggered my way back to the big hotel on the waterfront where we were staying, managed to hit the correct button on the elevator and fell into my bed for the rest of the afternoon.

That night, Ben Oswald took his announcer crew out to dinner. I got a call in my room at about five thirty inviting me to join them.

Outside the hotel's entrance was a big white bus-like vehicle, with green lettering along the side reading LOWCOUNTRY TOURS. There was no one sitting inside, so I went back into the hotel and checked the lobby bar. Three of the guys were standing at the bar, feet resting on the brass rail, sipping cocktails while the TV set behind the bar showed the day's sports highlights.

"Hack-man!" one of the guys at the bar called out to me when I walked in.

"Hey, Jimmy," I said, and went over to greet Jimmy Williams, the main color announcer at IBS. Jimmy had played on the Tour for about fifteen years before a shoulder injury sent him up to the booth. He had won a PGA Championship along with a handful of Tour events and had starred in a couple Ryder Cups. He worked the booth on the 18th hole along with his TV announcer partner, Van Collins, who was standing next to Jimmy at the bar.

"Hacker, you know Van, right?" Jimmy said, nodding at the man next to him, "And this is Billy Fairfield, the Voice of the Par Threes."

I shook hands all around. Jimmy Williams was now in his late forties but still had that flatbelly look of the former professional golfer. He also had a bushy head of blond hair cut improbably in an old mullet, which had been popular back before he starting playing on the Tour. I was surprised no one had ever told him he looked dated and stupid, but then again, it was only a haircut. His do must cost a fortune at the salon—because who does mullet cuts anymore?—but then, he could probably write it off as a tax deduction.

Van Collins was maybe twenty years older. He had been announcing sports for IBS for a generation at least. His familiar baritone had called college football, professional baseball and hockey games for the network before he moved over to handle the golf broadcasts some ten years ago. He was known as a pro's pro…always hitting his marks, seamlessly moving the telecasts between commercials, promos and live action. He was dressed in golf casual, a sweater tossed over his shoulders and his hair turned mostly to white. He had been nursing a tall Scotch at the bar, and after a desultory handshake and wan smile, he went back to it.

Billy Fairfield was tall and wiry with rimless glasses and eyes that never stopped darting around the room. He, too, smiled and shook my hand, but held back a bit. He seemed to be taking his cues from whatever Van Collins did.

"When did you get into town?" Jimmy asked me.

"Couple days ago," I said. "I've been scouting the town."

"Well, shit," Jimmy said. "You shoulda called me. I could have used a better partner today than old Van here. Jeezus, Collins, how many three-putts did you have?"

"Kiss my ass," Van said, not turning away from his

Scotch, as if he were worried it would run away and hide if he took his eyes off it.

"Where's the rest of the motley crew?" I asked.

"Oh, they'll be down," Jimmy said. "Oswald likes to be fashionably late."

"Up yours, Williams," said a brash voice at the door, and we all turned to see the Assassin, Ben Oswald himself, standing there. "How many goddam drinks you had already?"

"Not enough, Ben, not nearly enough," Williams said.

Oswald was wearing black jeans, a white Oxford shirt open at the collar and a pair of cowboy boots. He stared at me through his thick glasses. "I see you got the message," he said to me. "You know all these guys?"

Before I could answer, someone came around from behind Oswald. She was short, she was rounded in all the right places and she was quite blond, in a color not usually found in nature. She tossed her locks back with a flip of her head and came walking right over to me, hand extended.

"I don't think I've had the pleasure," she said. "I'm Kelsey Jenkins. Nice to meet you, Hacker."

I shook her hand, and didn't mention that we had met some years ago that weekend I covered the LPGA event down in Miami. The weekend that ended with the murder and suicide of Big Wynnona Stilwell and her husband Harold. I figured Kelsey had been so traumatized by those events that she had forgotten meeting a stud muffin like myself.

Kelsey had joined the IBS crew a couple of years ago. And while some of the old timers thought adding a female voice to the weekend broadcasts of men's golf was sacrilegious, the viewers got used to watching her work. Oswald most of the time sent her out to follow one of the leading groups and do the fairway reporting—checking the lie, checking the distance, predicting the shots to come. Other times, he sent her to work one of the towers on the concluding holes. Either way, she had turned out to be a competent and interesting announcer.

"We all here?" Oswald said, looking around.

"Waiting on Parker," Jimmy said with a laugh. The others all smiled. He looked at me. "There's always one straggler," he said, "And ours is Parker Long."

"Is Kenny Craig not coming?" Van Collins piped up from the bar.

"Oh, yeah, the Professor," Oswald chortled. "Can't forget him."

"I'm right here," said another voice, and Craig walked in. Short and a bit on the pudgy side, Craig was the main swing analyst, the master of slo-mo, the guy who could dissect someone's swing right down to the toenails. In addition to his work with the network, Kenny Craig worked as a swing coach with a half dozen or so Tour players. He knew a lot about the golf swing, hence his moniker.

"OK, everyone into the bus," Oswald said. "If Parker doesn't show up in five minutes, we're leaving him."

The guys at the bar settled their tab and we all walked back outside. Kelsey Jenkins fell in next to me and whispered "He always says that, but he's never left anyone behind for dinner."

We filed into the bus and everyone took a seat. The bus held about forty seats, so there was plenty of room. Once we were all seated, the bus driver cranked up the engine and revv'ed it a few times. As if on cue, Parker Long came out of the hotel, looking a bit rushed, and swiftly got on board. We all rewarded him with a round of derisive applause. The driver pulled the door closed and pulled away.

"Right," Oswald called out. "I hope you all like seafood, 'cause we're going to a place that serves the best in the South. It ain't fancy, but, well, you'll see."

The bus driver followed Abercorn through the heart of the historic district, passed by Forsythe Park and its huge, multi-layered fountain spewing white foamy water, and took a left to the east on Victory Drive. There were still some large brick mansions facing on Victory, but the houses in the neighborhoods behind looked more like normal-sized suburban ranches.

We drove past an area filled with the usual mix of big box stores, through a few more suburban neighborhoods and then, just before the road crossed a bridge over the Wilmington River, turned hard right down a narrow little road on a bluff above the river. A little bit further down, we passed a sign that said Welcome to Pinpoint.

"Anybody know the most famous person who hails from Pinpoint, Georgia?" Ben Oswald called out from the front of the bus. "How about you, history boy?"

He was, of course, referring to me. Luckily I knew the answer.

"Unless you're thinking of someone else, I'd say it has to be Supreme Court Justice Clarence Thomas," I said.

"Give that man a cigar!" Oswald said.

The bus slowed down to a crawl. The street was barely wide enough for the bus and the verges were covered in white beach sand mixed with crushed oyster shells. To the right, we passed some scruffy looking one-story houses, shaded by the trees, yards encased in chain link. To the left, the greenish water of the river seemed still. Along the bank in the distance were some weathered wooden docks crowded with working shrimp boats, their derrick arms raised upright and their nets hanging neatly. Looking out over the marshes from the road, I felt I was in central Kansas: the horizon stretched out endlessly over the brown and green grasses, broken here and there by collections of trees that indicated where higher land had survived amid the eternal tidal flows.

"This is a workingman's town," Oswald said. "The open ocean is maybe five miles thataway..." he pointed to the east, "...but to get there, the boats gotta run about ten miles through the marshes, following the green snake. But be glad they do, because the shrimp and crabs they serve at this place probably arrived at the docks an hour or so ago."

The bus pulled up in front of a gray house with a sign that announced it as Fiona's Seafood Shack. It looked kinda shacky, with some white plastic tables and chairs set on a patio in front.

"Don't look like much," Oswald said. "But just wait."

We climbed off the bus and went inside. The cinder-block room was filled with plywood tables with square holes cut in the middle. Underneath each hole was a fifty-five gallon plastic trash can. Customers sat around the tables and huge trays of boiled crabs and shrimp were brought out, along with wooden blocks and small wooden hammers: you used the hammer to crack the shells of the crabs, dug out the meat and tossed the empty shells into the hole in the table.

"Mistah Ben," called out a large black women standing behind the counter at one end of the room. "Bless your heart!"

"Hiya, Fiona," Oswald said, waving at her. "We got about eight, and everyone's hungry."

"Y'all done come to the right place, then," Fiona said. "Sit yourself down and we'll get you fed right up!"

We seated ourselves around one of the large tables. Some of Fiona's crew brought out some pitchers of iced tea, plastic glasses filled with ice and the hammers and planks. The floor was poured concrete, the cinder block walls were painted lime green, the lighting overhead was fluorescent and there was a jukebox against one wall that flashed colors. I went over and pumped in a few quarters and pushed the right buttons and the doleful opening chords of James Brown's "It's a Man's World" echoed through the room. Some of the other diners, mostly black folk, nodded their approval.

"Righteous," said one old man sitting near the juke box. He was wearing a paper bib and his face and fingers all seemed to be coated in crab juice. But he was smiling.

It wasn't long before the rest of us were similarly decked in seafood detritus. Fiona brought us several large metal trays loaded with boiled blue crab, several more with boiled shrimp and dishes full of cole slaw, french fries and hush puppies, cocktail sauce and drawn butter. For a long time, there was nothing but silence from our table, except for the sounds of wooden hammers cracking crabs open and humans sucking the delectable meat into their gaping maws.

Ben Oswald finally sat back with a deep sigh of contentment and looked around the table proudly.

"Best goddam food south of DC," he said. "And I'll kick the ass of anyone who says different."

That kind of narcissistic pronouncement was like waving a red flag in front of an angry bull to me, but I decided to let it pass. One, I was too full of fresh shrimp to argue, and two, I realized that being the boss-man was important to The Assassin. He was, of course, just another dipshit who happened to know how to make good golf TV, but so what? I kept my trap shut and thought that Mary Jane, at least, would have approved of my newfound maturity.

Oswald turned his gaze on me.

"Whaddya think, Hacker?" he said. "Best seafood you ever had?"

"Best seafood of its kind," I said, borrowing the qualifying phrase from what Gary Player always says about whatever golf course he's standing on. "Bar none."

"Goddam right," Ben growled. "Kelsey? You had enough?"

"Way too much, Ben," she said. "Thanks."

"Goddam right." He took a few sheets from the carton of wet wipes that Fiona's crew placed on the table and wiped down his hands, arms and face, then passed it around.

"OK," he said as the rest of us hosed ourselves down. "I want everyone at the course tomorrow at one p.m.," he said. "Which means those of you going off golfing need to leave early and get back in time. You got that, pro?" He was looking right at Jimmy Williams, who just smiled that 100-watt smile of his and nodded.

"Meeting at one, rehearsal at two," Oswald continued, looking around the table. "We're just three weeks from the Masters. We gotta start handicapping these fuckers, y'know? Tell the folks who's playing good, who's not. Van, you got all that?"

Van Collins, the head announcer, nodded solemnly. He was staring at his tall plastic glass which was filled with ice, water and what I suspected was Scotch that had come from Van's own hip flask. Van seemed to be a big fan of Scotch.

Oswald went on. "Billy, you're on seventeen. Parker, sixteen. Kelsey and Kenny are the rovers. Any questions?"

I raised my hand.

"Hacker?"

"They got dessert here?"

Tony Sciutto was already in the coffee shop when I came down at eight the next morning, a half-eaten plate of scrambled eggs, grits, hash browns and bacon in front of him. I plopped down across from him in the booth, introduced myself and shook his hand. The waitress brought over a pot of coffee, filled my cup and refilled Tony's.

"Sorry, Hacker," he said, not looking sorry in the least. "I'm an early riser, so I was getting a little hungry."

"No apologies necessary," I said. "Go ahead and eat. I'll catch up."

He picked up his fork and went back at it. Sciutto was probably in his late forties. His hair was black and trimmed short. His complexion was olive, with dark shadows of whiskers evident on his cheeks, even though he had apparently shaved already earlier in the morning. He was wearing jeans and a somewhat faded old golf shirt.

The waitress came back around and I ordered. Tony kept eating. A couple of the other members of the IBS crew walked past our table. I could tell who they were because both were wearing T-shirts that said "IBS" on the front.

"Shooter," one of them said in greeting as they walked past.

Tony nodded but didn't stop eating.

"Shooter?" I asked.

He looked at me and grinned. "Old nickname," he said. "It's a riff off my last name and what I do, so ever since I got into TV, people have called me that."

My waffles arrived about the same time he finished his eggs, so I dug in while he sat back with a sigh and sipped some coffee.

"So," he said."Whaddya got?"

I grabbed the file folder I had brought down from the room with me and tossed it across the table at him. He opened the folder, took out the six or seven pages I had written the night before and began to read.

"Not sure it's a script in the format you're used to, since I have no idea what format that is," I said. "But I think you can get the gist of it."

I ate my waffles while he read. And the three strips of bacon that came with them.

He finished and looked at me over the tops of the pages.

"That's pretty damn good," he said. "I can work with this. And Becky Ann will make it sing."

"Really?" I said. "You're not just telling me that to make me feel good on my third day on the job?"

"Oh, Christ no," he said. "I was fully expecting to have to completely wing this segment. But this is good stuff. Oswald will like it, though he'll never say so. You can tell he likes something if he doesn't insult you to your face, but says something nasty about an innocent bystander instead. He's a piece of work, Ben is."

"Great," I said. "When do we get started?"

"No time like the present," he said, standing up. "Besides, we gotta get out to the Plantations by one. Otherwise that asshole will say something insulting to both of us."

AFTER A BUSY morning shooting video at various places around town, Shooter and I rode the IBS bus from the hotel out to the golf course just after noon.

I was still amazed at how Shooter had taken my skeleton script and turned it into something. I was also amazed that he had made me do the stand-up in front of the camera. He called it laying down the tracks. That had not been something I'd even thought about doing. As they say, I have a great face for radio. But he just told me to shut up and read my lines. Which hadn't been hard, since they were literally my lines.

He had used a small handheld camera about the size of a shoebox. I had held a wireless mic for the audio that was captured in his little shoebox. We had done four or five locations, one or two takes each, and then he had smiled at me and said "That's a wrap!"

"It is?" I'd said.

"I'll give the raw footage to Becky Ann, along with your script and by this time tomorrow, she'll have a nice four-minute segment," he said. "You thought of a name for this yet?"

"A name?"

"Yeah, you know...'Hacker's History' or something like that."

"I think Fractured Fairy Tales is taken," I said.

"Holy crap," Shooter said. "Those were great. Rocky and Bullwinkle, right?'

"Good memory," I said.

Our bus pulled in to the Club at Plantation Pines, one of the many fancy real estate developments that dot the Lowcountry coast from Nag's Head to Jacksonville. Lots of piney woods, black lagoons, green fairways with bright-white bunkers … all surrounded by fabulous McMansions: five-car garages, acres of rolling green lawns and the obligatory pool in the back. I used to wonder where all the rich people who could afford living in these places came from, but decided that was one of the mysteries of the age. They all come from somewhere, brimming with cash and looking for that luxurious respite from a busy, stressful world. Of course, the stress follows them inside the gates, but they don't know that until they've moved in.

The bus took a side street away from the magnificent brick-and-gable clubhouse with its landscaped entrance drive and four-story USA flag out front, and took us down to the television compound. Here, on a three-acre field of flat, treeless ground, IBS and its contractors had rolled in about a dozen trailers which were now parked cheek to jowl. Off to one side, a bristling array of satellite antennas pointed up into space.

We embarked from the bus and Shooter led me through the maze of wooden walkways, rimmed on both sides with thick black cables, to the collection of trailers at the center of the field which contained the control rooms and other facilities for the TV crew. One of them held the canteen and that's where we went first.

"Don't know about you, but making TV makes me hungry," Shooter said and led me inside. Two trailers had been parked side by side and opened up to create a double-wide space. Along the back, white-coated chefs were busy putting hot food of various kinds into the steam trays on the line, and members of the crew lined up with trays and plates to load up. There were burgers and dogs, various kinds of pasta, fresh veggies, salads, desserts and more.

We got in line, grabbed our plates and trays and went though, loading up for lunch. We grabbed some chairs at the long tables that stood against the wall. Shooter went over to the drinks station and got us each a tall glass of iced tea.

"Mazeltov," he said as he sat down.

"Sciutto a Jewish name?" I asked.

He grinned. "Naw," he said. "I've just worked in New York too long."

"Hey, Hacker," said a voice behind me. I turned around and saw Digby Allen standing there. He gave me an awkward little wave.

"Hiya, Digby," I said. "How's it going?"

"Good," he said. He turned and kept walking. Talkative fellow.

I turned back to my lunch. Shooter nudged me.

"You know him?" he asked.

"Yeah," I said. "Met him up in New York."

"Strange dude," he said.

I shrugged. "Who isn't strange?"

Shooter grinned at me. "Yeah, I guess," he said. "Still that one has a rep with some of the crew."

"A rep?"

"Well, let's just say it wouldn't surprise some of us if they found a bunch of dead kittens underneath his bed," he said. "Just sayin'"

"Dead kittens?" I said. "Yeah, that qualifies as creepy."

Shooter was about to say something else, when Arnie Wasserman stuck his head in the door of the canteen and yelled "Talent group meeting, five minutes. Trailer 33B. Five minutes."

"It's showtime," Shooter said, and we got up and left.

Trailer 33B was the main control room for the broadcast. I followed the other talent into the room. One of the long walls was covered almost from end to end with banks of TV monitors. I counted more than thirty screens, each one labeled with either a number or a name, which I assumed was the cameraman, and some of them had both. There was one large monitor in the center of the wall, directly opposite the center of the rows of controls—all glowing with the colors of the rainbow—where the directors sat. I figured that large monitor showed the program feed which went out to the satellites and eventually appeared on TV screens all around the country.

The tech crew had taken their places at the various boards and controls. Ben Oswald sat in the middle, directly opposite the large main monitor. His leather chair, on plastic wheels like the others in the room, was the largest and plushest. There was nothing in front of him but an empty white blotter. On either side of his position, there were assistant directors with their own specialized control boards, computer screens, and telephones. The assistant director to Ben's right hand was the guy who mashed the buttons to select which camera's shot would go out to the world. The guy on the left would be in charge of the Chyron graphics, the scoreboards, and any other informational screen that Oswald might need during the telecast. I didn't know what the other assistant directors in the main row did, but I assumed they talked to the cameramen, the talent in the booths, and called up the replay tape after good or bad shots. There were some seats behind Oswald, back against the wall opposite the monitors, where the production people sat. And the shorter end walls of the trailer were also utilized with desks set perpendicular to the main set-up. I saw the replay guys taking up positions there, ready to cue up any shot Oswald wanted to show again and get it ready for broadcast.

Oswald entered the trailer, with Arnie right behind. Ben sauntered over to his seat at the center and sat down. Arnie stood behind him, his ever-present notebook open and ready. Wasserman had dressed down here in the South, and today was wearing starched denim and a long-sleeved cotton shirt in bright pink. Oswald was dressed in his usual frumpy pants and a shirt. He had either given up on the idea of dressing for success, or he just didn't care anymore.

"Awright people," Oswald called out from his high-backed leather command chair. "Listen up. We're gonna do a live shot rehearsal from two to three. I want everyone in their place and ready to go at 1:55. You all know your places. Let's be sharp, on the ball. Right? Let's do it."

That was the full extent of the meeting. The announcers turned and filed out of the control room trailer, heading for their assigned places on the golf course: talent to the towers and the fairways, camera and sound crew to their stations. Shooter left. He told me he was shooting approach shots on sixteen. I just stood there.

"Hacker!" Oswald's sharp eyes missed nothing. Especially me. "Where the fuck are you supposed to be?"

"Beats the crap outta me," I said.

"Jesus Christ on stilts," Oswald exclaimed, throwing his hands up in dismay. "Arnie! Tell this idiot fuckwad where he's supposed to be."

He turned back and started firing directions at the group of assistant directors who had taken their seats and were playing with the buttons and slides on their control boards, heads down, looking busy.

Arnie Wasserman glided over to me. He looked into his notebook and nodded to himself.

"You're supposed to be working on your history segment," he said. "But of course, Shooter is busy. So maybe you should be working on your script?"

"The segment's in the can," I said. "We shot it this morning. Recorded the audio tracks. Becky Ann has the film and the script."

He looked at me, lips pursed, eyebrows raised. I don't think he was expecting that.

"Really?" he said.

"Done and dusted," I said, smiling at him. "Maybe I could just sit in here and watch how great golf television is made."

He looked at me closely to see if I was trolling him. I mostly was, but I did want to see how it all worked.

"OK," he said finally and motioned at a nearby empty chair. "Sit there and keep quiet."

I mouthed the words *Yes, boss* at him and sat down.

At five minutes to two, the overhead lights in the control room were turned off. But with the multiple screens on the wall and the glowing colors from the control boards, there was enough light to see what was going on. The main monitor showed the IBS logo, while the other monitors were jumping around as the cameramen sought some actual golfer to focus on. It was Wednesday, so the morning pro-am was finishing up, and some other players were out playing a few holes, getting ready for the start of the tournament tomorrow.

Just before the top of the hour, one of the assistant directors announced "thirty seconds." He gave another warning at fifteen seconds, then ten. Then he counted down: "five… four…three…" He then held two fingers aloft, then one.

"Music and roll tape," Oswald barked. Both of the assistant directors flanking Oswald touched a few buttons and we heard the familiar musical intro that IBS used, and the main monitor, now bordered in red to indicate it was live, showed the IBS Sports logo. Aerial shots of the golf course, taken from a helicopter fly-by on a recent bright sunny morning, filled the screen while the studio announcer's prerecorded voice told the viewers that they were watching the PGA Tour on IBS. Shots of some of the more famous players in attendance danced across the screen.

"Standby camera two," Oswald said. I looked up at the bank of monitors and found Camera Two: it was showing the front of the Plantation Pines clubhouse.

"Standby Van," Oswald said. "Intro and Camera Two in three … two … now!"

At his command, the clubhouse shot filled the main screen and Van Collins' dulcet baritone welcomed viewers to Savannah for the playing of the Southern Plantation Open which, he told us, was an important run-up to the Masters, just three weeks away. Oswald ordered a series of shots of the golf course while Van and Jimmy Williams began talking about which players seemed to be reaching the peak of form, and which ones seemed to need some extra work before heading up to Augusta.

"Standby sixteen," Oswald said. "Parker, that's Justin Thomas. Van … send it to 16…"

The main announcer finished up what he was saying and then said "Let's go out to sixteen…"

"Sixteen-A," Oswald said and the camera shot from the fairway showed Justin Thomas and his caddie talking as they sized up his next shot. Parker Long began narrating the scene, telling us how far Thomas had left to the green and what the wind was doing.

"Standby ten," Oswald said, "Kelsey, you're up."

Thomas hit his approach shot and the camera followed it to the green.

"Closer, Sammy, tight in," Oswald said as the ball landed on the green. The camera zoomed in and we watched the ball bounce twice then check back and rolled to about fifteen feet from the hole."

Parker Long, in the booth, said "He's got a great look at birdie there. Let's go to Kelsey on ten. She's got Billy Sommers."

"Ten," Oswald ordered and the camera shot flipped over. Kelsey started talking about what an excellent season Sommers had going so far, and said he was really looking forward to playing in his first Masters in a few weeks time. Sommers was lining up his putt while she talked, and he stepped up and hit the putt.

"Tight," Oswald said and the camera zoomed in again. "Tighter!" We watched as the screen showed the ball creeping up to the edge of the hole, stopping there momentarily, and finally dropping in. There weren't a lot of people in attendance on a Wednesday, but the ones who were there cheered lustily anyway.

"Replay?" Oswald said.

"Got it," one of the assistants on the side of the room called out.

"Cue it," Oswald ordered. "And run replay."

Kelsey said something about how well Sommers was putting and that this effort demonstrated how his touch was still there.

While we watched the putt again, Oswald was looking ahead for the next shot. He quickly scanned the banks of monitors, found a player ready to make a shot, and had both camera and announcer ready for his segue.

Just in the first ten minutes, I found myself impressed with how seamlessly Oswald was able to move around the golf course, finding the next player and the next shot. Almost every one of the thirty or so monitors, each connected to a camera, showed a player either getting ready to hit a shot, hitting a shot, or reacting to a shot he had just made. Oswald was able to find, amid all those images and events, a narrative story line that progressed from one to the next without interruption. It was quite a performance. Ben Oswald was in his element, the Svengali making the story happen right before our eyes.

For the next hour, I watched in amazement as Ben Oswald choreographed the cameras and announcers and replay tapes almost perfectly to show the golfers playing their way around the course. Four or five times, when one of the production assistants in the back of the room signaled, he announced commercials, and one of the announcers would say "We'll be back to Plantation Pines right after this message."

It all looked quite effortless and easy, but I knew it wasn't. But this was why IBS paid the Assassin whatever he wanted. I couldn't see any mistakes. But when the hour was over and rehearsal was called, Oswald threw a pencil across the room at one of the assistant directors, a young woman on one of the replay controls.

"You fuckin' missed that putt," he muttered. "It looked to me like Barnaby rushed that putt, left the face open. But you missed it. Left poor Fairfield with his thumb up his ass trying to describe it. Television is a goddam visual medium, you idiot."

"Sorry, Ben" she said, turning a little red.

"Yeah, you are sorry," he snapped. "Get the fuck with it or get the fuck out."

The woman turned red but said nothing. I figured everyone who worked for Ben Oswald must be on some kind of chemical assistance, or he would have been murdered years ago.

At the end of the rehearsal, Oswald stalked out of the trailer. Arnie Wasserman stepped forward. "Good job everyone," he said. "Let's make sure we do it just as good tomorrow. Two o'clock call. We're on-air at three-thirty. See ya then."

Nobody answered. There was no collective 'yeah, awwright' response from the team. They all kept their heads down, finishing up with whatever buttons they had to push.

Had I still been a golf writer with a newspaper column and a readership, I would have written something about how Ben Oswald was the kind of leader who inspired an '*esprit de corpse*' from his team. That made me smile. Then I realized the only audience I had who I could share my wordsmithing brilliance with was my wife, Mary Jane. That made me sigh.

9

The next afternoon the golf tournament got underway. I took up my position at the back of the control room. A little after five, an hour or so after the telecast started, Ben Oswald told Van Collins, the head announcer, to intro my history segment.

"OK Van," he said, "Let's cue up this Hacker crap. See what he came up with. Hide the women and children."

When the live feed came back from a commercial, Van's dulcet tones filled the speakers in the room.

"We here at IBS are excited to introduce a new segment to our regular golf broadcasts," he said. "We call it Hacker's History of Golf featuring noted golf writer and historian Pete Hacker. Here's his first contribution …"

"Music," barked Oswald, and the soundtrack began. "And…run tape."

The famous picture of golfer Bobby Jones, dressed in a soaking wet jacket, hair plastered against his skull, wearing an exhausted expression, filled the screen. And my narration began.

In 1929, the great Bobby Jones had one of his most embarrassing losses as a competitive golfer. He was at the peak of his career and, like dominant golfers to follow like Hogan and Nicklaus and Woods, he was expected to win every tournament he entered, even though he remained an amateur.

So in September of 1929, when Jones—the two-time defending champion-- ventured west to play in the U.S. Amateur held at the ten-year-old golf course at Pebble Beach, California, everyone assumed that the title was not in doubt—Bobby Jones was going to win, it was just a question of by how much.

And the tournament began playing out according to form. After two rounds of qualifying stroke play, Jones indeed led the field. But in the first round of match play, the unthinkable happened. A young kid from Oklahoma, a caddie no less, beat the great Jones one-up. The two-time defending champion was gone. Mighty Casey had struck out.

Jones didn't play another competitive round of golf for six months. With time on his hands, he did go down the road at Pebble Beach and played at the new Cypress Point Club, and was so impressed that he immediately sought out the architect of that course, Dr. Alister Mackenzie, to come work with him to create the Augusta National Golf Club in Georgia.

It wasn't until February of 1930, a new decade, that Jones again got his clubs out, when he came to Savannah, Georgia to play in the Savannah Open against a good field of professionals. They played four rounds at the Savannah Golf Club, which claims a pedigree back to its founding in 1792, just about seventy years after General James Oglethorpe had founded the new colony of Georgia and laid out the grid-like streets and parks of old Savannah.

And after a spirited weekend of golf ... Jones lost again. This time, it was professional Horton Smith who nipped Jones by a single shot.

Few people today remember the 1930 Savannah Open. But they should. Because that was the last tournament Bobby Jones ever lost. 1930, of course, was the year of Jones' great Impregnable Quadrilateral, or what today we call the Grand Slam. 1930 was the year he never lost again.

Jones went to Scotland in May of that year and won the British Amateur at St. Andrews. Two weeks later, he captured the British Open by two shots at Royal Liverpool in Hoylake.

After a ticker-tape parade down Broadway, Jones went out to Interlachen in Minneapolis and won the U.S. Open by two, and in September, at the famous Merion Golf Club in Philly, he beat Eugene Homans in the final round to capture the Amateur title he had lost the year before.

And then he retired as a competitive golfer.

Nobody since 1930 has repeated Bobby Jones' greatest accomplishment, either by winning the old Slam of the two Amateur and Open titles in the same year, or in the modern version, which is winning the four major professional titles. In a few weeks, the only person this year with a chance to duplicate Bobby Jones' greatest feat will be unveiled, when we find out who wins the Masters.

But his journey that year started right here in Savannah, Georgia. So if you believe history can repeat itself, pay attention this week ... not to the one who wins the title here in Sunday. But take a look at the runner-up. And wonder.

And maybe go plunk down twenty bucks on the second-place guy this week with your favorite bookie or your local sports betting shop. Because you never know... stranger things have happened in this royal and ancient game.

SHOOTER WAS RIGHT. Becky Ann Billingsly had taken Shooter's video shots, a bunch of historical footage and my narration and created a great three-minute segment. She had found lots of historical stuff on Bobby Jones, and mixed it with the shots we had taken a day earlier, in Savannah and at the Savannah Golf Club, and added some dramatic music in the background. My voice did the narration, but it was only at the end that I was shown on screen. I thought I looked like a dork, but then I always think that when looking at a picture of myself. But otherwise I was pleased.

When my piece was over, they went to a commercial. The control room was silent.

"Where did you learn how to dress?" Oswald said finally. "Christ on a stick, you never heard of an iron?"

That was all he said. They came back from commercial and he was quickly engrossed in doing his maestro thing, calling for the next important golf shot to be brought to the screens of the viewing audience, and telling the announcer how to set the stage.

I heaved a silent sigh of relief. One of the replay editors caught my eye and gave me a smile, a nod and a brief thumbs-up. I guess I was now, officially, a TV guy.

I felt my cellphone vibrate in my pocket. I knew better than to let in ring out loud when I was sitting in here. I fished it out and saw it was Mary Jane calling. I got up, went outside and answered.

"Was that my handsome husband I just saw on TV?" she said. "It looked just like him."

"Yeah, I think it was," I said. "Did I look like a dork?"

"Are you saying that I married a dork?" she said. "That's kinda insulting."

"Ben Oswald said my shirt wasn't ironed," I said.

"No, I don't expect it was," she said. "You should ask him for a wardrobe consultant. That'll fix his little nasty wagon."

"So, you saw the whole thing, right?" I said. "What did you think?"

"I made sure I got home early today so I could watch," she said. "You told me it would likely run in the first hour. I thought it was good. History, Savannah, Bobby Jones, the Masters, the Grand Slam. You touched all the bases."

"I think you mixed your sports metaphors there, toots," I said. "But thanks. The video editor did a great job."

"No," Mary Jane said, "The writer did a great job. As usual." She paused. "When are you coming home? The kids miss you."

"Sunday night," I said. "I'll probably get in late. Gotta go through Atlanta and anything can happen up there. Tell DJ to save up some extra poop for me."

"Not a problem, there," she said. "If I'm not still up when you get in, wake me up," she said. "I've never kissed a TV star before."

"And I've never made love to a groupie before," I said. "I hear it's extra hot."

She made a purring sound and hung up.

I went back into the control room and sat down in my chair on the back wall. The golf tournament wasn't very interesting—it was the first round and nobody was exactly setting the place on fire. Still, Oswald and the crew tried to show a lot of players making a lot of shots, and they kept returning to show the top ranked players in the field, even the ones struggling on the day. I'm sure that Neilsen or Gallup or somebody has ironclad research that shows your average TV viewer would rather watch Tiger Woods at 12 over par than Joe Nobody who's made five birdies in a row.

The afternoon passed quickly. I was still fascinated by the interplay and coordination going on in the control room, and beginning to learn how the thing came together. It all still focused on Ben Oswald. The cameramen knew the shots he liked. The announcers knew the comments he wanted to hear. The replay people were constantly busy rewinding and cuing up tape in case Oswald wanted to see a particular shot again. The guys on the Chyron kept the stats and scores flowing across the bottom of the screen. It all worked like a well-oiled machine, at least for the folks watching at home, or sitting at the bar of a hundred country clubs.

And then the well-oiled machine threw a rod.

We were scheduled to telecast until six o'clock. That was the inalterable deadline: it was just the first round and our local affiliates has newscasts to broadcast and ads to run.

By five-thirty, most of the A-level players were off the course. One of the benefits of being a leading money winner or a past tournament winner is that you don't get the earliest or the latest tee times. The dew sweepers in the morning and the sunset closers in the afternoon all tend to be the young, the hopeful and the no-names on Tour.

So at five-thirty, the only players left on the course were about ten players no one, including me, had ever heard of. So Oswald had his crew of announcers start talking among themselves while he threw a few shots up on the screen.

"Van," he said, punching through to his main announcer in the booth behind the 18th green, "Let's talk about the Masters. We got twenty minutes to fill. Everybody join in."

For the next few minutes, all the announcers were chatting with each other about who was hot, who was not. Who always played well at Augusta and who hadn't made the cut there in years. The kind of stuff golf fans eat up.

After about fifteen minutes, Oswald mashed his talk button.

"Parker? Are you still awake?" he said. "You care to join in?"

There was silence. He tried again.

"Earth to sixteen," Oswald said. "We're handicapping the goddam Masters. Your participation is required, dammit!"

Silence.

"What the fuck," he said. "Did Parker Long decide to go home early? Benny? Are you still there?"

"I'm here, boss," Benny the cameraman on sixteen said. "But my platform is right above the booth. I can't see if he's in there or not."

"Jeezus X. Christ," Oswald was seething now. "Parker? Can you hear me, you fricking idiot?"

Silence.

Oswald spun around and his eyes fell on me, sitting quietly against the wall.

"Hacker," he said. "Get your ass out to sixteen green and find out what the hell's going on with Parker Long. Now!"

I did what I was told. From the area where the TV trailers were parked, it wasn't a long walk over to sixteen green. The last three holes all bent around the TV compound to some degree. So it took me less than five minutes to get to the green. I saw the squatty TV tower behind the green: it was constructed out of metal tubes all bolted together like an Erector set, rising about fifteen feet in the air. Dark colored plastic had been wrapped around the tower to disguise all the metalwork and hide the cables.

Benny the camera man was standing on the top of the tower, where a plywood platform had been constructed. Beneath him, two rectangular windows provided the view and muted the sound of the announcer sitting inside at his wooden desk. But I couldn't see inside.

I went around to the back of the structure and climbed up the metal ladder steps that continued up to the rooftop deck. Halfway up, I pushed through the plastic opening and went inside.

Parker Long was in there. He was sitting upright in his wheeled office chair, wearing his headphones with the mic attachment in front of his face. There was a TV monitor, a notebook and a sheaf of papers spread out on the plywood shelf that functioned as his desk. He was facing out the windows looking at the green. But he wasn't moving.

"Parker?" I said and went closer. There was an acrid smell of something burning in the air. I went up and looked at his face.

His eyes were open and staring. His mouth was arranged in a grimace. A silent scream. His two hands were clenched on the plywood desk, fingers tightly contracted in an odd shape. I reached over and felt for a pulse on the front side of his neck, where the carotid artery runs up next to the windpipe. Nothing.

I could hear something buzzing softly, insistently. I wasn't sure what it was. Carefully, I reached up and removed Long's headphones. The buzzing got louder. I held one ear pad up to my ear.

"You stupid goddam lazy bastard…" Ben Oswald was in full meltdown. "Wherever you've gone, Parker, I will hunt you down like the dog that you are! You'll never work on my network ever again after this, you sorry piece of puke. Goddam it, answer me!"

I found the button labeled "Internal" on the desk in front of Parker, and mashed it down. "Uh, Houston," I said into Parker Long's microphone piece, "We have a problem."

10

For most of the broadcast crew, the next few hours unfolded in what must have seemed chaotic, frustrating and endless circumstances. That's what happens whenever the police are investigating a suspicious death, which Parker Long's certainly was. But I'd been through the drill before, so I just wrapped myself in my invisible patience cloak and let it all play out.

When Ben Oswald had gotten the word in the control room that one of his announcers was dead in his greenside booth, he immediately threw the program back to New York. There were just five minutes left in our allotted time, so the IBS newsroom took over and did a recap of the day's news, which mostly involved the announcers listing the many ways the President was personally destroying the country.

Oswald arrived at the tower above the sixteenth green about the same time as the first cops. The Savannah PD had a number of officers assigned to the golf tournament for crowd control, traffic and the like, so when they caught the call, a couple of the senior officers on the grounds were sent over to see what was up.

Benny the camera guy had closed down his equipment on the platform above my head, then climbed down the ladder and stuck his head inside the narrow space of the announcer's station.

"What the hell's the matter with him?" he said, staring at the motionless figure of Parker Long.

"He seems to be dead," I said.

"Jesus God," the camera guy said, and he got out of there as fast as he could. I thought I heard him retching down below.

Oswald's curly head of hair thrust through the doorway next.

"The fuck is going on?" he thundered as he entered. Then he looked at Parker closely. "Fuckin' A," he breathed. "He's dead, isn't he?"

"I believe that's what they call it, yes," I said.

Moments later, a very large black man, dressed in the dark navy field uniform of the Savannah police, climbed in through the doorway. He took a close look at Parker Long, felt for a pulse, shook his head, and reaching up to the microphone affixed to the epaulet on his left shoulder, muttered in a report with various number codes. Then he turned to look at us.

"Who found him?" he said.

"That'd be me," I said. "The director..." I nodded at Ben standing next to me, "...couldn't raise him late in the broadcast and sent me over to see what happened. I climbed up here and here he was." I nodded at the body in the chair.

"Did you touch anything?"

"I took his headphones off," I said. "Nothing else. Benny the camera guy stuck his head in. I think that's him yorking in the bushes down there."

The officer nodded. Then he sniffed, his face scrunching up.

"What's that smell?" he asked.

"Don't know," I said. "Smells like something burning. I noticed it when I got in here."

The cop pulled out his eight-inch flashlight and clicked it on. He flashed it around the desk, then bent over and shined it underneath.

"See anything?" I asked.

"Mmm," the cop said. Noncommittal. We heard sirens outside. Two more cop cars had arrived.

"Gentlemen," the officer said, "I'm going to ask you two to leave the crime scene right now. But we're going to need a full statement, so if you'd please stick around for a while until I get can an officer to take it, I'd appreciate it."

"Crime scene?" Oswald was stunned. "What crime? What do you think happened?"

"Sir," the cop said, "I don't know what happened. We call it a crime scene until we know what happened. We will investigate. You guys are with the TV network, correct?"

We nodded.

"OK, then. I want you to go back to your TV compound and wait until I can get an officer over there for an interview. We'll need to talk to the camera operator and anyone else who might have been in contact with the victim."

"Victim?" Oswald wasn't giving up. "You think there was foul play here? Goddamit, I'm the executive producer and I need to know if ..."

"Sir!" The officer was out of patience. "Please do what I asked. Return to your compound and wait for my officer. Is that clear?"

It was. We climbed out of the tower and headed back to the compound of trailers.

Oswald got on the phone to New York. IBS corporate would want to know that one of their announcers had died during a live broadcast. They would especially want to know if that death had been caused by someone else. I suspected that within half an hour, either some corporate lawyer from New York would be on a private jet heading for the Lowcountry, or, more likely, some white shoe lawyer from one of the leading firms in Atlanta, on retainer from IBS, would be heading our way. At least his Gulfstream could get down here in an hour or less. Just another reason to sit tight, say nothing and wait. That was the drill.

Back at the trailer park, the rest of my colleagues gathered in bunches and buzzed as they gossiped and swapped theories about Parker Long's death. Ben Oswald disappeared into the trailer that held his office on the road. After about an hour, Arnie Wasserman came into the main control room and announced that the police were about to begin taking statements from the crew. We were encouraged to tell them everything and anything we knew, especially anything we had seen that day concerning Parker Long. When he left, everyone went back to gossiping.

Four cops walked in, including the large black guy who came out to look at the body in the tower. He saw me sitting quietly against the back wall and waved at me to follow. I could feel the eyes of everyone else follow as he led me out of the control room. He went over to the canteen trailer and paused at the top of the wooden stairs that had been set up for the crew to use.

"We've taken over this space for the questioning," he said. "One, they got coffee. Two, lots of chairs and tables."

"Good call," I said. "Might be a few stray brownies or cookies laying around too."

"One can always hope," he said and we went inside.

The Savannah cops were pretty sophisticated. There was already a crew inside, setting up a video camera and a bright light on a tripod. The camera was aimed at an empty chair, next to another chair set up for the interrogator. They were apparently prepared to videotape all the crew as they were questioned.

The big black officer led me over to the coffee urns and we each poured ourselves a cup. He saw me looking at his nameplate, pinned above his badge, which read Connor. He stuck out a beefy hand.

"Delbert Connor," he said. "Savannah PD."

I told him my name and what I did. The guy manning the video camera nodded at Delbert and we went over and took our seats. The lights were bright in my eyes, and a bit irritating.

"Can you adjust the lights down a bit?" Delbert said. "We're just asking questions here, not trying to torture anyone."

"Right, captain," said the video guy, and he jumped up and adjusted the light a bit.

"OK, Mr. Hacker," Delbert said. "For the record, can you tell us your name, your occupation and how you came to discover the body of Mr. Parker Long?"

I went through my story. Delbert nodded here and there. The video guy just looked at either the camera or the floor.

"You told me before that you smelled something burning when you first went into the booth," Delbert said. "Can you elaborate on that a bit?"

"When I came into the announcer's space and found that Parker was dead," I said, "I was aware of a burning smell in the room."

"What kind of burning smell? Paper? Leaves? Firewood?"

"No," I said. "More pungent that those. Kind of acrid. Like maybe something plastic was on fire. Chemical-like."

"Was there any smoke?"

"No," I said. "It was just an odor in the air. I think you caught it when you came in a few minutes later."

"Right," the cop said. "Did you know the victim?"

"Not very well," I said. "I've only been with the network for a few weeks, and this is actually my first tournament on the crew. I met him last night for the first time when we all went out to dinner."

"I see," the cop said. "So I expect you don't know anyone who'd want to see Parker Long dead?"

"No," I said. "I'm afraid not."

"Anyone on the crew who was mad at him for any particular reason?"

"Not that I know about," I said. "He apparently was congenitally late. But that's the only thing I heard."

"Explain."

I told them about the dinner the night before for "the talent," and how everyone had joshed that Parker was always the last one down.

"OK, thanks Mister Hacker," Conner said. "That'll do for now. Of course, we may have additional questions for you. You in town for the whole weekend?"

"Yeah," I said. "I'm supposed to fly out Sunday night." I paused. Then went for it.

"You think he was murdered?" I asked.

"What makes you think that?" Conner said.

"Something about that acrid smell," I said. "It's the only unusual detail, except of course that Parker Long croaked.

I mean, he was fine, doing his job, announcing golf…until he wasn't. If someone got him, it was quick and it was silent. That burnt smell could have been wires. Electrocution. Somebody coulda zapped him, which could have caused that smell, and then removed the wires and skedaddled into the crowds. Pretty easy."

Delbert Connor looked at me with fresh interest, head cocked to one side.

"That's a pretty detailed analysis of a crime scene from a guy who covers the golf tour," he said. "I think it's a really good idea for you to stick around this weekend."

I laughed. "Before I got into golf," I said, "I worked the police beat up in Boston. Saw dozens of crime scenes. Know the drill. Know cops. So I know you smelled what I smelled and you are thinking the same thing. You've probably combed the area beneath the tower for wires, burned or not. Plus dusted everything in that room for prints. You'll only find mine on Parker's headset, which I took off his ears. And you'll find out from the rest of the crew that I was sitting in the control room for the entire time of the broadcast. But don't worry, I'm not going anywhere. You need me, I'll be right here."

Delbert Conner looked at me with that level cop stare. He was hard to read, as are most cops, but I knew he didn't like me for the crime, if in fact there had been a crime.

"Right," he said. "Here's my business card. You think of anything else, you call me. Thank you for your information."

He nodded with his head at the door and I left.

11

Later that night, I called home.

"Hi, honey," I said when Mary Jane picked up my call. "I think I've done it again."

"Oh, crap," she said. "I don't like the sound of that. Have you been arrested for homicide?"

I laughed.

"Have I *ever* been arrested for homicide?" I asked.

"It's been threatened once or twice if I recall," she said. "Why don't you tell me what happened."

So I did.

"It's a good thing I love you so much," she said when I was finished. "Otherwise I might believe that you are a dead body attractor. So tell me, how many police officers have you pissed off today?"

"Not a one," I said, trying not to sound proud about it. "My man Delbert Connor actually likes me, I think."

"Well, that's progress," she said. "What are the chances that Officer Connor will let you leave town on Sunday to come home?"

"I can't see why he wouldn't," I said. "I didn't do anything wrong. Ben Oswald sent me over to see why Parker wasn't talking anymore. I discovered the reason: he was dead.

We don't know how or why, yet. So I think I'm in the clear. I've got about twenty alibis."

"Well, thank goodness for that," she said. "The kids would miss you if you got locked up for a stretch in the Georgia state pen."

"You would too, right?"

There was silence on the line. Which continued on longer than it should have. Finally, Mary Jane giggled.

"Of course, you big jerk," she said. "Come home. All is forgiven."

"I didn't do anything," said. "So I don't need forgiveness."

"Well, maybe not for whatever happened to the dead guy," she said. "But overall your slate is far from clean."

She made some kissing sounds and we hung up.

I was thinking how lucky I was to have an understanding wife, sort of, when there was a rap at the door to my hotel room. I opened the door. Ben Oswald was standing there, nervously shifting back and forth and looking frazzled.

"Hacker," he said, "As you know, we're down a man for the weekend. I want you to take over Parker's spot on sixteen."

"Are you insane?" I said. "I've never done any broadcasting before. Well, except for yesterday. But all I did was whatever Shooter told me to."

"Jeezus, Hacker," he said, shaking his head. "All I'm asking you to do is sit in the booth up there, watch what's going on and talk about it. How hard can that be? And I'll be in your ear the whole time, telling you what to say and when to say it."

"Why don't you just hire a talking parrot then?" I said. "Be easier than trying to train me."

"If I could, I would," he said. "But we've got a broad-cast tomorrow afternoon, and we're up against it. I need some-one, and you're it."

"Swell," I said. "This has got disaster written all over it."

"Look," he said, "I just put in a call to Billy Joe Bo-sworth. He's filled in for us a couple of times in the last year or two. He's a little corn pone, but he's not bad. The viewers seem to like him. If he can get over here from Texas tomorrow, I'll put him with you at sixteen. Between the two of you, we might be able to pull this off."

I knew Billy Joe, of course. So did every golf fan. The Boz. He was from San Angelo, Texas, which as everyone knows, is where the fictional Tin Cup was from. But unlike Kevin Costner, Billy Joe had an honest-to-God Texas twang and the country-boy persona to go with it. He had played the Tour for about ten years, won two or three events, and charmed the socks off fans with his countrified similes and yee-haw enthusiasm. But I could see Oswald's strategy clear-ly: with Billy Joe's nonstop observations and my own mea-ger contributions, we might just be able to make it through a weekend of golf without looking stupid or ignorant.

"Yippee-o-ky-yay," I said. "I'll give it my best shot."

Oswald looked relieved.

"Great," he said. "Thanks."

He turned and walked away down the hall. I closed the door. "And good night to you, too," I said to myself.

I sat on the bed and thought for a while. First, I thought of all the things that could go wrong. I knew the TV guys did lots of preparation. Each week, the announcers all were given thick notebooks with facts and figures about the players in the field, and statistics about how they had played the course at Plantation Pines in the past, and personal anecdotes they had collected over their years of experience. I also knew, based in part on my observations while watching the production over the last couple days, that the "talent" was called that because they were good at talking while thinking on the fly. And having Ben Oswald or one of the assistant directors yapping in their ears the whole time. I was flying cold and alone here, Billy Joe or no Billy Joe. I felt my stomach do a little nervous flip-flop.

Then I thought about what could happen if we pulled this off. Maybe IBS would hire me full time. That would go a long way towards helping with the new house problem waiting for me back in Boston. And it would make me a TV star. People would come up to me in public and ask for my autograph. Golfers would slap me on the back and tell me how brilliant I was. Women would throw room keys at me, or maybe their underwear. Hey…it could happen.

My reverie was interrupted by another rap on the door. I opened it. Ben Oswald again.

"One more thing," he said. "Your existing contract is still in effect. So in addition to this new assignment, I need you to keep doing those history segments. I liked the one we ran today. New York says the initial feedback was positive."

"Aw, gee, stop all the compliments…you're gonna make me blush," I said. "I take it I'm still getting paid the same amount?"

He looked at me, appraisingly.

"I'll talk to New York," he said. "If this works out, we can probably do a contractual addendum. Get you a little more."

"Swell," I said. "My newborn son will appreciate that."

"You got a new kid?" he said. "I didn't know that."

"Yeah," I said. "He was born last October. I was two under par on the thirteenth green at Brookline when Mary Jane went into labor."

That made him smile. "Hope you finished the goddam round," he said. "Two under at Brookline ain't something you quit on." But he was just kidding. I could tell by how his eyes went a little soft around the edges. "I remember where I was when my two were born, too."

"I didn't know you had kids," I said.

"Yeah, well, we're not that close," he said. "And they're mostly grown up now. I wasn't a very good father, being away most weekends doing TV shows."

"Yeah," I said. "I expect that would be hard. But I'm sure they understand."

"I'm not sure they do," he said. "But there's not a goddam thing I can do about it now."

He turned and walked away again. Mister Happiness.

THE NEXT DAY, I got out to the golf course by late morning. I'm not sure why: there isn't much one can do to practice for talking about golf. Announcers don't go out to the putting green and repeat "Hoo, boy, Johnnie, that putt had a little extra sauce on it" about six times, playing with emphasizing different words to see which one sounds best. At least, I had never seen nor heard of one.

But I did run into Van Collins in the canteen. He was munching on a salad and sipping some iced tea while he read the sports page of the Atlanta *Journal-Constitution*. I grabbed a cup of coffee and sat down next to him.

"Hacker," he said, peering at me over the top of his paper. "I hear you're making your virgin voyage with us this afternoon. Nervous?"

"Yeah, a little," I said. "I've always wondered how you guys avoid saying 'fuck' and 'shit' when you're on the air."

He chuckled. "That's easy," he said. "If you even think of those words, Ben Oswald will reach through the wires from the control room and choke the very life out of you. Knowing that, it's actually pretty easy."

"Great," I said. "That's one potential worry dispensed with. Here's another: what if I have to pee?"

He shook out his paper, folded it in half, laid it on the table and smoothed it out. The man liked his newsprint wrinkle free.

"You get the assistant director's attention, tell her that you gotta go," he said. "Next time a commercial break comes up, she'll give you the word. You got three minutes to get down to the Port-A Potty and back. But if you pee before the show, like your mother always said, you can generally make it through the afternoon. I've heard stories about guys taking milk jugs up to the booth with them, but I've never gone there."

"Not a big milk drinker," I said, "So I guess I'll just hold it."

"I heard Billy Joe Bosworth is flying in," he said. "Word of advice…don't let him start to ramble. He can tell a story that goes on for hours if you let him. This is TV. Keep it short and sweet and toss the ball down the line to the next guy."

"Right," I said. "Short, sweet and pass the ball."

He smiled at me. "You'll be fine," he said. He paused. "I hope."

WITH HIS LAST words ringing in my ears and causing my insides to cramp up, I went outside. The day was warm and sunny, and the wind was light. There was a good crowd on hand for a Friday, and the air was filled now and then with the cheers announcing that someone had made a nice birdie putt somewhere out on the course.

I saw Delbert Connor in his well-pressed navy uniform talking to a couple of others who looked like detectives outside one of the TV trailers. I went over. He saw me coming and broke away from his conversation before I got close enough to listen.

"Morning, Captain Connor," I said. "How's the investigation going?"

"It's going," he said, shaking my hand. "But like most investigations, it's not going in a straight line."

"Care to tell me what that means?" I said.

"Not particularly," he said, but he smiled kindly.

"Do you have a cause of death yet?"

"Yeah," he said. "The victim was electrocuted. Some kind of high current zapped him."

"Really?" I said. "Was that accidental or on purpose?"

"We don't know yet," he said. "We've impounded all the equipment and our crime lab rats are going over it right now. Hope to have something to go on by tonight."

"I'm supposed to do the broadcast from that booth this afternoon," I said. "Do I need to worry about getting zapped?"

"I don't think so," he said.

"Think?"

He chuckled. "Well, one theory is that there was some kind of equipment malfunction," he said. "If that's the case, we've taken the equipment away and sent it to the lab, so you should be okay."

"And theory two?"

"Ah," he said. "That theory says that there was a bad actor involved. If that theory is true, then he, or she, might still be out there."

"Oh, great," I said. My stomach did another lap.

"But if that theory holds," he said, "Then the bad actor was pissed off at Parker Long, not you. Of course, the bad actor, if there was one, might have some kind of problem with all IBS announcers, or people who like golf, or men in general. Under any of those assumptions, you could very well be in mortal danger."

"You really know how to assure a guy, don't you?" I said.

"Just doin' my job," he said, and doffing his captain's hat, he walked away.

12

I met Billy Joe Bosworth at the TV tower on the sixteenth green. After grabbing some lunch from the canteen within TV City, which is what I had come to call the confusing collection of trailers, I joined the pre-production meeting of the talent, held in Oswald's office trailer.

"OK, people," Oswald had said to us once we had assembled around a conference table. "We're going to open with a tribute to Parker Long. The storyline is that he died suddenly at the end of yesterday's broadcast. And that he'd want the show to go on."

"Is that true?" asked Van Collins. "I mean the part about him dying suddenly."

"As of now, yes it is," Oswald said. "We don't yet know *why* he died suddenly, but hopefully the cops will have an answer about that soon. If any of you want to chime in during the show with your own personal memories, feel free. This is a tough time for all of us, and our viewers expect us to talk about it."

He had looked around the table, daring anyone to say something. Nobody did. So he waved us away and we split up to take up our stations around the course.

I had walked out to sixteen. Just as I arrived at the tower, a golf cart drove up, and the Boz got out.

He was in his late forties now, but still looked like the flatbelly kid I remembered from his Tour days. Blond hair, broad shoulders, narrow waist. He was dressed in dark slacks and a golf shirt. He pulled his wraparound dark glasses off when he saw me and came up with his hand out and a big grin creasing his face.

"Hack-Man!" he said, "Great to see ya! How's your Momma n' them?"

I shook his hand. His grip was strong.

"Momma's dead," I said, "But the family is good. You?"

"Ah, hell, Hacks," he said, "Wife and kids are better than a hound dog without the ticks. Sheila's so glad to get me out of the house for the weekend, I'm a little worried she's got a new stallion out waitin' in the barn. Haw!"

I chuckled and motioned for him to go first climbing up the ladder to the broadcast room. He scampered up like a monkey and I followed. Tony Sciutto poked his head over the edge of the platform above us and waved. He'd been assigned to take over the camera on the sixteenth tower. I guess Benny from yesterday was still upset with Parker's death. Shooter had his headphones on and was apparently busy getting his big camera ready for the broadcast.

Inside, the room was stuffy. The wraparound bunting that covered the entire tower scaffold was excellent at cutting off any movement of air. I noticed that two chairs had been set up in front of the plywood shelf that functioned as a desk. The top of the desk was covered by two big TV monitors, a couple of laptops, two thick notebooks full of player stats, and a couple of electrical outlet strips. There were two small plexiglass windows overlooking the putting green below the tower, but the way the desk was set up I don't think anyone planned to look through them—we were all slaves to the TV screen and its flickering image. Somebody had also placed a drink cooler underneath the desk, and there was a box of snacks—chips and cookies—against the wall.

We heard the entrance flap on the back of the tower flop open and turned to see Digby Allen climbing in. He had some headphones in his hand.

"H-h-hi guys," he said. "Gimme two secs and I'll have you all set up and ready to go."

Billy Joe sat down on one chair. I remained standing and watched Digby. He put the two headphones down on the shelf and crawled underneath. He rooted around, found a wire with a long metal jack on the end, and fed it up behind the shelf. I reached over and held it.

"Th-th-thanks," Digby said. He continued rooting around until he found a second jack and passed that one up as well.

He stood up, took the jacks from me and plugged them, one after the next, into a metallic box that had been screwed down into the plywood behind the two monitors.

"These are your audio units," Digby said. "Connects your headphones to the system. You can adjust the volume here…" He pointed to a knob on the unit. "If you want to talk to Control, you hit this button…" He showed us. "When that button is depressed, whatever you say goes over the intercom only. Not to broadcast. You should also hit that button if you have to sneeze or cough or something. It's like the kill button. Got it?"

"Got it," I said. "Is this the same kind of equipment that was in here yesterday? Have you tested it for shorts?"

Digby chuckled. It sounded more like a giggle.

"Same equipment, different box," he said. "The cops took the other one away for testing."

"So, you're sure these are safe?" I asked.

"Pretty sure," he said. And giggled again.

But he took one pair of headphones, put them on his head, grabbed the cable that dangled from it and plugged the jack into the audio control unit. I waited for a bright flash and for Digby's hair to catch on fire. But there was nothing.

"Sixteen to control," Digby said into the mic. "Test, test." He listened, nodded, then took the headphones off and handed them to me. "Good to go," he said.

While this was going on, Billy Joe picked up his own headphones, plugged them in and put them on.

"Git along little doggies," he said into his mic, after mashing down the intercom button. "This is William Joseph Bosworth Junior coming to you live and in living color from sixteen green. Over and everlovin' out."

I heard someone who sounded raspy and angry like Ben Oswald utter a long string of curses along with an order to shut the hell up.

I adjusted my microphone, which swooped out from the headphones on an adjustable boom, mashed the intercom button and said "Hacker here. Ready to go."

"Stand by," said a voice in my ear.

"Okay, guys," Digby said. "Call me if you have any problems. Have a good show."

Boz ignored him. I waved my hand. Digby disappeared out the flap.

"Hope you know what you're doing," I said to Billy Joe, "Cause I'm flying blind here."

"No worries, Hack," he said cheerfully. "This is easier than hunting armadillos. And those little bastards just sit there and let you blow their heads off."

"Right," I said. I opened one of the notebooks and began reading some of the stuff that had been provided by IBS' statistics team on the dozen or so players who were near the top of the leaderboard after the first round. There wasn't much that could be called top secret: mostly just hometowns, family names and ages, years on Tour, wins and earnings to date and things like that. In other words, the color was mostly gray.

"You call the balls and strikes," Billy Joe said, "I'll do the brilliant analysis."

"Okay," I said.

"But feel free to jump in whenever you want," he said. "I mean, you covered these guys for years, right?"

"Right," I said. "Years."

At the stroke of three, our main monitor screen went dark. Then, with some doleful music playing softly in the background, the voice of Van Collins, somber and deep, said "Welcome to the Southern Plantations Open. Today, the hearts of all of us here at IBS are heavy. Yesterday afternoon, as our broadcast came to an end, our colleague and brother Parker Long, who has helped us cover the PGA Tour for the last seven years, passed away at his broadcast station overlooking the sixteenth green."

A photo of Parker, showing him smiling as he sat behind a broadcast desk similar to the one Boz and I were sitting at. He looked natural and happy, headphones over his ears, wires extending out like umbilical cords.

"Our thoughts go out to Jennifer Long and their three kids. We'll be bringing you more news and stories about Parker as our tournament coverage continues this afternoon. He would have been the first to tell us that the show must go on. So we will continue to show you the golf tournament today, despite our feelings of loss and sadness at the passing of our friend and colleague. Jimmy? Your thoughts?…"

Jimmy Williams, our main color guy, started in on a story about the first time he met Parker Long, at the Bob Hope Classic back in the early 20-oughts. I checked the monitor showing the video Shooter was capturing of the group of three players walking up onto the sixteenth green. Matt Kuchar was one of the three, and he began marking his ball and fixing his ball mark.

I hit my intercom button. "Kuchar's ready to putt. He's four under today, three out of the lead," I said.

"I can fucking see that, Hacker," Oswald growled back. "We only have thirty-two monitors here, you stupid ass. I'll tell you when I need you to talk."

I didn't say anything, but inside my head, I called him a few names that even the New York Times wouldn't see fit to print.

Williams finished up with his long and mostly boring anecdote, and Van Collins, ever the professional announcer, made a smooth segue.

"We'll be talking more about our memories of Parker throughout the broadcast today," he said. "But for now, let's get back to the golf. Out on sixteen, Matt Kuchar is getting ready for a birdie putt. Our Pete Hacker is there, along with former Tour champion Billy Joe Bosworth. Fellas?"

"That's right Van," I said. "Kooch is looking at about twelve feet for birdie. He's four under today and steadily moving up the leader board."

"Aw, heck, Hacker," Boz chimed in, "Let's call it five under. This one he's got is going in. Guys like Kuchar pay the rent with putts like this. I got a hundred this one drops like a Marine recruit at Parris Island. Whaddya say, Hack?"

"Are you betting on live TV?" Oswald was almost screaming. "Jesus H. Christ with a shish-kebab. You can't do that, you moron!"

I smiled.

"I'll take that bet, Boz," I said. In my ears, I heard Oswald begin a long string of obscenities, interspersed with promises to have my testicles tied in knots before being set afire with a blowtorch. I ignored him.

Kuchar ambled around the green like he does when sizing up a putt, stood over the ball and sent it on its way. Shooter zoomed in from above as the ball neared the hole, and had a tight close-up when it fell in. The crowd around the green broke out in cheers. So did the Boz.

"Hu-Ya!" he yelled. "How's about them green apples, Hack? Been on the air all of five minutes and I'm up a hunnerd buckaroos! Is this a great country or what?"

"Good call, Boz," I said. "But the day is still young."

"I'm fining both of you buttwipes a hundred dollars each," screamed Oswald in our ears. "Go to fourteen. Kelsey?"

Boz and I looked at each other and grinned. He held out a fist and I bumped it with mine. Stickin' it to the Man.

A few minutes later, Jordan Speith was in the threesome playing the sixteenth. Oswald threw us the shot as he got ready to hit his approach from the fairway.

"Speith's got one seventy-five," I said, as one of the fairway spotters reported that number in my ear. "He's got an eight-iron. Jordan's struggling today. He's three over for the round and right on the cut line at one-over."

"Jordon's been struggling for a year or two now," Boz said, shaking his head in the booth next to me. "I wish I knew what it was. For a stretch there, he was golden. In the hunt most every week. Nowadays he ain't. Lotta talent left on the table, Hack."

Speith hit his shot. He pulled it a bit and it fell into one of the greenside bunkers.

"He'll be disappointed with that shot," I said. "Eight-iron from the fairway and he pulls it wide left. Not good."

"Not good?" Bosworth said. "That was stinkier than my lil girl's diaper after she ate all my burritos. Someone needs to a light a fire under that boy, and soon."

"Careful, Boz," said the voice in our ear. "No talking about shitty diapers on the air."

Oswald cut away to show someone putting on fourteen, but came back to us for Speith's bunker shot.

"Here's Speith in the bunker on sixteen," I said when we were back. "He needs to make a couple good shots on these last three holes, or he'll be back in the Big D for the weekend."

Speith's bunker shot ran about twelve feet past the hole.

Next to me, Boz began humming "Turn Out the Lights," a song made famous by Dandy Don Meredith during Monday Night Football years ago.

"That party's over," he said. "I'd say ole Jordan is homeward bound, Hack."

"Looks like it," I said. "What is it about golf? One day you're on top of the world, the next, you can't put two shots together to save your life."

"She's a fickle bitch, golf is," Boz said. "Cain't never figure her out, nor depend on her. Which is what I said about my first wife. Or was that my second?"

"OK," Oswald said in our ears. "You guys are officially on notice. Any more of this amateur hour and you'll both be swimming home. In a box."

I was asked to send the feed up ahead to the seventeenth, so I did. I looked at Boz.

"He mixed his metaphors there," I said.

"Aww, Benny boy is ninety percent hot air," he said. "I'll bet the people watching at home are liking this shit."

I hope so, I thought to myself. But I thought they might.

13

"Have you seen your press clippings?"

Mary Jane came into our bedroom wearing nothing but a robe, carrying two cups of coffee and a newspaper tucked under one arm. DJ was on his back next to me, making happy noises and trying to suck on his toes. Victoria had been bundled off to school already, but my wife had called in sick. Shirker. But one with a good union.

I sipped some coffee and glanced at the front page. The Middle East was threatening to blow up, the Chinese were unhappy about a new round of tariffs and, as usual, the President had said or done something that the media determined to be the worst thing ever said or done. In other words, situation normal.

"Sports page," Mary Jane said impatiently as she lay down on the bed, grabbed our son, opened her robe and attached him to one of her breasts. I watched with a small degree of jealousy. But then I remembered what had happened when I awoke a few hours earlier, before anyone else in the house was up. The best part of having to travel for work was the reunion when I got home.

I picked up that section of the paper and scanned the page. Bart Concannon's column that morning was full of short and pithy takes on the world of sports news. And midway down his column I read this:

MAKING TV GOLF FUN AGAIN. Did you watch the golf tournament this weekend? It started off sadly when former Tour player turned IBS broadcaster Parker Long died suddenly in his booth on Thursday afternoon. But IBS brought in a couple of ringers: Billy Joe Bosworth, a.k.a. 'the Boz,' and Boston's own Pete Hacker, longtime golf writer for the Journal. Assigned to Long's former station on the sixteenth hole, these two were hilarious, betting on putts, talking trash about the players they were watching and generally keeping the audience in stitches. I'm told longtime executive producer and director Ben Oswald wanted to sack the funny pair ... until the overnight ratings came in and showed that the watching fans loved this new and decidedly ungolf-like style. I agree. It's long past time that staid old golf tournaments got a little shot of fun, and Boz and Hacker might be just the way to go.

I read the piece twice. Mary Jane noticed the frown that creased my forehead.

"What?" she said. "He liked you. He really liked you."

I managed a weak smile in her direction.

"Might not have been the best idea to go completely wild on my first run out of the box," I said. "Oswald was barely talking to either one of us by Sunday. I'm half expecting a call today telling me my services are no longer needed."

"But I thought Concannon said the ratings were good," she said, shifting DJ from one breast to the next. He went at the new one with gusto, but I could tell he was moments from falling asleep.

"If the Assassin doesn't like you, I don't think it matters too much what the ratings say," I said. "He's kinda the main man around IBS."

"Well," she said, "He'd be crazy to let you go. I don't know anything about golf and even I was laughing on Sunday. You guys were hilarious."

"There will be blowback," I said. "There are a lot of sticks in the mud in golf. Did I ever tell you the story about Bill Murray?"

"The ghostbusters guy?" she said, pushing DJ into the center of the bed between us, where he stayed, his little eyes closed, and soft little baby snores highlighted his exhalations. "No, I don't think so."

"Well, a bunch of years ago he played in the Pro-Am at Pebble Beach," I said. "And he was a big hit—he joked around with people in the gallery, mugged for the cameras, did his usual funny stuff. And on the last hole, he dragged a woman out of the gallery, brought her into a bunker and danced her around until she fell down in the sand."

"Oh, my," she said. "I'll bet the PGA Tour wasn't happy about that."

"Good guess," I said. "Well, a couple of days later I was down in Florida playing in some corporate event and one of the guys in my foursome was one of the lead dogs on the PGA Tour board of directors, some big muckety muck CEO type. And he was telling everyone how he had gotten on the phone to the commissioner and told him to get that sonofabitch off the air and never let him back on. Ever."

"Not a Bill Murray fan, I guess," Mary Jane said.

"Not a fan of humor," I said. "It runs deep in the PGA Tour family. The next time someone in that organization laughs out loud will be the first."

My cell phone buzzed from the bedside table. I answered it. It was an old friend from ESPN. He told me ESPN wanted to interview me and the Boz on SportsCenter that night. To talk about the new wave of golf broadcasters. I told my friend I'd get back to him.

"What?" Mary Jane wanted to know. I held up a hand. Then I called IBS in New York and eventually got through to someone in the promotions department.

"I just had a call from ESPN," I said. "They want to interview Bosworth and me about covering golf in the New Age or something."

"I know," the woman said. "They called us, too. I'm trying to get Boz a flight to New York. What's your schedule look like? Can you get down to Bristol?"

"My schedule?" I looked over at Mary Jane.

"We're having dinner tonight at PawPaw's" she said.

"I can't do it tonight," I told the IBS woman. "I've got a dinner date with the leading mobster in New England. But any other time is fine, unless I end up at the bottom of the Charles River wearing cement overshoes."

"Ha ha," she said, "You are such a kidder. No wonder people like your schtick."

"Schtick's are for kids," I said and rang off.

I looked at Mary Jane. "I guess they did like me," I said.

"You betcha," she said. She got out of bed and dropped her robe to the floor. "If you can get DJ into his crib without waking him up, I believe I can demonstrate how much I like you, too."

We drove out to Milton, about fifteen miles south of Boston, later that night, to have dinner at the palatial estate of my sorta-kinda father-in-law. Carmine Spoleto was of that indeterminate age known as "over eighty," but he still controlled the operations of the Boston Mob with what I imagined was an iron, if slightly liver-spotted, fist.

Mary Jane was not his daughter, but had been his daughter-in-law until that dark morning when Carmine's son had been ambushed in a Charlestown tenement by some rivals. He had not come out alive. Carmine had stepped up to help Mary Jane and her infant daughter Victoria survive. And a few years later, when I came along, he had accepted me as part of his family. If not his Family. Which was fine with me, since I am somewhat allergic to Charlestown tenement buildings anyway.

PawPaw, as Victoria had called him since she was small, doted on his granddaughter, and I hoped he was happy with his new grandson as well. Mary Jane did not let him spoil Vickie, but Carmine had told me that her college tuition was taken care of. And the wider Spoleto family, consisting of Carmine's six daughters, had welcomed Mary Jane, the kids and I into the fold for all holidays and special events. Which were frequent: it seemed like one of the extended Spoletos were having a christening or a confirmation almost every week.

Tonight, it was just the four of us, Carmine, and the five or six tough guys who served as his bodyguards at the big estate overlooking a broad tidal marsh that extended out to the east where it joined up with Boston harbor.

Tiny Tony, one of Carmine's goombahs, was busy in the kitchen. There was a huge pot of tomato sauce—otherwise known as 'gravy'—bubbling away on a back burner. Tiny, wearing a starched white apron stretched around his prodigious girth, the source of his ironic name, was grilling some sausages with red and green peppers, and watching over another big pot of boiling pasta.

"Buona serata, Hacker," Tony said when we came in, giving the sauce a stir. "Howsa that little *ragazzo* coming along? Sleepin' through the night yet?"

"Antonio," I nodded at him. "Not quite yet, I'm afraid. Still likes his three a.m. feeding."

"Don't blame him a bit," Tiny said with a big smile. "He's still a growing boy."

Mary Jane came in with the ragazzo on her hip, and a tote bag filled with diapers, chewable toys, changes of clothing and a few jars of baby food. Tiny Tony went over and chucked him under the chin and made little woo-woo noises. DJ rewarded him with a big grin.

"I think he likes me," Tiny said. "Wait until he tastes my cooking. He might ask me to take over as his daddy!"

I took the spoon out of the gravy, blew on it and tasted it. It was heavenly.

"Hell," I said, "I might have you move in as my daddy if you'd cook like this every day."

"Hey," Mary Jane said with a frown. "I heard that."

The old man came tottering in to the kitchen. He had that uncertain gait that most elderly have, like his knees were going to collapse inwards with his next step, but Carmine had a tough inner core, developed over the decades of rubbing out his enemies and breaking the legs of malcontents. His thick glasses hung delicately on his large hooked nose, and the few wisps of stringy white hair he had left were draped hopefully across his pink bald skull.

Mary Jane had plopped DJ into a high chair and fed him some crackers, which he was gumming into submission. The old man walked over and chucked him under the chin.

"*Bello, bello,*" he cooed.

DJ grinned back at him, crumbs clinging to his chin.

Tiny Tony opened a bottle of wine and poured us each a glass. He put out a tray of antipasto, some nice slices of salami, pepperoncini, chunks of cheese, artichoke hearts, green peppers, and a selection of olives.

"Where's Victoria?" I asked as I sipped some of the wine and nibbled on the munchies.

"She's out front trying to talk the guys into showing her their guns," Mary Jane said. "She's at that age."

"You want I should talk to them?" Tiny Tony said.

"She's fine," I said. "Let her be."

Carmine pulled himself up to sit in one of the bar chairs set against the pass-through counter at the end of the kitchen. Tony put some of the antipasto on a plate and placed it in front of him, along with a glass of wine.

"How you doing?" Carmine said to me. "Still talking on the television?"

"Yeah," I said. "Did my first tournament last weekend."

"Yeah?" he said. "How did it go?"

"He was great," Mary Jane said. "The people loved him."

"Buono," Carmine said. "I guess that means you'll keep doing it, right?"

"Hope so," I said.

"Well at least all those unfortunate events of the past, the murders and the mysteries, the Russians and the bad business out in California ... all that is behind you now," Carmine said.

Mary Jane snorted. Softly, but a snort nonetheless.

Carmine heard it. And turned to look at her.

"What?" he said. "Has there been another killing in Hacker's world?"

I stepped in.

"Well, one of my television colleagues unfortunately passed away last week," I said. "I don't know if he was killed, or if he died from natural causes. The police are still investigating."

"I see," Carmine said. He frowned. "What happened?"

I told him. He listened without giving away anything.

"Perhaps he had the heart attack, no?" Carmine said when I finished. "Or something else medical in nature?"

"Perhaps," I said.

"You do not think so?"

"I don't know what to think," I said. "Not enough information yet."

Victoria came bounding into the room, ponytail flying and cheeks alight.

"Richie's gun is sooo cool," she announced, climbing up on a barstool next to Carmine. "He keeps it under his arm in a holster thing."

"You shouldn't bother Richie, or any of the guys," her mother said. "They've got a job to do."

"Yeah," Vickie said. "Shootin' people!"

"Ricardo has a weapon so he doesn't have to shoot people," Carmine said, frowning at his granddaughter. "It's a serious thing, not a toy."

"Whatever," Victoria said. But she smiled up at her grandfather, and he smiled back at her. They had a bond, those two.

"If Hacker's job gets extended, we might be able to find a bigger house," Mary Jane told her semi-father-in-law. "This little guy isn't going to be little forever, and we're gonna need another bedroom in a few months."

Carmine sipped some wine, closing his eyes as he savored the taste.

He turned to look at me. "I told your wife that if you need some help, you just need to ask," he said.

"Thank you, Carmine," I said, and I meant it. "But you've done so much already for my family. I can't ask you for a house loan, too. I think this job will work out. Time will tell."

He looked at me through his rheumy eyes, taking my measure, not for the first time in my life. Then he nodded.

"Si," he said, "*Capisco*. I understand. A man must make his own way in life. Provide for his family. But I am happy to help if I can. A man like me must also take care of his *famiglia*. And you are part of my family, so I am duty-bound to help you in any way I can. And I will."

"*Grazie mille*," I said. "Let us talk about this again later. See what happens."

Carmine Spoleto looked at Victoria, trying a small bite of the salami to see if she liked it. He looked at DJ, still gumming and humming at his cracker. And at Mary Jane and I. He smiled, and nodded.

"Very well," he said. "We shall see what happens. And now, let us *mangiare*."

14

It was the Tuesday after the Masters—which had been won by Donal O'Leary, the Irish Flash from Cashel, an outcome that had reduced the worldwide stocks of Guinness by roughly half—when I joined the rest of the talent from IBS to play Conrad Gold's Hudson Links course up in Dutchess County, New York.

It was a sunny day, but there was a brisk and chilly wind out of the west. Winter was over, but it here in mid-April, it wasn't gone and while the grass was green, mostly, and the trees were just beginning to bud out, it was a day that required a few layers.

I don't know if any of the other guys on the crew took a helicopter from Manhattan up the Hudson River, but I drove over in a rented car from Boston. I took the Mass Pike out to the New York border, then turned south, past Poughkeepsie and Newburgh, staying on the eastern side of the river, until I hit the little burgh of Cumberland, where Conrad Gold had espied the land along the river, backed by some high rocky bluffs, where he built his club.

His Scottish architect, Clyde Stewart, had carved out his holes from the rocky shale and thick woods, adding in some revetted bunkers and finishing the course with three closing holes along the river's bank: a par-four, a par-three and a beast of a par-five closer, with water in play on every shot. I believe Stewart was trying for something dramatic.

Back from the river's edge a ways, but built atop a high bluff, Gold had constructed a Gothic-like series of towers in reddish granite for his clubhouse. There were several wings in this monstrous edifice, one which contained the dining room, one the exercise facility, and one, in the back, for the club's offices. The second and third floors were filled with overnight accommodations for members who got too loaded to drive the hour back to New York and needed a place to sleep it off.

I left Boston early enough to get there by about ten in the morning, leaving a couple of hours before our scheduled tee time of around noon. At a private club like the Gold Hudson Links, you don't need a formal tee time. Members just show up and play. It's good to be rich.

So I had enough time, once I'd arrived, to grab something to eat, change my shoes in the lavish clubhouse locker room, thickly carpeted, decked in heavy wooden lockers, a cheerful fire burning in the fireplace against the last of the morning's chill, and exchange looks with the twelve-point buck's head mounted above the mantel. He never blinked.

Van Collins and Jimmy Williams were kicking back in the locker room when I arrived, drinking coffee, reading the Times and not listening to the cable news on the four or five flat screen TVs hanging at various places around the room.

Oh, looky here," Jimmy chirped at me when I walked in. "It's the Robin fuckin' Williams of golf. Got any good jokes for us today, Hack?"

"Besides the one I'm looking at, you mean?" I said.

"Oooo," Van Collins said, looking at both of us over the top of the sports page he held in his hands. "Isn't it a little early in the day for a death match?"

"Awww, I'm just pulling his chain a little," Jimmy said.

"Though you do have a bit of a green hue, Williams" said a voice from the back of the locker room. I turned to see Kelsey Jenkins brushing her hair at one of the sinks back there. "A little jealous, maybe? New boy makes good?"

"Isn't this the men's locker?" Jimmy called out. "Who let the girl in?"

"Kiss my ass," Kelsey said. "What century do you live in?"

"The wrong one, apparently," Jimmy said with a chuckle.

Ken Craig, the Swing Doctor, Billy Fairfield and Greg Cunningham wandered in and began changing their shoes.

"Is the Boz going to be here today?" I asked.

"Why, you need his moral support now?" Jimmy said. "Can't make the funnies without a straight man?"

"Wait," I said, "I thought I was the straight man."

"I think you're both retarded," Jimmy said.

"We call them developmentally challenged now, you fucking oaf," Kelsey said. "Geezus."

Collins shook out his newspaper. "Boz isn't coming," he said. "Management decided buying him a ticket to come preview the course for the PGA Championship was an unwarranted expense."

"So he can just sit in his little booth and make shit up with Hacker," Jimmy said. "Perfect."

"Man," Ken Craig said, "Somebody got up on the wrong side of the bed this morning."

"Oswald coming up?" I asked next.

"Don't think so," Van said. "Got some meetings with the suits to take care of. He might get here for dinner tonight."

"I need to go hit some balls," I said. "Been a couple months since I've had a club in my hands. Anyone else?"

"Yeah, I'll go with you," Kelsey said, zipping up her wind jacket.

The range at Hudson Links was located just behind the main clubhouse. The hitting stations made a long semi-circle beyond a broad sidewalk, and the crew had set up our bags on white wooden frames every ten feet or so. A lovely pyramid of new white Titleists waited for us to come start belting them down the long grassy sward of the range, which was dotted with round putting-green targets and colored flagsticks.

While I was glad to get away from the atmosphere in the locker room, which was rapidly turning toxic, it really had been a few months since I'd swung a golf club. Having a small baby at home tends to put a crimp in your golf game, as most new fathers eventually discover. I did some stretching at first, trying to get loose in the cool air, and took out a few irons to swing together, using the extra weight to unlock my back and legs, still stiff after the long drive across Massachusetts that morning.

Kelsey apparently wasn't as stiff as me: she began hitting some sand wedges at the nearest target green, about fifty yards away. It had been more than ten years since she played on the LPGA Tour, but she still had that wonderfully rhythmic swing, and her wedges flew low, hard, and in control, landing on the practice greens, jumping forward once and then sitting down hard on the second bounce.

"Swing looks good," I told her as I continued to stretch.

"Oh, thanks," she said. "I live in Port St. Lucie now, and I've been working with Johnny Hanlon," mentioning the name of one of the golf gurus then in favor. He's helped me out a lot. Of course, it doesn't hurt to be able to play all year round."

"Tell me about it," I said. I pulled out my pitching wedge and began hitting some half-speed shots, just trying to get a rhythm and make solid contact. The first few felt a little squirrelly, but eventually I started using the center of the club-face, and that felt pretty good. The golf swing is like riding a bicycle: it can be wobbly at first, but eventually you remember how it all works.

I switched to a nine-iron and made a few full-swing shots. Same rhythm, same thought: hit it in the middle of the face. Surprisingly, it worked. Kelsey was in the hitting station to my right, so she couldn't see my swing unless she stopped and looked, and she was busy going through her own warm-up. But she did call to me.

"The sound is good, Hacker," she said. "Don't know where they're going, but they sound good."

I laughed. "Is there a box on the scorecard where you get extra credit for a good-sounding shot?" I said. "I might need that against Jimmy today."

"Oh, you'll need way more than that, Hacks," Jimmy said, coming up to us and, finding his clubs leaning against one of the hitting stands, rooting around inside the pockets for a glove.

"What's the game, Jimmy?" I asked. "I thought we were just going to play teams."

"Oh, we can play any team game you want," he said. "But I want you straight up. Match of cards? Even up?"

"Fine with me," I said.

The other guys eventually came out to the range. I was hitting some nice three-woods now, having worked my way up through the irons. Amazingly enough, I was still hitting them mostly with the center of the clubface. One of the first lessons I learned when I played on the Tour, all those many years ago, was not to fiddle around if the swing was working. If you were hitting them sideways or thin or fat, well, you could and should try to make some kind of adjustment. But if you were hitting them solid and square, don't do anything. What are you gonna do, hit 'em *squarer*? Don't think so.

"Nice swing there," said a voice behind me, after I hit another sweet little three-wood off the deck, the ball flying low and hard, with a nice little controlled draw, well out there past the 275 yard sign.

I turned. A short, swarthy guy was standing there, dressed in well-pressed tan slacks, and a navy-blue Hudson Links windbreaker over a white turtleneck and golf shirt. He had a surprisingly deep tan for mid-April. He stuck out a hand.

"Danny Abbate," he said. "Head pro. Glad to have you with us today."

I shook his hand. "Thanks," I said, "Looking forward to seeing the course."

"Just so you all know, there's a lot of activity out there," Abbate said. "We're in full-go mode at the moment for the PGA Championship. Building the grandstands and hospitality tents. We've got most of the fairways roped off already. So you'll likely hear some banging and might have to dodge around some trucks and cranes here and there. But everyone in the work crews knows to keep off the golf course proper if possible."

"Got it," I nodded. "Everything on schedule so far?"

"Pretty much," the pro said. "The weather this spring has been helpful. We had a little snow at the end of March, but it wasn't much, and only delayed us for a day or so. We'll be ready."

"Well let's get going then," Jimmy Williams chimed in. "What are we waiting for? None of us are getting any younger."

"We're just waiting for Clyde to get here," Abbate said. "He's on his way up from the city. We thought it would be helpful for you guys to have me and Clyde along to talk about the course while you play."

"I'm sure it will," I said. I turned back to my practice. I wanted to whack a few drivers before I went to the putting green.

"Hey Danny," Jimmy called out from a few stations away. "Make sure you put me and Hacker together, will ya? We got a little side match going."

"Will do," the pro said with a grin. "We're not really busy today, so if you guys all wanted to play together as a group, I'm not gonna call the USGA on you."

I laughed. "Naw," I said, "You go ahead and pick the groups. We'll be fine."

A couple of us made our way, a few minutes later, over to the putting green. Here at Gold's Hudson Links, they had installed a huge rolling acre of putting green and beyond that, routed around some small trees, hedges and park benches, they had built one of those putting courses—18 holes with actual miniature fairways, bunkery places, thick rough and even some water hazards. I'd seen courses like that in Europe in a few places, and had some fun trying my luck playing them. Only a place like Conrad Gold's pleasure emporium would have the budget to install and maintain one.

I was hitting some putts when another golf cart came zipping up and a big burly barrel-chested brute of a man climbed out. He was wearing tan corduroy plus-fours with dark green woolen knee socks, a heavy woolen sweater and a royal green tam o'shanter which matched the color of his socks, and which contrasted nicely with his bushy red beard and did nothing to contain a wild head of frizzy red hair.

"Ach, lads and lassie," he said, his brogue thick enough to walk on. "Sorry I'm late. New York is a big city, is it not? At least we ha' a braw day for it."

Clyde Stewart, the course architect, went around and shook everyone's hand. Then Danny Abbate came out and announced who was playing with whom. Jimmy and I were assigned to the second foursome, along with Kelsey and Stewart.

The first group—Van Collins and the other three guys—made their way down the hill to the first tee. We were all riding in carts, but the club had a forecaddie, decked out in his white Augusta-like coveralls, to go around with us, helping us look for lost balls, read the greens and otherwise keep us organized. And moving.

"You going to hit any balls?" I asked Stewart.

"Nae, lad," he shook his head. "Gawf is in me blood. Wasting time in practice is of no use to me."

I shrugged. Different strokes for different folks, as they say.

"So, Hacker," Williams said as we waited for the group ahead of us to clear the way on the first tee. "What do you think, hundred a side? Birdies an extra twenty-five, eagles fifty?"

One of Hacker's Rules for Golf, developed over many years, is that the guy who proposes the bet has the most to lose. It's simple psychology, really. Jimmy Williams thought he was top dog at IBS. And he deserved to think that: he had won several PGA Tour events, including two majors, in his career. That got him bragging rights, certainly over little ole me.

But the Boz and I had suddenly leapt into the public glare. People were talking about us, how we did a golf tournament. They weren't talking about Jimmy Williams, except perhaps to contrast his usual style with our new, brash way of broadcasting golf. I'm sure that pissed him off a little. Maybe made him feel a touch insecure. I don't know. So he probably thought a good and thorough thrashing of me on the golf course would help restore the equilibrium, at least in his world.

Me? I could find no good reason to give a major crap about a match against Jimmy Williams. My reason for coming this brisk spring day was to familiarize myself with a golf course I had never played, so I could make some halfway intelligent comments about it when the PGA Championship was played here in another six weeks or so. Otherwise, I'd rather be at home in Boston's North End, taking my kid for a walk.

So I was really not all that interested in playing along with Jimmy's little swordfight scenario. I'd gladly sign an affidavit to the effect that he was a better golfer, and had a larger dick. No biggie for me.

"Whatever," I said.

The forecaddie told us the fairway was clear. Jimmy motioned at me to go first. "Tee is yours, Hack," he said. "For this hole, anyway."

I smiled, teed my ball and took a look down the fairway. The first hole at Hudson Links was a straightaway par four, a healthy 470 yards or so, playing downhill in the general direction of the river off in the distance. There was a nest of bunkers on the left side and another big one on the right, but the latter was way out of my range. I aimed at the right-side bunker and hit a nice controlled little draw that came back to the center, hit on the fairway and bounced away down the hill.

"Ach, laddie," Clyde Stewart said. "Ye hit that one jest like the bloody architect designed it!"

"Good shot, Hacker,' said Kelsey, who was waiting to hit from one of the more forward tee boxes.

Jimmy Williams was uncharacteristically silent. He was next to play, and he tried the opposite attack: he started his ball down the left and tried to cut it back to the center. But it didn't cut, and it dropped out of sight into one of the bunkers.

"Fuck," he said. "If I could find the bloody architect, I'd kick his sorry ass."

Clyde thought that was funny, and was chuckling when he hit his own tee shot. Kelsey followed and we were off. Kelsey and the forecaddie drove the carts and the three of us walked.

"It's lovely country up here," Stewart said. "Very ancient rock formations, millions of years old. And the river here runs as deep as anywhere along its length. If we were in Scotland, we'd call it the Firth of Hudson, even if there's no tidal flow way up here."

"How'd you meet Conrad Gold?" I asked.

"He was planning to build a fancy new club along the River Clyde west of Glasgow," Stewart said as we marched along the fairway. "I went to meet him for that job. But the finances fell through, as they often do, and the project came to naught. But we seemed to hit it off fair well, and he hired me to do a course in the south of France and then this one."

Kelsey hit her second—for which she needed a hybrid iron club—and Jimmy climbed down into the bunker for his second. He had about 170 yards left, but had to get over the front lip, which meant he'd probably have to lay up. He took a more lofted club and managed to get his ball to the front edge, just off the green.

Clyde hit his ball, then came over to where I was standing.

"He's a strange wee man, Conrad," he said. "But he knows the gawf. Knows what he wants as well. After I did the first routing here, on paper, he came and walked the ground with me. Naught but trees and weeds and brambles, but he could see the holes. Even with naught there, he understood. So he was tellin' me to move a green twenty feet left or add a tee box there. Quite impressive, really."

I pulled a seven-iron and made a nice relaxed swing. The ball flew down the hill and ended up hole high, about twenty feet to the left of the hole. It was just like on the practice tee—I had a good rhythm and, by not trying too hard to do anything, I hit the ball square on the clubface. Makes it an easy game.

Jimmy chipped up to five feet and, after I had missed my birdie, he sweated over his putt. But he made it, and did a little celebratory dance before plucking his ball out of the hole.

"Nice putt," I said. "Hope you can keep that stroke going."

"Keep your mouth off my game," he growled.

We played on in the breezy and cool morning. Clyde Stewart, despite his aversion to practice and warming up, played a very respectable game, especially around the greens, where he was deft with chipping and pitching, and ran in enough putts to keep most of the bogeys away. By the time we made the turn, he was two over, about the same score as Kelsey Jenkins, who was also playing good golf, save for the seventh hole which she doubled when she found herself trapped behind some trees. She birdied one of the par threes, after a lovely four-iron over a blue-black pond to about three feet.

There was a lot of pre-tournament construction going on in the background. Workers were laying plywood and block foundations, erecting metal scaffolding and installing long rows of aluminum bleachers. Later, others would wrap the scaffolds and bleachers in dark plastic to hide "the bones" and make the structures look neater. The workers mostly ignored us, save for a couple of cat whistles at Kelsey. She smiled at them and raised her middle finger in their general direction.

I was playing par golf, probably because I wasn't even thinking about my score. I had somehow stumbled upon a rhythm back on the practice tee, and I just kept hitting shots with that same relaxed, even, unhurried tempo. My drives found the fairways, my approach shots found the greens and I two-putted everything. I don't think I was ever in the rough or a bunker on the front side, and missed just one green, but even then was able to putt it from the fringe. Pretty ho-hum, although I was enjoying myself, but I put that down to the company. Clyde Stewart kept us all loose with his rambling tales of courses he loved, European players he knew and occasional stories about how Conrad Gold had made him move this green thirty feet further up a hill, or bring a water hazard closer to the edge of a green. It was interesting to talk about shot values and think about how the best pros in the world would play this course in six weeks.

But my steady and unexciting play was driving Jimmy Williams slightly crazy.

"Another goddam par," he said when I tapped in a ten-incher on the long ninth. "Do you ever make anything else?"

"Bob Jones used to say Old Man Par was the main opponent," I said, picking my ball out of the hole. "Not the other guy, not the course…just Old Man Par. Beat him and you win."

"You're supposed to beat him, not bore him to death," Williams said. He was one down for the front nine, after he had bogied the sixth.

The chef had set up a charcoal grill outside the clubhouse, and had a selection of burgers, fat sausages and assorted kinds of salad waiting for us. I was starved and loaded up.

Jimmy looked at me. "Aren't you worried about eating too much, throwing your game out of whack for the back nine?" he said.

I rummaged around in the cooler filled with ice and pulled out a bottle of beer, a locally brewed IPA. I popped the cap and took a long pull. Then I smiled at Jimmy.

"What, me worry?" I said. I heard Kelsey chortle.

We all heard the chop-chop of a helicopter approaching the club overhead. We all looked up and saw the bright gold fuselage with the dark tinted glass bubble at the front of what we assumed was one of Conrad Gold's corporate fleet of copters. This one slowed, circled a bit, then headed for a helipad on a grassy level just below the front facade of the clubhouse. It made a perfect soft landing, the engines gave out a final roar and then went silent, and we watched as the blades continued to go round and round. The side door slid open and the unmistakable bald head of Conrad Gold climbed out. He looked up the hill, saw us, and waved.

"That guy knows how to make an entrance, doesn't he?" Jimmy Williams said.

15

Gentlemen," Conrad Gold said, when he had climbed the hill up from the helipad and joined the group of us sitting around in our golf carts, munching on lunch. "I hope you left some food for me. I'm starved."

He went over to the barbecue and helped himself to a burger with all the fixings and a canned soft drink. He came back and sat down in the cart next to Kelsey. He nodded at her.

"I meant 'gentlemen' in the broadest sense," he said.

"No offense taken," she said. A woman who knows how to choose her battles.

"How have you found the course so far?" Conrad continued, as he chewed. "Think it will present a good test for the PGA?"

"Lots of elevation change," Van Collins said. "Every shot seemed uphill or down. Add in some May weather and they might have a hell of a time out here."

Gold nodded, wiping some mustard off his chin with a napkin. "True enough," he said. "The back nine is quite a bit flatter, as the holes are mostly down along the river. But there is water to be found on almost every hole, right Clyde?"

"Oh, aye, Mister Gold," the big Scotsman said. "Plenty o' places to get off the straight and narrow."

Gold looked at me.

"I enjoyed your, er, *unique* commentary the other week," he said. "Are you planning to continue with that? Or has the network asked you to tone it down?"

"Be kinda hard to tone down who I am," I said. "Probably holds true for Boz as well. No, Ben Oswald hasn't told either of us to change anything we're doing. So we'll probably keep doing it."

"I see," Gold said. "Well, like I said, I found your banter quite amusing. At least it's different."

"That's me," I said. "Mister Different."

"You guys finished?" Jimmy Williams chimed in, probably upset that no one was talking about him. "I'm ready to hit the back nine."

"Well, let's get to it, then" Collins said. "You gentlemen ready?" He didn't apologize to Kelsey for his gender assumption.

Most of us were, so the first group headed to the tenth tee. Kelsey went inside the clubhouse to visit the ladies room. The rest of us went to the tee to watch. Clyde Stewart announced he was going to join the first group, with Van Collins, so he could expiate on the golf course with him for a change. Conrad Gold announced he would ride back and forth between groups.

The tenth was a long par five, running from virtually the back porch of the clubhouse all the way down to the Hudson River. Like a ski jump, the fairway descended down a gentle slope, dropped over a lip and fell even more steeply for fifty downhill yards or so, and then flattened out and continued on in a straight line for another two hundred yards. If you could poke it out there around 300 yards, your ball would carry over the lip and keep running for another hundred. To the right, a rocky cliff crumbled down in a boulder-filled scree almost to the edge of the fairway, while a stand of brushy forest bordered the left side. There were imaginative nests of bunkers dropped in here and there, just where one's shots might land. I looked at the scorecard and noticed that there was a pond situated right behind the green. Something to think about if you decided to go for the green in two with a fairway metal. Those are notoriously hard to stop, especially coming downhill and downwind, so you'd have the thought, in the back of your mind, of the ball running over the green and into the pond.

Clyde Stewart saw me looking at the card and smiled at me.

"I was thinkin' o' the last hole at Gleneagles Kings," he said to me. "Long, flowin' down the brae. But I thought addin' that wee pond would put the fear o' Old Nick in some of them."

"Does the green slope front to back?" I asked.

"Oh, aye, that it does," he said with a grin.

"You're a sadistic bastard," I said.

"Aye, that I am," he said. "I should be ashamed. But, strangely, I am not."

The first group teed off and headed down the fairway, Clyde in tow. Somebody had magically produced a gold-painted golf cart with a fake Rolls Royce nose on it, luxury seating and wraparound plastic windows for Conrad Gold, and he climbed in and immediately called someone on his cellphone. There was a little practice putting green just behind the tee box, and I went over and stroked a few putts while we waited for the fairway to clear.

There were several piles of building materials stacked next to the putting green, and someone had spray painted a bright green line along the edge to indicate where the stands would begin. It looked like the practice green would be covered up by the bleachers for the tournament.

Jimmy Williams was strangely quiet during all this. I guess he was still mad about being one down for the front nine, which meant I was up a hundred. He was chatting quietly with our forecaddie.

"OK, Hack," he called finally when the group ahead had cleared out of the way. "Let's get it on."

I still had the honor, so I aimed my driver down the right edge of the fairway, put today's relaxed and easy swing on it and watched as the ball drew back nicely to the middle. It hit and rolled but stayed on our side of the ski jump lip.

Jimmy was next, and he teed his ball a little higher than normal and put a Godzilla of a swing on it, barely managing to stay in his shoes and not fall on his face. His ball shot down the fairway, high and far, bounced twice and disappeared over the lip, no doubt running for miles.

"Hope you didn't hit Van," I said. "He wouldn't like that."

"Aw, screw him and his golden voice," Jimmy said, hitching up his pants like Arnie used to do. "I got all of that one."

Kelsey, from the middle tees, hit her drive down the middle and we set off.

I played conservatively on my next shot, hitting an easy four-iron to a little over a hundred yards short of the green. I didn't think I could get a three-wood to the green anyway, and I didn't want to take on Clyde's devilish risk-and-reward trap on the green. I figured I could put a lot of spin on a wedge for my third and hopefully get the ball close to the hole.

Kelsey followed my lead and laid up on the long hole, but Jimmy had about 260 yards left on a slight downhill lie and he was going for it, tossing caution to the winds. The forecaddie told him about the front-to-back slope of the green, but he was undeterred.

"I didn't come all the way up here to lay it up," he muttered, teeth clenched. He took out his fairway metal club, took aim and let it rip. Because of the downhill lie, the ball came out hot and low, screaming toward the green, where the group ahead was still putting out.

Three of us yelled "Fore!" and we watched as the guys on the green all ducked and covered and then watched as Jimmy's ball landed about ten yards in front of the green, bounded up onto the green and began running. And running. And running. It shot past the hole and disappeared off the back edge, into the water. Van Collins gave us the over-and-in sign.

"You have got to be kidding me," Jimmy said, moaning a little. "I just hit two of the greatest shots of my life and I'm in the water! What kind of crappy golf is that?"

"I'll note your displeasure when Mister Stewart's next payment is due," Conrad Gold said from his wrapped-in-plexiglass golf car.

We all laughed, but I could tell by the dangerous shade of red that was gathering on Jimmy's neck that he was pretty pissed. And likely wounded. It'd be hard for him to get himself back in the match now, unless I totally crashed and burned.

I hit a nice three-quarters sand wedge and watched the ball bounce twice and sit down hard, about ten feet to the left. Possible birdie, easy par. Life was good.

"Old Man goddam Par," Jimmy muttered, more to himself, and stalked away toward the green.

When we reached the last four holes, I was three-up on Jimmy who was now bitching and moaning about every shot.

I'd say he was toast, but I knew that Clyde Stewart had likely designed the last four holes to be the concluding crescendo to his golf course, the final test of nerve and skill where the champion would be determined.

Fifteen was a short little dogleg left filled with all kinds of interesting trouble. The fairway ran level from the elevated tee for about 270 yards and then turned sharply to the left and downhill for a hundred yards or so. But there was a narrow creek running across the fairway at the turn, and that creek fed into a marshy, reed-filled pond to the left of the green. The creek bed was filled with rocks and brush and bushy grass to make it visible from the tee.

It was a classic risk/reward kind of hole. If you were feeling your oats, you could try to drive the green, even though you'd need a controlled draw around the corner, but not too much of a draw or the marshy pond would come into play. Or, you could lay up off the tee with a mid-iron, get as close to the rocky creek as you dared, and then feather a wedge down the hill to the green, which sat atop a ten-foot ledge over the river's edge. There was a small but deep little bunker right in front, adding yet another thing to think about.

I was still in my effortless zone, so I pulled out a five-iron and laid it out there short of the creek. I wasn't chasing someone to win the PGA Championship, so making a four on this hole would be fine with me. And a three was always possible.

Jimmy Williams, on the other hand, was leaving nothing in the bag. He consulted with the forecaddie on a good line, then took his driver and smashed it down the hill and around the corner to the left. We lost sight of it once it turned the corner.

"Whaddya think?" Jimmy asked as it flew out of sight.

"Won't know till we get down there," the caddie said. "But I think the angle was good. You should be dry."

"Long as I can make a bird," he said, teeth clenched.

Kelsey also played the percentages and laid up. When we got down to the corner, we all had good views of the green below us. I couldn't see Jimmy's ball anywhere, and he and the forecaddie scurried down to look for it, probably thinking his day's tip depended on him finding it on dry land.

I hit a nice wedge to about ten feet, and Kelsey was also on in regulation. When we arrived at the green, Jimmy was standing in ankle-deep rough about twenty yards short and right of the putting surface.

"I wanted to let that rough grow between now and the tournament," Gold said, getting out of his cart to watch us play. "I'd love to see it a foot high, but the tournament staff from the PGA will probably make us cut it back to six or seven inches."

Jimmy had his sixty degree wedge out and tried an explosion shot to knock his ball onto the green. But the grass grabbed the club, its speed died and the ball plopped forward maybe five yards and nestled down in the deep stuff again.

He let out a bellow of frustration, took a couple steps forward, took a quick stance and just made an angry hotheaded slash at the ball. This time, he caught it cleanly and we all watched as his white ball arched against the deep blue afternoon sky before dropping, with a nice splash, into the Hudson River.

Jimmy looked like he wanted to send his wedge in swimming after it, but, though he reared back, he managed to control himself and stopped. Then he shook his head, looked up at us and smiled.

"I believe my goose has been cooked," he said.

"Shit happens, Jimmy," Kelsey said, going over to him and giving him a little hug. "We love you anyway."

When we walked over to the sixteenth tee, set on the riverbank, we found a short dark man in slacks and a windbreaker standing there, looking intently down the fairway. Standing next to the man was a small black-and-white border collie who was completely fixated on what his master was looking at. I followed the man's gaze and saw a gaggle of Canada geese down the fairway. They were poking their beaks into the turf grass, looking for something to eat.

Conrad Gold came up beside me.

"Watch this," he said, a smile on his face.

The man raised his hand in the air. The dog went on point, quivering in concentration, every fiber of its body straining to be let free. The man dropped his hand and simultaneously gave out a low whistle.

The dog took off as if shot, bulleting its way down the fairway. The geese saw him coming a long way away and by the time he reached the spot where they had been foraging, they had long since taken flight, honking in displeasure as they circled out over the Hudson River. The dog made a couple of circles, sniffing the ground, then turned and began to trot back towards us.

"Folks, this is Willie McLeod," Gold said. "Finest dog trainer in Dutchess County and the man who keeps my fairways clear of goose crap."

"Not me, Mister Gold," Willie said, "It's Bullet that does the work."

Bullet returned to his master's side, and was rewarded with a bit of a dog cookie. His tail wagged furiously while he scarfed it down, then he sat attentively by Willie's side and looked at us, head cocked, deciding whether we were worth chasing.

"You know, I wondered how you kept the geese off the course here," Kelsey said. "They must love this place."

"It's a big problem with course owners up here," Gold said. "The numbers in the Canada geese population have been rising for several decades now. The number of natural predators is down and the environmental people won't let us shoot them, which would be fast and effective. So I just get Willie and Bullet to do goose patrol and so far it's been pretty effective."

"We were up on seven and eight a while ago," Willie said. "Canada geese are herbivores and they pretty much love anything they find growing. So we gotta keep after them, keep them moving along."

We turned back to golf. Sixteen was a good long par four along the river. The tee had been built atop a concrete platform sticking out into the water, and the tee shot called for the players to thread the needle between a nest of sand on the right, and the river all down the left. The second shot was similar, but this time the green had been installed sticking out into the water. The only strategy that would work on this hole was two straight shots. On a Sunday afternoon in the PGA Championship, executing those two shots with all the pressure riding would be an interesting test of one's fortitude.

"Did you have any trouble getting approval for that platform where the green is?" I asked Gold, standing next to me. "It doesn't look like a land form known to nature."

"Trouble?" he said with a chuckle that didn't sound like a happy noise. "Only about three years of litigation with the Audubon Society, the Save the River crowd and I think some native American tribes. I don't know if you'd call all of that 'trouble.'"

"So how'd you convince them to let you do it?"

"We agreed to call it a 'dock,' which was permitted under the law," he said. "Then I made a donation of a few million dollars and transferred title of a buffer zone for a park that runs from the river just north of eighteen all the way up to the top of Hannerty's Bluff up there…" He nodded at the tall, rocky hill that rose to the east above the river. You gotta do stuff like that these days to get anything built."

Naturally, I made my first bogey of the day, driving into the next of bunkers on the right. I had to lay up coming out, lofted a wedge onto the small and rolling green and got down in two. Jimmy made a regulation par. I noticed his swing was slower and more relaxed now that our match was pretty much over. As a result, he drove it down the middle of the fairway and rifled a mid-iron right at the flag.

Seventeen was Clyde Stewart's variation on the island green concept. The green was bounded by the river on three sides, and the entrance was defined by a visually arresting series of tall boulders that looked like they had rolled down the hillside and come to rest on the water's edge.

"Did you move those there?" I asked Gold, who laughed.

"I did not," he said. "It was the power of a receding glacier approximately 20,000 years ago which dropped them there. I liked the idea of having to hit over them. Even though they really don't come into play for any normal shot into this green."

The hole played about 190 yards from our tees, and Jimmy hit a four-iron into the breeze. It was a lovely shot and the ball tracked the flag all the way. The rest of us followed his lead and we all made par on the hole.

The last hole at Gold's Hudson Links was a monster par-five back towards the clubhouse visible up on the bluff.

Again, the river was in play the entire length of the hole, lurking there on the left as we played north. Today the wind was against us every inch of the way, so it took all of us three long shots to get home. I hit driver, three-wood and eight-iron, and my approach just crawled onto the front edge of the green, leaving me a long putt to the back where the pin was.

"This is an unusual northerly wind today," Gold said as we stood on the green and looked back down the fairway. "Usually, it's helping a bit out of the southwest. That means someone behind a shot or two would be tempted to give it a go trying to get home in two. That last little inlet in front of the green might well get a lot of action in the PGA."

"It's a nice piece of work," Jimmy said, clapping Conrad on the back. "There's some holes out there that'll give the boys fits."

"I hope so," Gold said.

We made our way back up to the clubhouse and unpacked the carts. Heading into the locker room, Jimmy handed me some folded bills.

"Three hundred," he said. "Well played."

I held up my hand. "Why don't you keep it?" I said. "We'll play again, and the outcome will probably be quite different. Let's keep a running total and at the end of the season, we'll take the crew out to dinner or something. Deal?"

He paused, thinking. Then he smiled.

"Good idea, Hacks," he said. "I'll get your ass next time for sure."

"Yeah," I said, "You probably will."

16

We met for dinner that night in the "Chairman's Room," a private dining room centered by a large round table that seated 20. There was a fire burning cheerfully in a granite hearth and the room was paneled in deep stained mahogany with brass sconces and a deep green carpet.

We only took up about twelve of the place settings, but Conrad Gold took his place at the center, in the largest black leather chair, and the rest of us spread out around him on both sides. We had enjoyed cocktails and hors d'oeuvres downstairs in the cocktail lounge before Gold led us up the dramatic winding staircase to his private dining room lair on the second floor.

Two waiters in starched white waistcoats poured the wine and the club's head chef, dressed in his pristine white chef's coat, black-checked pants and wearing a tall toque, came in and announced the evening's menu.

"We are starting tonight with some bacon-wrapped seared Long Island scallops in a lemon-sage reduction, and some pork pot stickers in a soy and orange sauce, followed by your choice of roast duckling, rack of lamb or steak Diane, flambeed to order with a mustard garlic aioli sauce," he told us.

"Desserts to follow so please leave some room!" He bowed and returned to his kitchen.

Gold held up his wine glass.

"Thank you, ladies and gentlemen, for coming today," he said. "I hope you enjoyed the golf course. We are looking forward to seeing what the world's best golfers can do with it in a few weeks. *Salude!*"

We drank. Van Collins, our lead broadcaster, was our unofficial spokesperson, and we let him respond.

"Thank you, Conrad," he said, nodding at our host. "I think we all learned a great deal today. I know I appreciated having Clyde Stewart on hand to explain some of the architectural strategies that went into the course design. But thank you for having us here today. If I can ask a question, when did you first think that this course was worthy of holding one of the world's major championships?"

Conrad Gold smiled. The light from the chandelier above the table reflected off his bald pate, which glistened.

"I would say it was when I told Jack Cunningham, who was then the president of the PGA of America, that I would guarantee his organization twenty-five million dollars if they awarded the PGA Championship to this course," he said. "Jack just nodded at that, didn't gasp, didn't frown, and that's when I knew we'd get the tournament."

The rest of us looked at each other, with more than one or two raised eyebrows. We all knew, of course, that the PGA of America was pretty much an organization for sale. It is, after all, the trade organization of golf professionals…the ones who work at country clubs and municipal daily fee courses alike, selling shirts, balls, clubs and tee times. Giving lessons to hackers and running the annual Member-Guest.

Once upon a time, the PGA of America had also op-erated the professional golf tour, but by the end of the 1960s it was obvious to everyone that the Tour needed professional management. And independence. The club pros from the PGA of America just didn't have the expertise in sports marketing or management to run a major competitive sports league.

So the PGA Tour had branched off and become the worldwide moneymaking behemoth it was today. They left the PGA of America with two small bones: the annual PGA Championship and the biannual Ryder Cup Matches. At the time of the split, nobody gave much thought to the Ryder Cup's future potential. Up until the late 1960s, the USA side always won the event, on both sides of the Atlantic, usually by huge margins. It wasn't much of a sporting spectacle…it was mostly boring.

And the PGA Championship was still trying to find its footing as one of golf's four major events. It had originally been contested in match play, the only major in that format, which made it interesting and different from the Masters and the two Opens. But the PGA of America decided to change the tournament over to stroke play, like the others, because it believed that the all-important TV money would disappear if they couldn't promise a dramatic Sunday afternoon show-down featuring the best players. In match play, there's always a chance that Joe Nobody and Fred Whodat could ride a hot streak into the finals amid the sounds of TVs clicking off all across the fruited plain.

The PGA of America got lucky with the Ryder Cup. The European Tour took off in the 1970s and '80s, and it was Jack Nicklaus who suggested to Lord Acton that his Great Britain and Ireland team be expanded to include all the good new players from Germany (Bernhard Langer), Spain (Seve

Ballesteros) and elsewhere into a new Team Europe. When the feisty Euros began actually winning against the once-dominant USA team, the Ryder Cup took off as one of the great spectacles of sport and began making the PGA of America buckets of money.

The PGA Championship used to follow the U.S. Open around the same basic rota of famous old clubs: Winged Foot, Oak Hill, Baltusrol, Hazeltine. But they had to talk those clubs into extending invitations: the tournament tied up the course in the middle of summer and while the PGA got the TV revenue, the clubs got little other than a little more notoriety. Nobody was happy.

So the PGA of America went in a new direction: they pretty much announced they were for sale. They began awarding their major event to newer courses around the country. Newer courses which were far more willing to pay big fees to get the national attention the PGA Championship could bring.

One of the first was Shoal Creek in Birmingham, Alabama, a hellish place to play a golf tournament in the heat of August. But the developer of that real estate development with a golf course got the right money in the right pockets and landed the event in 1984. (Of course, the PGA of America got a little more than they bargained for when it became known that Shoal Creek didn't have any members of color. They quickly found a suitable local gent to draft into the club and life and the tournament went on.) A few years later, the PGA was played at Oak Tree in Edmond, Oklahoma, a course owned by a couple of PGA of America members who were building a network of clubs and real estate around the country. Again, serious money changed hands.

That inspired the organization, after a few years of selling its major championship to the highest bidder, to begin bidding itself. The PGA of America began investing in building residential real estate projects with championship golf… and then arranged for those courses to host the PGA Championship. Valhalla in Kentucky, owned in part by the PGA, landed two PGA Championships. It was good business, albeit a little cynical.

And here was Conrad Gold, proprietor of a worldwide chain of upscale golf developments, telling us that he had bid, and won, a major tournament for the price of $25 million. None of us at the table were surprised, except maybe at the price tag. Some of my colleagues might have been gobsmacked; I thought it was pretty low.

"Is that the going price of the PGA Championship these days?" I asked.

Gold looked at me with a smile. "I have no idea," he said. "That was the number I threw out there, and they accepted. Make of that what you will. I'll make make some of it back on my share of the concessions and ticket sales."

The waiters began bringing out the food, and we all concentrated on eating for a while.

"How many members do you have here now?" Jimmy Williams asked.

"I think we're up close to 450," Gold said. "I can get you the exact number. Two-thirds are New York metro residents. The rest are what we call national members. They have official domiciles outside the metro area. And we have a few dozen international members as well, most of them reciprocal members from other Gold Clubs around the world."

He paused as the main courses were brought in.

"We have twenty-five guest rooms on this floor for members who wish to spend the night," he continued. "And our long-term plan calls for construction of some villas along the riverfront. Some of those will be sold to members, but the club will retain title to a handful so that members can stay there if they wish. I think some of you are planning to spend the night with us, yes?"

Several of us murmured our assent. I was planning to spend the night in luxury before heading back to Boston's North End and DJ's diaper duty.

"Who do you like for the PGA?" Kelsey asked. "I can't decide if length or shot-making will be key here."

"Hopefully both," Gold said, sipping some wine. "We'd like to think the course demands an all-around game. But I don't keep up with the Tour enough to tell you who I think is going to do well here. We'll have the usual field of stars from around the world, so I'm expecting it to be a good show."

Kenny Craig, the Swing Doctor, and Bill Fairfield, one of the tower announcers, began tossing names back and forth. We all had a fun fifteen minutes or so arguing our favorites and non-favorites. I think most of us at the table agreed that Tiger was officially past his use-by date. Which probably meant he was one of the favorites.

Another chef wheeled in the dessert cart when the plates had been cleared and we all demurred before capitulating and ordering up something chocolate, caked or, in my case, a big piece of strawberry rhubarb pie with a scoop of vanilla ice cream.

I was sitting next to Van Collins and I heard his phone go off. Almost simultaneously, the phones of Jimmy Williams, Kelsey Jenkins and Ken Craig began buzzing. I laughed.

"Breaking news," I said.

Van Collins excused himself and went out into the hall to answer his. The others ignored theirs, more interested in dessert. A minute or two later, Collins came back into the dining room. He looked shocked, blood drained from his face.

"Arnie Wasserman is dead," he announced gravely.

There were gasps around the table.

"What happened?" I asked.

"He was shot late this afternoon," Collins told us. "An apparent robbery or mugging. He was on the way home after work, stopped at a local market on the upper West Side and someone shot him in the head."

"They get the guy?"

"Not yet," Collins said. "Police are looking for the perp now."

"Holy crap," Kelsey said. "That's awful."

Conrad Gold looked confused.

"Did I know this Wasserman?" he asked.

"He was Ben Oswald's chief assistant," Collins told him. "He kept the production side moving. He seemed pretty indispensable. This is going to cause some big problems for us."

"Well," Gold said, "I'm sorry to hear about this. My condolences for your loss. Please tell Ben that if there's anything I can do, just let me know."

The dinner broke up. After news like that, talking about golf seemed pretty insignificant.

17

I called Mary Jane from my luxury suite. It had a big queen-size bed with a canopy, a seating section with a sofa and two chairs and a 48-inch flatscreen TV mounted on the wall, a small kitchenette with a fridge, microwave and coffee maker, a luxurious bathroom and a balcony overlooking the Hudson River valley. My balcony had a hot tub on one end, water bubbling away with wisps of steam rising into the chilly air of evening. Had I been there with Mary Jane and a bottle of chilled Taittinger's, I could have envisioned some fun possibilities. Alone, I dialed my phone, fully clothed and mostly sober.

"What's your opinion of hot tubs?" I asked when we connected.

"Generally good," she said, "Even though they have a reputation for spreading disease."

"How about chilled Taittinger's?"

"Again, good, although I've always preferred a good Dom Perignon. Why these interesting questions?"

"There's a hot tub on my balcony," I said. "I'm looking at it and was envisioning being in it with you."

"Aww," she said. "How sweet."

"My visions were more carnal than sweet, I think."

"I should certainly hope so," she said. "Did you win?"

"Win what?"

"I don't know…I assumed there was some kind of match today and that means someone won and someone lost. Which was it?"

"I guess I won," I said. "But he was into it more than I was. We just had a fabulous Conrad Gold dinner and then got some bad news."

"Oh, no …one of you had to pick up the tab?" she said. I could hear the hint of mischievousness in her voice.

"Ha ha," I said. "No, we found out that Arnie Wasserman was shot and killed this afternoon down in New York."

"Oh, no," she said. "Who was Arnie Wasserman and has anyone blamed you yet?"

"Not so far as I can tell," I said. "He was Ben Oswald's aide-de-camp. Or go-fer. He did all the dirty work."

"So, he was the Assassin's assassin?"

I smiled. "Pretty good," I said. "Yeah, he was."

"Well, from what you tell me about Oswald, that means there's probably a long list of potential suspects," she said. "Not including you, I hope."

"I think I'm off the hook," I said. "After all, I was here playing golf all afternoon. I've got witnesses to the witnesses of my alibi."

"Thank goodness for that," she said. "So who killed him, if it wasn't you?"

"They think it was a mugger," I said. "Still haven't caught the guy. Seems to be one of those random Big City things. Kinda tragic."

"Well, I'm sorry to hear it," Mary Jane said. "Is this going to affect your job in any way?"

"Don't think so," I said. "I'm sure IBS will have someone new ready to insert into place in a day or two. Like Conrad said at dinner a while ago, 'No one is indispensable.'"

"Conrad?"

"Conrad Gold," I said. "He owns this place. Came up to have dinner with us."

"I can't believe you are sitting around talking with someone like Conrad Gold," Mary Jane said. "I mean, I see him on television all the time. He's always on one of the gossip shows. Stepping out with some scrumptious starlet or other. And he's always on the front page of the National Enquirer."

"You read the National Enquirer?"

"Only waiting in line at the supermarket checkout," she said. "Don't think I've ever actually purchased one. Conrad Gold seems to be one of the tabloids' go-to guys."

"I'm beginning to think he uses them as much as they seem to use him," I said. "He keeps his name in the public arena with his outrageous political comments and his dating habits. But that makes him famous for being famous, which I think he uses to his advantage in selling real estate at places like this. You know, if I buy a place at Conrad Gold's development, maybe there will be scrumptious starlets and other famous people hanging around. He actually strikes me as a pretty intelligent guy."

"Well, if he's turned dating scrumptious starlets into making millions of bucks, I guess one has to tip their hat," Mary Jane said. "Even though most of us non-starlets hate him."

"Once you get to know him, he's not all that hate-able," I said.

"Whatever," she said. "I've got some tests to grade. When are you coming home?"

"I'll head home after breakfast," I said. "Should be there when you get home from work."

"Excellent," she said. "We have leftover tuna noodle casserole. I made a big batch tonight."

"I had roast duckling tonight, so that actually sounds pretty good," I said.

"Roast duckling with Conrad Gold," she said. "Are you beginning to see why so many of us hate the man?"

We rang off. I looked at the empty hot tub, bubbling away on my balcony. But I turned away, and instead got ready for bed. No Taittingers.

In the morning, before I went downstairs in search of breakfast, I put in a call to Delbert Connor of the Savannah PD. I was a little surprised when he picked up the call. It was just before 8 a.m.

"Ah, yes, Mister Hacker," he said when I identified myself, "The case of the dead golf announcer."

"Right," I said. "I was just wondering if you've been able to pinpoint a cause of death for Parker Long? I know you were running a battery of tests."

I heard him shuffling some papers around on his desk.

"Yes," he said, "Here it is. The preliminary coroner's report came in about three days ago. It shows that Mr. Long was electrocuted."

"How?"

"That particular data point is not clear at this moment," Connor said. "Our investigation continues."

"Of course it does," I said. "Do you have any theories at least? How it happened that an announcer on a live TV broadcast could suddenly find himself zapped into oblivion?"

He paused. "Is there a reason why you are asking?" he said.

"Besides the fact that Parker was a friend and a colleague?" I asked. I figured he wouldn't know that I really didn't know Parker Long that well at all.

"And a member of a national broadcast media operation," he said dryly. "Perhaps looking for a scoop that will let out the news of this case before we are ready to release any."

"Oh, that," I said. "Well, yeah, there's another reason."

"Thought there might be," he said.

"Another member of our broadcast crew was shot and killed yesterday in Manhattan," I said.

"I've heard New York is a dangerous place," Connor said. "But my condolences nevertheless. What happened?"

"Apparently he was confronted and shot on the street," I said. "Assailant unknown, at least as far as I know."

"Where did this happen?" Connor asked.

"Upper West Side," I said. "I heard it was in or near the Fairway Market on Broadway."

I heard him scribbling notes.

"I know a few of the guys in NYPD," he said. "I'll give them a call later this morning and see what I can learn."

"You think there's a connection?"

"You know the old saying," Connor said. "Once is happenstance, twice is coincidence, three times is enemy action. Except for one thing."

"You don't believe in coincidence."

"How did you know that?" he asked.

"You're a cop," I said. "No cop believes in coincidence. It's against your religion or something."

"Furthermore, I don't know exactly why my victim died, whether it was an accident, an act of God or a violent attack," he said. "So I don't know what kind of connection you think there might be between my incident and the one in

New York. But I'll call and ask. All I can do at this point."

"Right," I said. "I understand." I paused for a bit, thinking. "Did you ever figure out what that smell was? The burning smell? We both noticed it."

"I can only surmise that the burning smell was somehow related to the electrocution," he said. "I've sent all the electronics equipment we impounded up to the state crime lab in Atlanta. Those guys are pretty good, but it'll take another couple of weeks before we hear from them."

"OK," I said. "Will you call me when you learn something?"

"Probably not," he said.

"If I call you back, will you talk to me?"

"I'm a public servant," he said. "Our goal is to serve and protect."

I figured that was as good as I was going to get from Delbert, so I thanked him and hung up.

18

The following week, I took the train down to New York again. There was a memorial service for Arnie Wasserman, and all of us on the broadcast crew had been told to be there.

"You get your sorry ass down to the city, and that's an order," said Ben Oswald when he had called me. "I want the entire IBS golf team to be there without exception. If anyone doesn't show, the *Times* and all the media gossipers in this fucking town will wonder what the problem is. I don't need crap like that at a time like this. So get your ass down to New York. Understand?"

"Got it, boss," I said. "The cops have any leads on who might have done it?"

"Naw, they're pretty much worthless," Oswald said. "Ever since this mayor decided he wanted to run for president some day as the progressive's progressive, he's been cutting the force down, telling them what they can and can't do, and letting out half the population of the prison on Riker's Island. He thinks this will win him votes, but instead, the city is on the edge of collapsing into anarchy. If it gets much worse, Mayor Dumbshit won't be elected dogcatcher, much less president."

"Great," I said. "I've always wanted to be in New York when it collapses into anarchy. Guaranteed to be a good time."

"Shut up," Ben growled. "No excuses. Be there."

So I caught an early morning Acela at South Station and arrived in Manhattan just before lunchtime. And I was starving, because the dining car had run out of breakfast food. Actually, it had never had any, since the amazing incompetents at Amtrak failed to deliver any, so they had none to sell. I did manage to score a cup of probably the worst coffee I had ever attempted to drink, so I was not only hungry enough to dare to buy a hot dog from the first street vendor I saw on Sixth Avenue, but I almost went into the nearest Starbuck's in a desperate search for caffeine. Luckily, I had second thoughts on both counts.

I had time to kill before Wasserman's memorial service was scheduled, so I walked over to Tenth Avenue and caught an uptown bus, riding past huge swaths of a city that didn't give a crap that I was hungry. Eventually, Tenth turned into Amsterdam and I got off at 86th street and made my way to the Barney Greengrass deli. Inside, I found a spot at the counter, ordered coffee and a hot pastrami sandwich and was soon feeling almost myself again. They brought me a slice of cheesecake and another cup of coffee and let me sit there unmolested while I scanned a copy of the New York *Post*. That tabloid paper is easier to read at a counter than the broadsheet *Times*, and I always liked the *Post's* golf writer better than the stuck-up asshole who worked for the *Times*. Nobody challenged my choice of newspapers.

Finally, it was time to make my way over to the B'nai Jeshurun synagogue, which occupied most of a block between Broadway and West End Avenue in an eye-catching and somewhat ironic Moorish-influenced facade with an impressive central arch over the front door. Inside, the main sanctuary was even more elaborate, with a magnificent decorated wall, a bank of stained glass windows on one side sending in some purplish light, and a dark ceiling overhead twinkling with faux stars.

Some of the other IBS people had arrived and taken chairs in the sanctuary. Because of the Jewish tradition, they had already had the official funeral for Arnie Wasserman, so for today's memorial service there was just a large framed photograph of him on a gold easel. In the picture he was smiling and, as usual, impeccably dressed. Alas, poor Arnie, I didn't know thee at all.

Standing at the back of the sanctuary, taking this all in, I saw Van Collins and Jimmy Williams lead a procession of my colleagues from the broadcast booth down the central aisle. An usher handed me a program for the service and a yarmulke, and I fell in with them. Then the Boz slipped in next to me. He gave me a wink and a smile.

"Yom Kippur," he said, in a whispered voice.

"I think you mean 'Shalom,'" I said. "Or maybe 'Gut Shabbes.'"

He just shrugged. I guess Yom Kippur is the only Jewish word they learn out there in San Angelo, Texas.

We took our seats. Kelsey Jenkins sat on my other side. There were about sixty people in attendance. A side door behind the altar opened and the rabbi came out, leading a procession of about six people, led by what looked like Arnie's parents. His Mom was weeping softly, dabbling at her eyes with a tissue.

"Those are the mourners," Kelsey leaned over and whispered to me. "Immediate family."

The family took up chairs in the front row and the service began. The rabbi began reading prayers, speaking in Yiddish, which the program told me were taken from the Psalms. Of course, not knowing the language, whatever comforting message they contained went right over my head, but I consoled myself by thinking that these words, or ones like them, had been spoken in such sorrowful situations for literally thousands of years.

After the prayers had been read, the rabbi began a eulogy, speaking this time in English. He told us Arnie had been a member of the congregation at this synagogue since he was a boy, and while the adult Arnie wasn't a regular at services, the rabbi knew that he was a faithful son of Israel. Arnie's Mom and dad put their heads together and wept silently.

When he finished his remarks, the rabbi paused, and said "It is a bit unusual, but one of Arnie's closest colleagues has asked if he might speak a word or two." He nodded in our direction, and Ben Oswald stood, his kippah pinned against his frizzy afro hair.

Ben walked up to the dais, took a sheet of paper out of his suitcoat pocket and turned to look at us.

"Arnie Wasserman worked for me," he began. "I hired him eleven years ago, right out of NYU. I hired him because he was smart as hell, sharp as a tack and took no crap from anyone, including me. Looking back now, I think I hired him because he reminded me of me."

We all tittered.

"I can't believe he's gone," Ben continued, voice wavering a little. "Things like this—" he waved a hand at the memorial photo, the grieving family and the people gathered around—"...tend to argue against the existence of a loving and caring God. But this is probably not the time or the place to have that argument." He turned and nodded at the rabbi.

"I just wanted to say that I loved the guy," he said. "We've been through a lot over these years. We had some fun. We had some fights. If I did something stupid, and I do that a lot, Arnie would tell me so. And I would listen. Because he knew right from wrong. He understood people better than I ever will. He was a good man. And I'll miss him."

The last sentence was spoken in a husky whisper, and he could say no more. He went back to his chair and sat down.

The service ended soon after. A few more people told us stories about Arnie. There were some more prayers and then the rabbi announced we were dismissed with a final blessing.

I followed my colleagues out of the synagogue and we stood on the sidewalk outside. There were two men waiting for us, dressed in suits. They looked a lot like cops. Because that's what they were.

One of them, forties, slightly overweight, thinning hair, went up to speak to Ben Oswald, who seemed to recognize the guy and shook his hand. The cop whispered something in Ben's ear and he nodded.

"OK people," Ben said, speaking to all of us from IBS, "This is Lieutenant Jefferies from the NYPD homicide squad. He wants to talk to some of you about Arnie. I've invited him back to the office where we can find a place to sit down. Lt. Jefferies and his assistant—" he paused and looked at the other cop who announced his name, Bob Delacroix— "...will be doing some routine interviews. Please cooperate with them the best you can. We all want to help them find the guy who did this. OK?"

We all murmured agreement. Ben hailed a passing cab and jumped in.

An hour or so later, I was sitting in a conference room with the other members of the announcers crew. I listened as they reminisced about Arnie Wasserman.

"Took me a while to warm up to Arnie, if you wanna know the truth," said Jimmy Williams. "I could never figure out who he represented. I mean, I knew he worked for Ben. But it always seemed like he was also tight with the suits on the 44th floor, y'know? I was never sure if he was asking me to do something because Ben wanted it done, or because the head of IBS did. Or if anything I told him would go no further than Ben, or shoot right to the top. Made me a little uncomfortable."

"The man is always the man," said Van Collins in his stentorian baritone. "People like Ben Oswald and Arnie Wasserman always pretend to be your best friend. But they get paid by IBS. That means they're always IBS' best friend, not yours. Good to remember that."

"Sounds like the voice of long experience," I said. Van looked at me and nodded.

Kenny Craig, the Swing Doctor, was drumming his fingers on the tabletop. "Did any of you guys hear any talk about Parker Long getting axed?" he said. "I mean, before he died."

There were muted gasps of disbelief around the room.

"Where did you hear that?" asked Kelsey Jenkins.

"I had a call the week before Savannah from Parker's wife," he said. "She told me Parker had heard from his agent, and it upset him no end. He wouldn't tell her what he said, but he had told his wife about a conversation he had overheard a year earlier, when he heard Ben talking to someone at IBS about possible personnel changes."

"There's a lot of assumptions in that scenario," Kelsey said. "Could have been something completely different. Van, you hear of anything like that?"

Van Collins sat quietly for a moment, hands folded calmly in his lap.

"You all know that there are things happening in the industry, right?" he started. He looked around at everyone, and most of them were nodding. "The TV contracts between the PGA Tour and all the networks are up for renewal. Nobody knows whats going to happen. Disney is supposed to be making a big play—that means ESPN and all its sub-networks. CBS, NBC and Golf Channel …Fox and its USGA contract … all of this is under consideration and the big money boys are slugging it out right now."

"Yeah, so what?" Jimmy said impatiently. "What does that have to do with us, or with Parker Long?"

"So," Van continued, "IBS is the weakest sister of the bunch. There's talk that we may get shut out of golf entirely. There's also talk that we may be in line to take over someone else's share. So IBS has to demonstrate that our golf programs are popular and attract a growing audience. And *that* means that every aspect of our operation is under a microscope. From the talent in the booth right down to the lowest technician … If someone or something is not performing at peak efficiency, out it goes."

"So they *were* thinking of canning Parker," Kelsey said, aghast. "My God. How long had he been with the network?"

"Twenty-two years," Van said. "He started with me doing college football and migrated over to golf shortly after. Been a mainstay. But mainstays can get old and stale, and I suspect the upstairs suits thought it might be pasture time."

"Pasture time?" I said.

"As in, put out to," Van smiled at me. "Look, they want a younger, more diverse audience, like they had when Tiger was in his prime. I loved Parker Long like everyone else in this room, but he did not attract the younger and more diverse audience the suits are looking for. It's hard to hear, but none of us is immune. We all gotta get the axe sometime."

"You know what they say," I said, "The only things that are certain in life are death and axes."

That made Boz laugh out loud, and the mood in the room brightened a bit.

19

The New York cops came into our conference room, and we all sat up straighter. Cops have that affect on most of us civilians.

The one we knew as Lt. Jefferies took the lead. His partner stood behind him and eyed us all. He was a tall black man with stooped shoulders and a large belly. He was losing his bristly black hair to male pattern baldness. He was dressed in a coat and tie, tie pulled down from his neck, collar open. But despite his shabby appearance, the black cop had those bright, ever-alert cop eyes, which darted around the room, taking us in one at a time, sizing us up, making educated guesses about who or what we were. I smiled at him.

"OK," said Jefferies, "Detective Delacroix here is going to conduct interviews with each of you. Nobody in this room is considered to be a suspect in the death of Mr. Wasserman. But we need a little more background about him and how he interacted with his co-workers here at IBS. Even the most insignificant detail might be important, so I urge you to speak freely with the detective. Questions?"

"You think he was killed by someone at IBS?" I asked.

Jefferies turned to look at me.

"Why do you ask?" he said.

"You said you wanted to know about how he interacted with co-workers at IBS," I said. "Does that mean you think one of us killed him? Jealousy, rage or spite?"

"What is your name?" Jefferies said.

"Hacker," I said. "Correspondent and host of Hacker's History segment."

"Ah," Jefferies said. "I believe Mr. Oswald mentioned your name. Warned me about you. Along with someone named Bosworth?"

"Yo," said the Boz, raising his hand. "Guilty as charged."

"To answer your question, Mr. Hacker," Jefferies said. "We don't know who shot Mr. Wasserman. "That's why we want to speak with all of you. From these conversations, we hope some leads will develop."

"Got it," I said. "So I probably don't need to hire my good pal Al Dershowitz for this interview."

"I wouldn't think so," Jefferies said, "But that is entirely up to you."

"I'll wing it," I said.

"Brave man," he said, "Detective Delacroix is one of the department's best interviewers. If you've got a deep dark secret, he'll find out what it is."

"Oh, crap," I said. "It's the jaywalking, isn't it? I knew when I cut across Amsterdam that someone was watching."

Jefferies decided that our little repartee had gone quite far enough. He turned at nodded at Delacroix and left the room. The other cop pulled out a chair, sat down, and took a black notebook out of his suit coat pocket and a ballpoint pen from his shirt.

"Who worked with Wasserman the longest?" he asked.

"Probably me," Van said. "Going on eleven years now."

They started talking. I got up and went over to the credenza standing on the far wall and grabbed a bottle of water. The Boz came over and did the same.

"You really know Dershowitz?" he asked. "I see him on the news all the time."

"Naw," I shook my head. "Just dickin' with the guy."

We went back and sat down.

"How about you, Mr. Hacker?" the cop said, turning to look at me. "When did you first meet Mr. Wasserman?"

"Couple of months ago," I said. "In a meeting room not unlike this one."

"Impressions?"

"He was a nice dresser," I said. "Expensive clothes. Looked like good labels. Nothing cheap."

"That's true," Kelsey Jenkins was nodding. "He was always well turned out."

"OK," Delacroix said, jotting down notes in his book. "Snappy dresser. What else?"

"He was Ben's right-hand-man," I said. "Ben wanted something done, he turned to Arnie to do it."

"Such as?"

"When I was here that day, he and Oswald were talking about some problem, and Arnie was making notes in his expensive leather notebook. I assumed he was going to do what Oswald wanted."

"And that was?"

"Oh, I dunno," I said. "They were talking about a technical issue, a problem that wasn't getting solved. Oswald said something about replacing the person who seemed at fault, and Arnie wrote that down in his notebook."

"Who was that?"

"A kid named Digby Allen," I said. "He's on the technical crew."

"I know him," Jimmy Williams piped in. "Strange little dude, but he knows everything about our equipment."

"Strange, how?" the cop asked.

"Oh, you know…he's a little socially awkward, I guess," Jimmy said. "Kinda nerdy." He paused. "No, *very* nerdy. But Jeez, you got something that ain't working, Digby'll get it fixed in a hurry."

"So why did Oswald want to replace him?" Delacroix said.

"Good question," Jimmy said.

"There had been a problem with a piece of equipment," I said. "It broke down or didn't work right about five times. It was Digby's job to make sure it worked, but the company which provided that equipment hadn't done anything to fix the problem, and Digby kept getting blamed."

"I see," the cop said. "Does this Digby person still work for IBS?"

"Gee, I think so," Jimmy said. "I saw him in Savannah."

"Yeah," I said. "I helped him, umm, deal with the problem and I think it got cleared up."

"How'd you do that, Hack?" Jimmy was confused.

I smiled. "We called the supplier and told them to fix the problem, or else."

"Why would they do what you told them?" Jimmy pressed.

"Well, they might have thought they were talking to Ben Oswald," I said. "There was some talk of things being shoved into someone's colon."

Everyone sitting around the table chuckled, except Det. Delacroix.

"You're a piece of work, Hack, that's for sure," Jimmy said, shaking his head.

Delacroix stayed for another thirty minutes or so, asking more questions. He got most of the same kinds of answers: everyone knew Arnie a little, but mostly professionally. And nobody was close to him. He was management. The Man, as Van Collins called him.

The detective finally snapped his notebook shut and stood up.

"Can you tell us anything about the crime?" I asked. "How it happened?"

He shrugged. "It was about five-thirty in the afternoon," he said. "Mr. Wasserman had just picked up a few things at the grocery store on Broadway and was walking south, in the direction of his apartment. He lived on West 71st, down past West End Avenue. Somebody came up behind him and put a bullet in his head."

"No witnesses?" I said. "On Broadway in broad daylight?"

"Oh, crap no …we've got plenty of people who saw it," he said. "But nobody could come up with a definitive description. Which is more than a little strange. All we got is that it was a white man, about five-ten, wearing a blue parka or jacket."

"No security cameras?" I asked.

Delacroix smiled. "That only happens on TV," he said. "The grocery store has sidewalk cameras covering the entrance and pointing in both directions, and we saw the victim leaving the store, but he was just out of reach of the video coverage area when the incident occurred. We got nothing on film."

"Hmm," I said, "That's interesting. Where did the shooter go?"

"He walked south about twenty yards, turned the corner on 73rd Street and disappeared," Delacroix said.

"Maybe it was a ghost," Kelsey said.

"Be as good a guess as any we've got right at the moment," he said.

"You know we had another incident a few weeks ago," Van Collins said. "We lost one of our colleagues, Parker Long down in Savannah. During a broadcast."

"Yeah," Delacroix said. "Oswald told us about that. And I've had a call from someone down in Savannah. Haven't had time to call him back yet."

"So you won't think the two deaths are connected?" I said.

"No indication of any connection at this point," he said.

He nodded at all of us and left.

"They oughta go talk to Jennifer Long," Kelsey said. "Find out if it was true that IBS was going to let Parker go. It might be important."

"Do you know her?" I asked.

Kelsey nodded. "Yup," she said. She held up her phone. "In fact, I was going to call her while I was here in the city and see if she wanted to get together."

"She lives in New York?" I said.

"Parker was born in Manhattan," Van Collins said. "The wife had a good job in the insurance business. Lifelong city people."

I looked at Kelsey. "Why don't you call her?" I said. "See if she's up for some company. We'll go ask her ourselves."

"Isn't that messing with police business?" Kelsey said.

"You heard Delacroix," I said. "They don't think there's a connection between the two deaths. So, no. It would just be a couple of Parker's old colleagues dropping by to pay our respects."

"You're a sneaky one, Hacker," she said, but she dialed her phone and walked out into the hallway to talk.

"Well, I'm out of here," Van said. "I guess we'll see you fellas in Memphis next weekend."

The others got up and began to leave. I looked at the Boz.

"You heading home?" I said.

"Yeah, the missus wants me back tonight," he said. "I got a seven o-clock flight back to Abilene."

As they all cleared out, Kelsey came back in.

"Bingo," she said, smiling. "I got Jennifer. She's invited us to tea in an hour."

"Excellent," I said. "Let's go."

20

Jennifer Long lived in a lovely pre-War apartment house in the Gramercy Park neighborhood, not too far from Madison Square Park, which does *not* contain the sports arena, but is a lovely green oasis in the middle of the city and sits in the shadow of the Flatiron Building.

Kelsey and I taxied over to the East 20's and Park Avenue, found the building and passed muster with the liveried doorman, who called upstairs, and got the okay from the tenant to load us onto an elevator for the quick ride up to twelve. You could tell we were in the high-rent district by the fact that there were just three apartments on each floor: one to the left, one to the right and one in the center.

A pleasant looking gray haired lady waved to us from the left wing of the building when we exited the elevator. Jennifer Long looked to be in her sixties. She was dressed in a gray wool suit, black slip-ons, a soft white silk sweater draped over her shoulders. There were two yappy little corgis tumbling around at her ankles.

"Kelsey, dear," she said, waving us inside. "How good to see you again."

Kelsey gave her a hug and introduced me. There was a long entrance hall which opened into a broad rectangular space illuminated by four arched floor-to-ceiling windows facing south. We were high enough that the afternoon sun flooded in.

In the center of the big rectangle was a large U-shaped seating group in white leather with colorful fringed pillows tossed here and there. Two other upholstered chairs flanked the fireplace on the wall opposite the arched windows. To the right, a large dining table with a beautiful floral arrangement in its center stood, and I sensed the kitchen was located back to the right. To the left, the end of the rectangle was covered in dark stained built-in bookshelves, filled with colorful volumes. A small French desk sat diagonally in the corner and a couple of Louis XIV chairs flanked a side table and reading light.

"Wow," Kelsey said, looking around, "This is amazing."

"Oh, thank you, dear," the older woman said, smiling. "Parker and I found this place more than forty years ago. We've always felt very lucky to have lived here. Our two girls adored the place. It's very convenient."

She motioned to us to sit down, and we played with the yappy dogs while she went into the kitchen, returning with a tray filled with things for tea. She put the tray down on the large coffee table and began pouring out cups for each of us.

"It's so good of you to come for a visit," Jennifer said, passing us a cup and motioning toward a plate of sugar cookies on the tray. "I miss talking to all of Parker's colleagues from the network. Such an interesting group!"

"I understand you were in the insurance business," I said.

"Oh, yes, I was," she said, smiling at me. "Retired now. But I was in senior management at Robinson and Crump.

They used to call us the American Lloyd's. We wrote huge policies on airliners and container ships, things like that."

"Guess that's more lucrative than an auto policy with State Farm," I said.

She tittered. "Oh, yes, indeed it is," she said. "Your typical commercial airplane, like you ride on to go to another city, is insured for tens of millions. We would typically insure a company's entire fleet. You can imagine the sums involved."

"And luckily, they hardly ever crash," I said. "So you must have come out smelling like a rose."

"Robinson and Crump did quite well," she said, nodding. "And one reason those airplanes don't crash is because of companies like ours, which make sure they obey the rules and take the steps necessary to keep from crashing. More tea?"

I shook my head, while Kelsey stuck her cup out for a refill.

"What brings you to the city, dear?" she asked Kelsey.

"We had another death in the IBS family," Kelsey said. "Arnie Wasserman was shot and killed last week. We came up for his memorial service."

"Oh yes, I did hear about that," Jennifer said. "What a shame."

The way she said it didn't sound like she was entirely distraught at the news.

"So some of us were talking after the service for Arnie," Kelsey said. "And Kenny Craig mentioned that you had said something to him about Parker being told he might get laid off. I wonder if you can tell Hacker and me anything more about that?"

"Ah, yes," Jennifer took a sip of tea. "I myself don't know how accurate any of this information is…or was," she said. "But Parker came home, I think it was toward the end of last summer, and told me he had heard that the network wanted to make changes."

"Changes regarding Parker himself, or the entire division?" I asked.

"Oh, no, it was about Parker's situation," she smiled at me. "I don't remember him saying anything about anyone else."

"He had a contract, didn't he?" Kelsey asked.

"Yes, of course, dear," she said. "It was due to expire at the end of this year. We had agreed, Parker and I, to talk about his retirement at the end of this contract period. Our girls live elsewhere…Sally is in southern California and Betty is up in Seattle. Parker and I wanted to have more time to visit them, spend time with our grandkids."

"Well, if that was your plan, why was Parker upset about his retirement being discussed at the network?" I asked.

"Because he heard they wanted him dismissed at once," Jennifer said.

"Heard from who?"

She sighed, sipped some more tea, delaying. "It was that man, Arnold Wasserman," she said finally. "He ran into Parker late one night at the hotel bar where they were staying for the broadcast. He was, Parker told me, quite inebriated. Parker said Wasserman told him not to make any plans, that his contract was going to be canceled. He, Wasserman, was going to make sure of that. It was quite direct and quite insulting."

"What did Parker do?" I asked.

"He immediately went to see Ben Oswald, the very next morning," she told us. "Complained bitterly, about being spoken to in that manner, and that he was being told he was going to be fired. Oswald calmed him down, said it was all a misunderstanding."

"And he heard nothing else since then?" I asked.

"No, he didn't," Jennifer Long said, with a slight smile. "But I didn't let it rest. I called Parker's agent, who is supposed to be fighting for his client. I asked him what he knew."

"And?" Kelsey asked.

"He told me that it was true that the network had contacted him about ending Parker's contract early. He told the network there was no possibility that Parker would agree to such a thing. He threatened legal action. Since then…and this was last September I believe….we hadn't heard another word."

"And then he died suddenly," I said.

"Yes," his wife said, sadly. "Quite good fortune for the network, isn't it? Now they can move in whomever they wish to replace my Parker."

Kelsey looked at me. I shrugged.

"Well for right now, that would be me," I said. "But I don't know how permanent a situation that is. Van Collins told us there are a lot of changes looming in the background, throughout the industry."

"Oh, Van is a lovely, lovely man," Jennifer said. "He came up for the funeral, was lovely with the girls. A dear man."

I grabbed a cookie from the tray, and half listened while Kelsey and Jennifer talked about her daughters and grandchildren. Finally, Jennifer turned to me.

"May I ask why you are asking these questions about Parker?" she said.

"You may," I said. "I'm trying to determine if there might be any connection between Parker's death and that of Arnie Wasserman."

"But Parker was killed by some faulty electrical equipment," she said. "It was an accident. At least, that's what I understand from the police in Georgia. And Mr. Wasserman was shot in the Upper West Side. I don't see how there can be any connection between the two events."

"Yes," I said. "Neither do I. But the police down in Savannah are still investigating exactly how Parker died. The circumstances strike some of us as odd. Unusual. Out of the ordinary. So I'm just asking some questions, trying to see things that aren't clear."

"And you think that the International Broadcasting System had Parker killed to get him out of his contract and bring in new talent? You, in fact."

She gazed at me, eyes steely and determined. This was not some frail old lady pushover. She used to write multi-million dollar insurance contracts for airlines and shipping firms.

"Well, when you put it that way, no, I don't think that," I said. "But I'm still not convinced that the two deaths are entirely coincidental."

She kept gazing at me. I gazed back. There wasn't much left to say, so we had a gazing contest. It's not hard: you just lock your eyes with the other person's and don't say anything.

Something had to give, and it was Kelsey.

"We've got to run," she said, standing up. "Thank you so much for the tea and your time, Jennifer. I'm sure that if Hacker learns anything more, he will let you know at once."

I nodded, without letting my gaze drop. I wasn't going to surrender. But we got up, said our goodbyes and Kelsey and I left. At some point, the gaze-athon ended. I don't know who blinked. But it wasn't me.

Outside, we walked half a block up to Park Avenue.

"Why do you think the two deaths are connected?" Kelsey asked me. "She's right, you know. One's an accident and the other seems to be murder."

"An accident?" I said. "How many other TV broadcasters have died as a result of a short circuit with their equipment? Like in the entire history of broadcasting? Never happened to Edward R. Murrow, did it? John Cameron Swayze? Walter Cronkite?"

She thought about that for a minute.

"Yeah, OK, I get that," she said. "But who would want to kill Parker Long? He was a nice man. Nobody disliked him. You're not buying the idea that the network or Arnie Wasserman had him knocked off are you?'

"Nah," I said. I say an empty cab coming down Park and hailed it. It pulled in to the curb and we got in.

"I don't know why someone might want to knock off Parker," I said. "But there's a lot I don't know."

"Where to, buddy?" the cabby asked.

"Where are you off to next?" I said to Kelsey. "I'm heading back home to Boston. I think there's a six o'clock train I can catch."

"I'm spending the night in the city," Kelsey said. "Heading back down to Florida in the morning."

I gave the cabby directions and we rode in silence through the city, each lost in our own thoughts.

21

Van Collins said "Let's go out to fifteen and check in with the Dynamic Duo, Hacker and the Boz. Gentlemen?"

"Gentlemen?" the Boz said. "Is he talking about us?"

"Nah, can't be," I said. "I mean, you're here."

"Oof," Boz said, chuckling. "First shot of the day. Good one."

"Speaking of shots, here's Jason Day getting ready for his approach to fifteen," I said. " He's got one-eight-five. Has a nine-iron."

"Nine iron?" the Boz said. "Do they ever make these guys pee in a cup after the round? I'd need two nine irons and a wedge from one eight-five."

"Well, yes, I suppose you would," I said. "Most of the rest of us would just take an eight iron and be done with it."

"Well, Day's shot came up a bit short," the Boz said. "He's putting, but he'll need to make a full turn on that forty-footer. Say, Hack, my theory is that these guys do things like try to hit a nine-iron one-eighty-five because they think it impresses the chicks. You know, 'hey, babe, I hit my nine from 185. Wanna feel my muscles?'"

"Naw," I said. "It's the size of their bank accounts that impresses the ladies."

"Cynical," Boz said. "You are so cynical."

"Besides," I said, "You people at home shouldn't pay any attention to what clubs these guys are using. First, they're professionals, and you're not. Second, they all mess with their clubs, bending the lofts up and down over in the equipment trailer. So Jason's nine-iron might have the same loft as your six iron."

"And that, folks, is today's advice from a Hacker," Boz said. "Worth exactly what you paid for it, which was zip."

"The voice in my ear is telling me to go to seventeen, so take it away Doctor Kenny Craig!" I said.

"WHAT ARE YOU doing, Hacker?," my daughter Victoria asked me.

I was sitting in my living room, watched a recorded version of last weekend's broadcast from Memphis. I wasn't actually taking notes on my performance, but I was trying to watch myself with a jaundiced eye. The Boz and I seemed to have created something the people liked, and I was trying to figure out what it was. So far, all I could see was two idiots having a good time watching golf and talking nonsense. That people seemed to respond to that? That was their problem, not mine.

"I guess I'm doing homework," I told my step-daughter.

"Watching yourself on the TV is homework?" she said. "Where do I sign up for that? I'm supposed to be doing some math equations."

"And I'd be happy to help you with that," I said. "Except for the fact that I always got straight C's in math. Total numerical idiot."

She smiled at me. "That's okay," she said. "They're pretty easy ones. And if I need help, my Mom is a teacher."

"You are wise in the ways of the world, grasshopper," I said.

"What are you guys doing?" Mary Jane came into the living room, DJ on her hip. "We need to leave for Paw Paw's in twenty minutes."

Both Mary Jane and DJ were recently bathed and he was dressed in new, and therefore momentarily clean, clothes. MJ's wet hair was piled atop her head and she was wearing her robe. She dropped the boy on my lap and went back into the bedroom to finish dressing.

DJ squirmed around for a minute and then made a raspberry sound. It was one of the new party tricks he had recently learned: sticking out his tongue and blowing. It amused him no end, and when I made the sound back at him, he collapsed in giggles. So we played raspberry for a few minutes.

"Are all babies this disgusting?" asked Victoria, "Or is it just my brother?" But she was smiling. I suspected she wanted to blow a few raspberries herself. But that would be totally uncool for a hip twelve-year-old.

"Well, I didn't know you when you were this age," I said. "But I'll bet you were just as disgusting. It's what babies do best."

"Have you guys decided where we're gonna live next?" she asked, as DJ reached over and grabbed a handful of her hair. He held it in front of his face and blew a raspberry at it.

I sighed. "Your Mom has been working on that," I said. "The rest of us are on a need-to-know basis. Are you okay with the idea of moving? Not having teeny angst attacks or any-thing?"

"Looking forward to it, actually," she said. "Thanks to baby brother here, half my room is taken up with stuff that's not mine, including the litter box for Mister S over there."

She pointed at my cat, Mister Shit, who was sleeping peacefully on one of our dining room chairs. 'Dining room' being the thing we called the corner of our living room that was closest to the kitchen.

"Yeah," I said. "I guess it's time for the household to expand. I'm sure your Mom has a plan for that."

"Plan for what?" Mary Jane said as she came back in. She was now dressed and her hair combed and ponytailed. She looked like a million bucks. Only with nice curves.

"Our new location," I said. "The Vickster is ready to move."

"Well, the Vickster needs to go pick up the clothes on the floor of her room and get ready to go," Mary Jane said, pushing her daughter down the hall. "You, too, big fella."

AN HOUR OR so later we were all in Milton, gathered at the palatial estate of Carmine Spoleto above the marshlands that were part of the Neponset River basin. Carmine's three daughters were there, along with husbands and children, and so were the handful of goombahs that Carmine kept around the place for security. Tiny Tony was there, but wasn't cooking today. It was Easter Saturday and Carmine's daughters had scheduled the big family to-do for today, so we could all celebrate Easter in our own ways. The Hacker family intended to sleep late, go out for lunch somewhere and watch golf in the late afternoon. Although I was not hopeful baby DJ would be down with the sleeping late part.

The party self-separated as always: the male adults gathered in the living room with cocktails and munchies, to talk about the Red Sox, Wall Street and other important topics. The womenfolk congregated in the kitchen, from which several amazing smells emanated. They were slamming the wine pretty hard, and bursting out with occasional loud peals of laughter. We menfolk just assumed that one of us was the subject. And all the kids, ranging in age from sixteen on down, were sent upstairs where Carmine's goombahs had installed all the latest shoot 'em up video games on the huge TV in the video room.

After a while, Carmine pulled me aside.

"Go get your wife and daughter," he whispered to me. "I have something to show you."

We met him outside the front door. Tiny Tony had pulled up one of the black SUVs that Carmine owned. Tinted windows and I assumed armor-plated. The head of the New England mob can't be too careful.

"Where are we going?" Mary Jane asked. She was carrying DJ on her hip. "Do we need to get the car seat?"

"Get in, get in," Carmine said, waving her into the back seat. "We're not going far. The *bambino* will be fine. *Andiamo.*"

Victoria sat between her Paw Paw and Tiny Tony in the front seat. Tony drove us down the main driveway, but turned hard right just before the road onto a narrow lane that circled down behind the main house toward the marshes. In about a hundred yards, we pulled up in front of a two-story structure located on the shore. There was a narrow passage cut through the marshes leading up to the dock that extended out in front of the building.

"What is this?" Mary Jane said.

"This is my boat house," Carmine said. "*Casa de barca.*"

"I didn't know you had a boat," Mary Jane said.

"I don't," he said. "I hate boats. Come see inside."

There was a wooden stairway leading up to the second floor. Tiny Tony stayed with the car while we all climbed up, and Carmine unlocked the door. He stood back and motioned us to go in.

I heard Mary Jane's intake of breath as she looked at the place for the first time. It was pretty impressive. We entered into a little vestibule with hooks along the wall and trays for shoes and things on the floor, and beyond that was a combination living room, dining room and kitchen. The front of the space was all window wall overlooking the acres of marsh and river that stretched out into the distance. There was a deep, black leather U-shaped sofa and granite-topped cocktail table in front of a large TV, a light-wood dining table with six chairs and a granite pass-through counter from the kitchen, which was full of stainless steel appliances and wooden cabinets.

The walls were cypress planks, stained a light cherry and filled with nautical art and artifacts, oars and steering wheels and the like. A hallway down one side led to the back part of the house, where I assumed the bedrooms were. And over next to the kitchen was a black metal circular staircase which led up to a loft space overlooking the living room space and sharing the same window walls looking out at the marshes.

"My God," Mary Jane said, staring at all this, "I never knew you had this place down here."

Carmine shrugged. "It was here when I bought this place twenty years ago," he said. "I never used it much. Some of the boys would sleep down here when I needed them to be close by. Other than that, it's always been pretty much vacant."

Victoria ran over to the metal staircase and climbed up to the loft. I heard her muffled yell, and she leaned over the railing. "There's a bedroom up here," she called. "Plus a bathroom!"

Carmine smiled up at his granddaughter. "And two more bedrooms in the back, plus the master bath," he said.

Mary Jane and DJ went to look. I stayed. There was a wrap-around porch in the front that extended down one side of the building. There was a big propane grill under a cover in one corner.

"This is a great space," I said. "Really nice. Impressive. But I really don't think we can …"

"Hacker," Mary Jane called from the back. "You gotta come see this."

I went down the hall. There was a small room on the left, a big bathroom in the middle and a nice sized bedroom to the right. Mary Jane was standing with DJ at the French doors which opened from the bedroom onto the wraparound deck. She pointed. Outside the doors, on the end of the deck, was a big, brand new hot tub.

"Jeezus," I said.

"Does that mean you're having some of those carnal thoughts again?" she asked sweetly.

I went back into the living room. Carmine, looking like the cat who swallowed the canary, was perched at the pass-through, half sitting on a bar stool.

"What is this all about?" I said.

He shrugged. "This place is practically unused," he said. "The boys can bunk in the basement in the big house, if I need them. Your family needs a new home. This might work, yes?"

"I can't take this place from you for nothing," I said.

"Of course not," he cut me off. "I would never make such an offer. I am a businessman. Also, that would be insulting to someone like yourself."

"Well, I'm glad you understand," I said, nodding. "It's really a lovely place, but …"

"How much do you pay in rent now, there in Cambridge?" he asked.

I told him the number. He nodded.

"You will pay me the same amount," he said. "Every month."

Mary Jane came and stood next to me. DJ was looking around and cooing at things.

"That is a very fair offer, Paw Paw," she said. "Are you sure the other girls will be okay with us living here?"

He nodded. "Si, I have spoken to them," he said. "They all think it's a great idea. Plus, I will have family close at hand if, *Dio non voglia*, something might happen to this old man."

I assumed he was talking about a medical emergency, not the guns-and-bullets kind. He was, after all, in his eighties.

"So," he said, turning his rheumy eyes toward me. "What do you think? Do we have a deal?"

I looked at Mary Jane, who was flush with excitement. DJ was chewing on a red rubber ring, but he looked like he approved. Victoria leaned over the railing above us. "You better say yes, Hacker, or I'll never speak to you again!"

"OK," I said. "I guess it's a deal."

Carmine and I shook hands. Victoria shrieked and did a loud clumping happy dance a floor above. Mary Jane leaned over and kissed me. DJ blew a raspberry.

"I hope you will be very happy here," Carmine said.

22

The beginning of a major golf tournament week has always felt to me like the opening of a medieval jousting tournament, except that there's no Errol Flynn running around in green tights and a feathered cap. But there are the pennants snapping in the wind, the smell of freshly mown grass, the stands special-built for crowds of spectators, meat sizzling on the grills, smoke drifting off in the breeze. Add the Sheriff of Nottingham, Maid Marion and a couple of court jesters and it would be exactly the same.

A chilly rain was falling on Monday afternoon when the IBS crew arrived at Conrad Gold's Hudson Links. The banners were hanging limply and wet on their poles and the court jesters were all inside one of the dozens of hospitality tents getting hammered on bourbon and scotch. I saw a small handful of players on the practice tee, but most of the pros were staying inside and dry.

We had all met for lunch at the Cumberland Arms Inn in the burgh closest to the golf course and our hotel home for the week. Ben Oswald had outlined our schedule, which included daily production meetings which would include in-depth reports on the players and updates on the golf course. After those sessions were over, we were free, and encouraged, to attend some of the PGA of America functions and cocktail parties which would be going on all week. The PGA of America is divided into "sections" both within and without state lines, and it seemed like every one of those sections was planning a big party sometime during the upcoming week. Based on past experience, I was only interested in attending the Nebraska section steak fry on Wednesday night. They always had excellent connections with some of the ranchers from the state who sent over the best rib eyes and sirloins in the world.

Our little white bus took us over to the Gold Club on the bluff overlooking the golf course, and despite the dreary weather, we could see the golf course laid out in waiting for the tournament. Fairways were pristine, rimmed with gallery ropes and bright with electronic message boards. The air was wet and heavy, and the tension, which had not begun to mount, was still hanging in the atmosphere along with the rain showers. This was a Big Show, one of four held every year, and it felt like it.

Ben, Van and Jimmy went in to do thirty minutes with the press. Ben explained some of the technological doo-dads we had imported for the broadcast, talked about the miles of cable that had been laid, the numbers of workers that had set up the broadcast headquarters and the times we were planning to broadcast live. Once Ben covered the logistics, Van and Jimmy talked about other PGA Championships they had covered over the years, and who they felt was playing well enough at the moment to win.

I stood at the back of the room with the other announcers, the Boz at my side, and watched the reporters asking questions. It had not been all that long ago that I had been one of them. I knew that with the rainy first day, a lot of planned interviews and preview stories had been postponed or deep-sixed, and that made the press guys nervous and unhappy. Which is never a good thing for your press corps to be.

Bartholomew Hastings, the somewhat young sports writer for the New York *Times*, who covered most of the major golf events for the paper, raised his hand.

"Yeah, Ben," he said, "Would you care to comment on the recent death of your assistant, Arnie Wasserman, and how that has affected your coverage here this week?"

"Sure," Ben said, nodding. But I noticed his eyes narrow and a bit of color rose in his cheeks. "Arnie's death was a huge loss for all of us at IBS. He worked closely with me for the better part of eleven years. I miss him every day, both personally and professionally. I don't know how his passing will affect our coverage. We haven't done a major without him in all that time. But our crew is made up of professionals from top to bottom, so my expectation is we'll do the best job we can, and I think the viewers will be pleased."

The *Times*man wasn't finished.

"You also lost one of your announcers, Parker Long, at the tournament down in Savannah earlier this spring," he said. "Can you tell us please if there are any connections between these two deaths?"

The red spots on Ben's cheeks got a little larger.

"Yes," he said. "Both Parker Long and Arnie Wasserman worked for IBS and they were my friends and colleagues. That's the connection."

"No," Hastings said, "I mean any connections between the two murders?"

"We don't know how Parker Long died," Ben said, "And it is impertinent and, if I can say, more than a little disgraceful for you to imply that he was murdered."

"The police in Savannah still have that death under investigation," Hastings said. "So the question of how he died is still open."

"And you are assuming that he was murdered," Ben shot back. "Do you have any evidence of that?"

"No," Hastings said, "But the police…"

"So if you have no evidence, how can you assert that the deaths of Parker and Arnie are connected?" Ben said. "You can't. And it's disgraceful that you imply it."

"I'll note that you haven't answered my question," Hastings said.

"You can also note that I'm about ready to come down there and kick your ass," Oswald said. His face was now officially red.

"Nice, Ben," the reporter said. But he sat down.

The PGA press person took charge, asked for any more questions, and when no one was brave enough to ask one, she declared the press conference to be over.

Ben stalked out, waves of steam metaphorically rising from his head. Van and Jimmy stuck around, and some of the reporters gathered around them to chat a bit and hopefully pick up another quote or two.

I went over and sat down next to Bart Hastings.

"Have you heard anything I haven't?" I asked him.

He had been writing something in his notebook. He looked up at me.

"Hacker," he said, acknowledging my presence. I know I was supposed to feel both a thrill and a chill that the reporter for the hallowed New York *Times* knew my name, but I had known Bart for five or six years. Nice guy, a little standoffish like most New Yorkers, pretty good writer. He was in his late thirties, tall and lanky, with a full head of hair and a craggy visage. Like Abe Lincoln without the beard.

"I assume you mean in regards to Parker Long," he said finally, snapping his notebook shut.

"Yeah," I said. "Last time I talked to Capt. Connor down in Savannah, he didn't exactly know how Parker died. You hear anything different?"

"And why would I tell you if I had?" he said. "Perhaps the news hounds from IBS can find out."

"Well," I said, "I would think you'd tell me so as not to be the world's biggest asshole. I'm not a reporter anymore, Bart. We're not competing for scoops. I'm a TV guy now and Parker was one of ours. We'd like to find out what happened."

"Well then," he said, standing up. "I guess you'll just have to read tomorrow's paper. See you around."

And he left. With me sitting there thinking that he really was the world's biggest asshole.

I called Delbert Connor.

"Connor," came the gruff voice.

"Hacker here," I said. "What is the New York *Times* going to publish tomorrow about the Parker Long case?"

"No idea," he said. "I'm a cop, not a clairvoyant."

"C'mon, Connor," I said. "Hastings has something. You gave it to him. You and I have been friends longer."

He laughed at that. "Friends?" he said. "Good one."

"What did the state lab come back with?" I said. "How did Parker get electrocuted?"

"Look, Hacker, my 'friend,'" he said. "My investigation is still open and active. I can't tell you much."

"But?"

"The crime lab took Long's headphones apart, piece by piece," he said. "They found some…umm…*unusual* wiring inside."

"What does that mean?"

"Shorthand version: someone messed with the victim's headphones," he said. "The lab guys found some some of the internal connections in the headphones had been tampered with."

"Tampered with how?" I asked.

"They don't know for sure," he said. "But the state's tech guy told me that the headphones Parker was wearing would have returned a lot of static noise. Parker wouldn't have been able to hear very well. Lotta static, bad quality sound."

"It was deliberate?" I asked. "Not just some old headphones where the wires wore out?"

"According to the lab, it looked like someone had worked to deliberately interfere with the headphones," he said. "And then carefully put them back together to look like new."

"But would that kill him? Zap him with power?"

"Nope," Connor said. "That's the part they haven't figured out yet. There was nothing they could see that would send power back down the headphone wires and into the wearer. They ran all kinds of tests, but it never did that. But it's something they've never seen before."

"Is that what Bart Hastings is running with tomorrow?" I asked.

"How the hell do I know?" he said. "Why don't you ask him?"

"Because he's the world's biggest asshole," I said.

"We all have our crosses to bear, don't we?" Connor said and rang off.

I THOUGHT ABOUT what Connor had told me for a while. I couldn't think of any reason why someone would deliberately mess around with the wires. But I could think of someone who might know.

I grabbed a courtesy van down to the golf course and wandered over to this week's location for Television City, where there were thirty or so trailers parked cheek-to-jowl to hold all the electronics, studios, control rooms and more for the international group of television broadcasters including IBS. Technicians of various stripes were running around in barely controlled states of panic, checking cables and testing equipment, which all had to be ready to go on Thursday morning.

I found the trailers that belonged to IBS' technical crew and stepped inside the first one. It was a dark space with a narrow aisle down the middle and all kinds of lockers and containers on both walls, holding every imaginable kind of gear: wires and cables and connectors and pins and splitters and tools and ties and more. Down at the front of the trailer, there was a space for a work bench across the width of the trailer, and this part at least was well lighted. And sitting on a metal chair at the work bench, bent over a piece of circuit board with a welding tool, was Digby Allen, our resident techie genius.

"Digby," I said as I came up. "What's goin' on?"

He glanced up, eyes looking extra large as seen in reverse through one of those plastic magnifying glasses things he had strapped to his head.

"Hiya, Hacker," he said. "Hang on a sec."

He bent back down over his work and deftly soldered a wire to a brass connection on the edge of the circuit board. A puff of white smoke drifted up and away, its smell acrid in my nose. He looked at his work through his magnifying glasses, then nodded to himself. He took off the glasses and turned to me with a smile.

"How you doing?" he said.

"Good, good," I said. "Listen, I have a question. Technical question."

"Best kind," he said. "Shoot."

"I was just talking to the cop down in Savannah looking into Parker Long's death," I said. "He said that the state crime lab boys took Parker's headset apart. Said they found the wiring inside was messed up. They think someone did it deliberately."

"That would cause static," Digby said without missing a beat. "He'd get a lot of feedback and interference and stuff. Be hard to hear anything."

"That's what the crime lab techies said," I said. "Can you think of any reason someone would do that to a guy's headsets?"

Digby thought for a minute. Finally, he shook his head.

"Naw," he said. "The announcer would have a hell of time with something like that. Be a real problem."

"So who would want to mess around with Parker's headphones?" I asked.

"Dunno," Digby said, shrugging his shoulders. "Someone who didn't want Parker to hear very well. Nobody in this crew would do such a thing. That's crazy."

"Yeah," I said. "Crazy."

He turned back to his work bench and I left.

23

Tony Sciutto and I met for breakfast at the Cumberland Arms Inn on Tuesday morning to go over this week's *Hacker's History* segment for the broadcast. He brought with him Jenny LoBianco, a young sound technician who he said would be working with us. We all went through the breakfast buffet, got some hot coffee and I showed him the script I had written over the last weekend.

He read through the pages, nodding to himself here and there. Once or twice he marked the pages, scribbling some notes with a pencil. Jenny and I ate in silence. Finished, he put the script down.

"Pretty good stuff," he said to me, smiling. "I can work with this."

"There's a lot of reference to the PGA back in 1958," I said. "Do you think you can get some historical footage?"

"Shouldn't be a problem," Tony said. "I've already talked to the PGA's chief archivist. He says we can use anything he's got."

"The PGA has a chief archivist?" I said. "Did not know that."

Sciutto gave the script to Jenny, who immediately began reading it. She was in her late twenties, long brown hair pulled back into a pony tail. She wore blue jeans and a long sleeved polo, and a pair of black-rimmed eyeglasses.

She zipped through the script, lips pursed in concentration. When she was done, Tony gave her a series of instructions: who to call, what to ask for, when to have the material ready for Becky Ann Billingsly, IBS' crackerjack film editor. Jenny took all this in, nodded, and slid out of the booth.

We watched her walk away.

"Sound technician?" I said.

He smiled. "She wants to get into producing," he said. "I'm letting her get some experience with this segment. She's a smart kid. She'll do fine."

"Not bad looking, either," I noted.

He held up his hands. "Not the deal, here," he said. "I'm a happily married man, She was in a relationship that ended badly. Took it pretty hard. I'm just trying to keep her busy with stuff, keep her occupied."

"Boyfriends can be such cads," I said.

He frowned, lines forming across his forehead.

"In this case, the boyfriend got dead," he said. "Jenny was dating Arnie Wasserman. Semi-secretly, but some of us knew."

"Oh, shit," I said. "Yeah, I can imagine that's tough."

We agreed on a time to get together later that afternoon to shoot some of the stand-up parts of my script. The rest I would do in an edit booth at the tournament's Television City compound.

I wandered over to the practice range. Old habits. Before a tournament, the range is always a good place to pick up gossip, rumors or other innuendo that might turn into a good story for the paper. Or the airwaves in my case. The best stuff rarely comes from the pros themselves, although they will talk for hours about their golf swings, but from the caddies, managers, physical therapists, wives and girlfriends, all of whom can be found wandering around the range while their man hits seven-irons for an hour.

I was watching Jon Rahm crushing his driver, while I stood near the ropes next to the tubs filled with brand new Titleists and Callaways. There were a couple of volunteers filling those little cloth bags with thirty or so balls, which the caddies would come over and pick up.

"He's a big 'un, ain't he?" said someone standing behind me. I turned. It was Billy Joe Bosworth. He grinned at me, and nodded at Rahm, stilling hitting huge drives down the range.

"Ever think how much money you coulda won if you were his size?" he said.

"The woods are full of big hitters," I said. "According to Hogan or someone."

"Yeah, Big Jon hits 'em right down the pike," Boz said. "I think they call him CenterLine. Anyway, who is this Hogan of whom you speak?'

I laughed.

Charlie Zimmerman, one of the big wheels with the big player agent company, Player Reps Incorporated, or PRI, walked over. He was carrying a leather briefcase. Always working, these agent guys. Always on alert in case a dollar gets loose and runs squeaking for the underbrush.

"Well, well," he said, looking at the Boz and me, "If it isn't the Laurel and Hardy of golf."

"I'd like to think we are the Three Stooges of golf," Boz said with a straight face.

Zimmerman looked at him, eyebrows raised, then shook his head.

"Still an idiot, Boz," he said. "Don't ever change."

"Nyuk, nyuk, nyuk," Boz said.

Charlie turned to me.

"Did you see this morning's *Times*?" he asked. "Bart Hastings ran an interesting piece on IBS."

"I heard he was working on something," I said. "No, I didn't see it. Got all the fish wrapped up I need. What did he say?"

Zimmerman rooted around in his briefcase and pulled out a copy. "Here you go," he said. "All the crap they see fit to run."

It was a column, running down the left side of the sports front. *IBS REELING FROM RECENT DEATHS*, the headline began, *WEAKENED TEAM PREPARES FOR PGA*.

Executive producer Ben Oswald puts on a brave front, but the broadcast team from International Broadcast System's golf division is reeling from the deaths of two important figures in recent weeks.

Deputy executive producer Arnold Wasserman was gunned down on the Upper West Side two weeks ago, and longtime booth announcer Parker Long died in a still-unexplained incident during the company's broadcast of the Southern Plantation Open in Savannah in March.

While Oswald says he expects IBS's broadcast of the PGA Championship this weekend from Gold's Hudson Links course in Dutchess County, New York, to go off without a hitch, others say the network has been devastated by the deaths of the two men.

"I don't see how the quality of the broadcast won't be affected by these losses," said a longtime observer of the television industry. "You can't lose two important cogs

and still have your machine operate flawlessly."

Police are still searching for Wasserman's killer, but said yesterday they do not currently have a suspect in that case. As for Parker Long, there are more questions than answers about his sudden death during the tournament in Savannah. Police in Georgia have discovered some irregularities with the broadcast equipment Long was using, but would not comment when asked if those equipment irregularities led to the death of the longtime sports announcer. That case is still under investigation, the police said.

During a Monday morning press conference at Conrad Gold's luxury golf club along the Hudson River some 50 miles north of New York, Ben Oswald turned hostile when asked about Parker Long's death, and threatened bodily harm on this reporter.

I stopped reading and had to chuckle.

"'Threatened bodily harm,'" I said. "That's pretty rich."

Boz had been reading over my shoulder.

"Who is this 'longtime observer of the television industry' he's quoting?" he asked. "That could be anyone who's ever watched a TV set."

I nodded. "The new journalism," I said. "Hastings hopes the reader thinks he's talking about some professor at Columbia who's written forty-seven books about the television industry. But if it was someone like that, he'd just quote him directly. No need for protection. So the fact that he's using that qualifier—'longtime observer of the television industry'—is a clue that the person being quoted is anything but an expert. But Hastings got him to say the words he wanted to quote, and wrapped that quote around an empty qualifier. Or, it could also just be Hastings himself, making up the quote.

Hastings knows that no one will ever question him about it, and if someone did, he would get all huffy and claim the inviolate right to protect his sources. But of course, no reporter from the New York *Times* would ever do something like making up a quote and attributing it to some amorphous being."

"Of course not," Boz said. "Except for any day ending with a Y."

Charlie Zimmerman was watching us. "You guys don't seem like you're unable to operate flawlessly," he said.

"We are unquenchable," I said. I gave him back his paper.

"Speaking of which, Hacks, it's gotta be almost lunchtime, right?" Boz said.

"I believe you are correct," I said. "Let's go."

AFTER LUNCH, WE had a two-hour production meeting in Television City, which lasted approximately a hundred and ten minutes longer than it should have. When it was finally over, I walked back onto the golf course and, to clear my head, watched some of the late afternoon practice rounds finishing up. Those last three holes along the Hudson were fun: the players and their caddies were trying to figure out the proper attack strategies, and there were a lot of splashes going on while they did. Because it was Tuesday and just practice, everyone was in a relaxed and good mood, and there were lots of playful insults being hurled around the greens.

I watched as Ernie Els stood on the seventeenth tee, looking down at the island green for several long minutes. I was standing up near the green, but I saw Ernie turn to look at someone in the gallery behind the tee, laugh and hold out his club, as if to say *"OK, you give it a try, buddy!"* The spectator declined the opportunity and Els finally hit a shot to the middle of the green.

After watching the shot-making for a while, I wandered up the hill to stand in the area where the players and their caddies came off the 18th. During the tournament, the players would head into the official scorer's office, set in a temporary trailer near the basement entrance to the clubhouse. The caddies would wait outside, zipping up the bags and waiting for their man to come back outside and tell them what was next: back to the range, over to the putting green, forty minutes for lunch, or done for the day and we'll take the clubs home.

This caddy staging area was my second favorite spot, after the practice range, for gossip from the caddies. They'd tell me, in so many words, how their man was faring.

"Oh, geez," one would tell me, "He had four three-putts today. He's still trying to figure out the speed."

Another one would shake his had. "Army golf off the tee," he'd say. "Left, right, left."

I would know that neither of those players would likely be a factor in the weekend's event. You can't win on Tour, especially a major, if you're not driving or putting the ball well. Not going to happen.

And of course, the caddies of the guys who were driving and putting well would never tell you that. Not right out, in so many words. Superstitious, they'd dance all around it.

"Pretty grooved today," the caddie might say. Or "he's hittin' it pure." Or, "mistakes at a minimum." All ways of telling me that the player had brought his A-game, and might be worthy of consideration for the weekend.

Of course, sometimes the results were totally opposite of what the caddies were expecting. The guy hitting Army shots off the tee might make everything he looked at on the green and be on the leaderboard on Sunday afternoon. Or the guys hitting stripes on Tuesday might be found deep in the woods on Thursday and Friday and on their way home Friday night. That's golf.

I chatted with some of the guys while they packed up for the day. The players, instead of heading into the scorer's room, were mostly branching off into the clubhouse, where they'd sit around the locker room for a while to decompress, or talk about sports and women with their entourage: the agent, the physio, the driver, the private jet pilot, the security guy, the equipment man, the nutritionist and the assorted friends and relatives who turned up for these big events.

Big Ben, the English caddie named after London's big clock because he was about six-six himself, was sitting on top of a rock wall, the bag of his man, Sidney Williamson, at his side. He was taking in the scene with wry amusement, as always.

"How's Sir Sid playing this week?" I asked him.

He shrugged. "Some good, some bad, some other," he said. "Been playing pretty good golf the last month or so. He'll show up this week."

Translated from the caddie, that meant that Sidney's game was in proper order, and Big Ben his caddie fully expected to be playing on the weekend and positioned on the first two pages of the leaderboard.

"He looking forward to Troon?" I asked. The British Open, still a couple months away, was scheduled to return to Ayrshire this year. Sidney had played well there in the past, with a couple of top ten finishes.

Big Ben shrugged, his eyes followed a couple of cute young things down the sidewalk next to the clubhouse. "He's paid his entry fee," he said. Translation: *He'll be there and expecting good results.*

Art the Dart came over, plunked down his heavy bag and heaved a sigh of relief. Art carried for Billy Wollaston, the young pro from Fort Myers who was moving quickly up the money list this year.

"Man, this place is hilly as fuck," he said, moving his back and shoulder muscles around. "Think we can get a golf cart?"

Big Ben chuckled at that. "They turned John Daly down," he said, "Very much doubt if they'll give one to you."

"Yeah, you're probably right," he said. "Bastards hate us, don't they?'

He looked at me.

"Hacker!" he said, "How you likin' the TV gig?"

"It's OK," I said. "A bit different. But pretty much the same thing I was doing before."

"I hear ya," Art the Dart said. He was thin as a rail, with long hair tied in a pony tail behind his head. He got his name from his boundless energy around the course, never being able to stand still for long.

I was about to move on, when Art stuck out his hand and stopped me.

"Listen, Hack," he said. "I've been meaning to mention to someone from your network. That round down in Savannah, y'know…when Parker Long passed?"

"Yeah," I said. "What about it?"

"Well it just so happened that Billy was playing the sixteenth that afternoon," Art said. "And I remember seeing a light from up in the booth. I mean, Billy was lining up his putt, waiting for the other guy to finish, and I was just standing on one side of the green, holding the flag, and I saw this flash out of the corner of my eye."

"A flash?"

"Yeah, from up in the booth in that tower," he said. "Kind of a blue zap kind of thing. It was like one of those old camera flash bulb things you see on TV sometimes when a politician or a movie star walks out, y'know?"

"But it was from inside the booth?" I said.

"Yeah, pretty sure," he said. "I mean, I wasn't staring right at the booth or anything, right? But I caught a glimpse of it anyway. Thought it was a little weird at the time. Later, I heard that Parker had croaked about that time. And I wondered about it."

"You tell the cops?" I said.

He shook his head. "Nah," he said. "It was just a peripheral vision thing. I couldn't swear by anything. Just caught a glimpse of a flash."

"You see anything else?" I asked. "Someone going in or out of the tower?"

He shook his head. "Nah," he said. "Billy made his putt and then we were off to the next tee. Didn't think it was anything important."

"OK," I said. "Thanks. The cops think something went wrong with his equipment that day. The flash you saw might be connected to that. I'll tell the cop down in Savannah who's running the investigation."

"Yeah, sure," Art said, getting up and slinging the heavy bag over his shoulder. "If they want to talk to me, I'll tell 'em the same thing."

He strode away. I stayed put and thought about that for a while.

24

H acker's History, PGA Championship edition:
Back in 1957, the PGA of America staged its 39th annual Championship at the Miami Valley Country Club in Dayton, Ohio. This tournament is historically important because it was the last PGA Championship to be conducted at match play.

If you're trying to remember who won the last major of 1957, it was Lionel Hebert, who pipped Dow Finsterwald in the final, 2&1. If you're trying to remember who Lionel Hebert was, you're not alone. He had a brother, Jay, who also won the PGA, in 1960. And Dow Finsterwald would come back the next year and win the first PGA Championship played at stroke play.

But in 1957, change was very much in the air at the PGA. Since the end of the Second World War, the championship had been losing ground with golf fans. Ben Hogan, the cock of the walk in golf after the war, played his last PGA Championship in 1948. Like many of the touring pros of his day, Hogan didn't like playing in the dog days of August heat. He also didn't like match play, where one round against a nobody who started sinking putts could send you home.

And the way the tournament was set up back then, a player who made it into the finals or quarterfinals could expect to play more than 200 holes, all in the August heat.

Another reason the PGA lacked big-name talent in the field was the PGA's own rules. First, in order to be eligible to play, a golfer had to be an official member of the PGA of America, and to attain that membership, you had to serve a five-year apprenticeship, working part-time at a country club selling shirts, giving lessons and schmoozing with the members.

Five years! And in 1957, there were a handful of young, up-and-coming golfers trying to earn a living on the PGA Tour circuit. Guys like Arnold Palmer and Mike Souchak and amateurs like Billy Joe Patton and a 17-year-old Jack Nicklaus were not allowed to play the 1957 PGA Championship because of the apprentice rule.

Of course, the PGA of America also had a 'Caucasians-only' membership rule until 1963, but that's another story.

So the 1957 PGA Championship had a weak field, at an unknown golf course (which had contributed the usual $40,000 to the PGA in order to get the tournament) held in the heat of the summer. Also, there was no national television or radio coverage. It's no wonder the PGA lost its shirt.

All of that helps explain why the board of directors of the PGA voted later in 1957 to change the format of the event from match play to medal. They also had TV cameras in place in 1958 at the Llanerch Country Club in Haverford, Pennsylvania. They also made sure golf's matinee idol, Arnold Palmer, was in the field. He didn't win. In fact, Arnie never won the PGA Championship, although he finished second a bunch of times.

It would be another ten years, in 1969, that the PGA Tour officially split off from the PGA of America and went on to become one of the most successful and wealthy sports organizations in the world.

Today, the PGA Championship continues to search for relevance in the world of golf. It still has a weak field, because the PGA of America insists on reserving thirty or so places in the field to the club professionals in its ranks. It's moved the play dates from the heat of August to the cooler weather of May now, creating a major season that runs from the Masters in April through the Open Championship in July. And it appears to still be open to awarding the tournament venue to the highest bidder, which this year was Conrad Gold and his worldwide resort and club chain.

But it's still one of golf's four major titles. And that means the competition will be fierce, the tension on Sunday afternoon unbearable, and the winner will hold special place in golf's ongoing history.

"ARNIE NEVER WON the PGA?" Billy Ray Bosworth said to me. We were in our greenside booth above the 16th green. It was Thursday afternoon. The PGA Championship had been underway since just after 6:30 that morning. We were on the air.

"Nope," I said. "Total choke job."

I heard Ben Oswald start yelling in my ear.

"My executive producer is yelling at me," I told the viewers. "Apparently he thinks that Arnold Palmer should never be criticized, may he rest in peace."

"Well," Boz said, "He was kinda The Man."

"I agree," I said. "He was also one of the nicest men I ever met. But he never won the PGA, nice guy or not. And he had his chances. Finished second in 1964, 1968 and 1970. But he never delivered the final round heroics he needed."

"But he's still The Man, right Hacks?"

"Sure, sure," I said. "If that makes you feel better."

We continued doing our Boz and Hack show on sixteen. I noticed many of the players went with three woods or less off the tee on the hole, trying to find the sliver of fairway between the water on the left, and the sand and thick rough down the right. Then they had to work a mid-iron into the small green, water left and behind, two deep bunkers on the right.

There were a lot of balls in the water. Boz began imitating submarine klaxons…*dive, dive, dive*…every time a ball splashed. The soundtrack of our golf tournament was beginning to sound a lot like the *Hunt for Red October*. Ben Oswald, who I had noticed was yelling at us a lot less than normal, told Boz to knock it off. "Can the sound effects, you moron," he said on the intercom at one point, late in the afternoon. "You sound like you're in seventh grade for Chrissakes."

The sun was making its way over to Buffalo when we finally went off the air. Shadows drifted across the fairways and the color of the water took on a weird hue: half pink, half orange. When our monitor went black, we packed up, climbed down the ladder and made our way back to Television City. There was a mandatory post-round production meeting.

I was exhausted. You might think sitting on your tuckus for six or seven hours talking about golf and golfers would be easy, but it's not. I was drained. I wanted a cold beer, a hamburger and Mary Jane to rub my shoulders. In roughly that order.

The talent gathered in our trailer, falling into the chairs set around a big conference table. Everyone else looked beat, too. Ben Oswald finally strolled in. He looked like he was ready to go another ten rounds with Muhammad Ali.

"OK," he said, sitting down at the head of the table. "That was pretty good. Kenny and Kelsey? Good job on the fairways today. I heard a lot of good insight. Van, Jimmy? Nice work. Tight. As to you two clowns at sixteen? …"

"Thanks, Boss," Boz said. "We'll try to keep the quality high throughout the weekend."

"Quality?" Ben said. "I've had five calls from the network today, since we went on air. Four of them were passing on complaints about language from religious leaders. I think you offended every one of the world's major religions."

"Who was the fifth call from?" I asked.

"What?"

"You said you had five calls," I said. "Four were from various padres complaining about Boz."

"Hey!" Boz said. "You were there, too!"

"So who was the fifth one from?"

"The head of IBS," Oswald said. "He was laughing. Said you two guys were very entertaining."

"What did you think, Ben?" I asked.

"Do you care?" he said.

"Sure," I said. "You're the television guy. You've been doing this for decades. If you think we're screwing up, I want to know."

He sat there silently for a bit. Everyone was watching him. I was expecting an Oswaldian explosion without parallel, and felt my lower colonic entrance slam shut.

"I can't stand your act," he said, finally. "It goes against everything I've ever believed about good TV. You are brash, mouthy, you've made yourselves the story, not the golf. You insult the traditions of the game. You insult the warriors who have gone before us. You're snarky, impolite, smart-assy. I can't think of a single reason why I shouldn't fire both of your butts."

He stopped.

"But…" I prompted.

"But it seems to be working," he said, dropping his head in defeat. "The preliminary numbers are in, and the fans are eating it up. Fuckin' nighttime comedians are riffing off your stuff. Social media has gone crazy. Clips of you guys are getting tweeted and retweeted by the millions. You've gone viral."

There was a silence in the room that lasted for a few seconds.

"So is this a good time to ask for a raise?" I said.

Van Collins, the old man of the group, who had been listening quietly with his head bowed, snapped his head up and stared at me. Sitting next to him, Jimmy Williams' face broke out in a grin. Then Van began to laugh, a deep baritone sound that came from his gut. Jimmy joined in, and pretty soon, everyone at the table was howling. Boz pounded me on the back.

Ben Oswald sat there, silent, staring. He looked like he wanted to grab something or someone by the neck and start choking the life out of it. But after a couple minutes of laughter from the crew at the table, he couldn't help himself. He began to laugh, too.

25

Later that night, I called home. I'd had my beer (and a couple extra) and a burger and now I needed some wifely contact.

"So, how'd you like the show today?" I asked her.

I heard a long deep sigh. "You're kidding, right?" she said. "I spent all day with my band of merry fourth graders, who all think they're as smart as fifth graders already because it's the end of the school year; I had to take Vickie to a play date; I had to bathe, feed, and re-bathe DJ and he has a cold, and now I've got a couple hours of packing boxes left. And you want to know if I spent any time sitting around watching golf on TV?"

Her voice was beginning to rise in timbre. It hadn't yet reached the shriek stage, but it was getting close.

"I withdraw the question," I said. "Besides, you know it went well. I wouldn't have asked, otherwise."

"Good for you," she said. She sighed again. "I'm sorry, Hacker," she said. "It's just been a long day."

"Completely understand," I said. "I'll be home late Sunday, and we haven't got another broadcast for two weeks. So I'll take over the packing and moving part."

"That will be a big help," she said.

"DJ call out my name yet?" I asked.

"Not so I can tell," she said. "He did say 'blaaaad" today. That's pretty close."

"Kid's a freakin' genius," I said. "Mensa material for sure."

She laughed. I liked that sound. Mary Jane had a wonderful laugh.

"So, no new murders today?" she asked, a mischievous tone in her voice.

"Not yet," I said. "But there's still a couple hours left in the day."

She yawned. Loudly.

"Why don't you go to bed?" I said. "Try again tomorrow."

"Good idea," she said. "I was going to start packing up some of DJ's picture books first. The only one he's heavily into at the moment is *Goodnight, Moon*. I've started to hate that one."

"Screw the picture books," I said. "Get some sleep."

AFTER WE SAID our good nights, I decided to wander down to the inn's restaurant and bar for a nightcap. IBS had booked most of the rooms in the place, so I figured there'd be some friendly faces in the lounge.

I was surprised to find the place mostly empty. It was a little after ten and there were maybe eleven people in the place. Most were are tables, finishing up a late meal with coffee and dessert. There were three people sitting at the long wooden bar. Two guys, who I didn't recognize, were sitting together at one end watching a ball game, but on the far end there was just one young woman, sitting alone. Jenny LoBianco. She was staring into her half-finished pint of beer.

I slipped onto the chair next to her.

"Hey, Jenny," I said. "Mind if I join you for a quick one?"

She turned her head and looked at me. Her eyes were shadowed, her face strained. Then she shook her head and forced herself to smile.

"Oh, hi, Hacker," she said. "Sure."

I ordered a shot of Bowmore from the barkeep and when it arrived, I held it up. She picked up her beer and we clinked.

"That history segment came out pretty good," she said. "Oswald was pleased. He even told me that, if you can believe it."

"Wow," I said. "I hope he's feeling OK. If Ben is handing out compliments, he must be sick."

She smiled. "True enough," she said.

"You have any ideas how we can make the next one better?" I asked.

Her back straightened and her eyes brightened.

"Yeah, as a matter of fact, I do," she said.

"Lay it on me," I said, and sipped a little of my peaty Islay scotch.

For the next ten or fifteen minutes, Jenny LoBianco reeled off a dissertation on how to improve *Hacker's History*. She started with describing the demographic breakdown of our audience and how we could direct our segment to appeal to that demographic. She had a few topics in mind that we could develop for future segments and described how they should look and sound and feel. She spoke in the strange language of television production, all framing shots and cutaways and white values and other stuff I had no idea what she was talking about. I bounced a few ideas back at her, and she liked a couple of them. When I next looked up, it was past eleven.

I drained the last of my second wee dram.

"Shooter was right," I said.

"About what?" she said.

"That you were sharp," I said. "You really get this TV stuff. I'll ask Ben if he can assign you to work with Tony and me. Produce the segment. I think the three of us would kill it."

She beamed at me. "That would be great, Hacker," she said. "I'd love to."

I motioned to the bartender to bring me the bill for both our drinks, and she began gathering her stuff to go upstairs to bed. She had a small purse next to her on the bar, sitting on top of a stack of yellow legal pads, file folders and a big leather-bound notebook. When I saw it, I did a double-take.

"Holy shit," I said. "That notebook looks familiar."

She looked at it, then picked it up and held it in her hands.

"Yeah," she said. "It was Arnie's. I like having it around. It reminds me of him."

"Where did you get it?" I asked.

She held the notebook, rubbing its nubby surface as if it were an old friend.

"He left it at my place," she said. "That night …"

Her voice caught, and she couldn't speak for a bit. She was remembering.

"After work, we went to my place," she told me. "I didn't have anything in the apartment to eat, so he said he'd go out and pick some stuff up at the Fairway. Some wine. Something we could have for dinner. He …he never came home."

Her head dropped, and she began to weep, quietly, head down so no one could see.

"So when he left the market, he wasn't going to his apartment, he was heading back to yours," I said.

"Yeah," she said. "I live about five blocks from him, just off West End Avenue. I told all this to Jefferies at the NYPD."

"Did you tell them you had Arnie's notebook?" I asked.

She shook her head. "No," she said. "I don't…didn't want to give it up. I-I just like having it near. It feels like he's with me."

"I understand," I said. "Have you looked inside? Maybe there were some notes or something that might be important to lead back to whoever did this to him."

She shook her head again. "I've glanced through it. I can't see anything relevant," she said. "Arnie made a lot of lists, and there are many of them on almost every page. But there was nothing I could see."

"Can I take a look?" I said. "Maybe I can see something you didn't notice. New set of eyes."

Jenny shrugged and handed the notebook over. I opened it. It was your typical office organizer—the heavy leather case opened to a week-by-week calendar, with lines for each hour of the day and space to add more notes. There was probably an alphabetized phone list in the back. A couple of straps and compartments on the inside cover provided places where he could have inserted a calculator and maybe his cell phone. Everything in its place and a place for everything. The motto of those office organizer types.

The calendar pages were covered with lots of scribbled notes. Arnie seemed to have been a very well-organized fellow. As Jenny said, he made lots of lists. Most of the entries had something to do with work. Some I could tell were directions and suggestions from Ben Oswald. But there were other notes jotted down by themselves—phone numbers, one or two words underlined or circled that meant nothing to me. I flipped through the pages to the day he was shot. He had

had an eight o'clock breakfast with someone named Hillary and lunch with Ben Oswald.

Down near the bottom of that day's column, he had written "6—dinner with JLB." Jenny LoBianco.

Just above that, I read another entry: "4:30—D" followed by a question mark.

"Who is 'D?'" I asked her. "Dave? Debbie? Don? She shook her head.

"No idea," she said.

"He didn't come in that night and tell you anything about his day? Who he might have met with?"

She smiled. "No," she said. "He mainly wanted to kiss me. Then he asked what I had on hand for dinner. Said he was starving. We looked in the fridge, and he volunteered to go get us something. He left and I took a shower."

She stared off into the distance, remembering that terrible night.

"I waited and waited," she said. "When he didn't come back, I thought something had come up at work. He often got late night calls and had to go fix some problem or other. I called, but there was no answer, his phone went to voice mail. So I eventually ate some cereal and just went to bed."

Her head dropped, and tears began to flow again.

"I'm so sorry," I said. "It must have been awful."

She nodded, silent.

"I didn't find out what happened until I went into work the next morning," she said. "Everyone was stunned. People were crying. It was awful, one of the worst days of my life."

"Because no one knew you two were dating," I said. "That must have made it worse."

"Arnie wanted to keep it secret," she said. "He just didn't think an intra-office romance was a good idea for someone in his position. He had plans."

"Plans?"

She smiled, a bit sadly. "Arnie was ambitious," she said. "He knew about all the stuff going on with the network, all the negotiations about the new golf contracts. He wanted to move up."

"Like into Ben's job?" I asked.

Jenny shrugged. "There's been some talk, watercooler gossip, that Ben may be on the downhill side of his career," she said. "Arnie believed that if IBS got a good chunk of the golf contracts in the network negotiations, he might be able to pitch going after a younger demographic. Oswald has been in charge of IBS golf for a long time. But times change. Arnie wanted to be part of that change."

"Did Ben know all this?"

"I don't know, for sure," she said. "Arnie said Ben was totally on board, but I wonder. They've worked together for many years and they seem to like each other, but there's always been something there between them. I haven't worked here long enough to know what it is. But there is something. Or, was."

"Well, Ben Oswald has never been described as a warm and fuzzy guy," I said. "And I imagine in his years he's seen more than one or two young ambitious junior execs trying to work their way up the ladder."

"I suppose that's true," she said. Then she yawned. "I'm beat," she said. "See ya tomorrow?"

"Right," I said. "Sleep well."

She left and went upstairs to her room. I sat there for a while while the ESPN boys ran tape on the top baseball plays of the day, an amazing loop of great catches, scooped ground balls, fastballs painting the black and three or four monster smashes.

And while that was running, I was thinking about Ben Oswald and his young, ambitious assistant. Who wanted to move up. Maybe into the boss' chair. Oswald had probably seen that before, probably lots of times. I wondered how that made him feel. I wondered what it could make him do. Like maybe follow that assistant to a market on the Upper West Side and put a bullet in his head. Possible? Sure. Anyone who has observed the human condition knows that anyone could do anything to someone else. But was it likely?

I didn't have an answer for that. My gut was not telling me. It was sitting there dealing with two shots of a fine, peaty Scottish whiskey, and that was all it was willing to do at that moment.

So I gave up, and went to bed.

26

I woke up early Friday morning and made myself a cup of that execrable pod coffee that everyone seems to think is the greatest thing since sliced bread. I beg to differ, but I managed to down a cup of the stuff while I scanned the sports pages of the *USA Today* that the inn had slipped underneath my door.

Tommy Scannell had grabbed the first round lead of the PGA Championship with a smooth 65. The kid from San Diego was just two years out of college and had played the round like he was under hypnosis, hitting one good shot after another while draining a bunch of birdie putts. Could he do it three more days in a row? Anything is possible, but I would bet on the negative side and not just because I'm a cynical bastard. First round nobodies in the lead rarely go on to win.

After him was the horde, names known and unknown, about twenty players all bunched up within three shots of the lead and another cohort a few strokes further back than that. In other words, a typical major logjam. Everyone still jockeying for position, hoping to still be relevant and within hailing distance come Sunday afternoon. But the smart ones, the ones who would actually be there on Sunday afternoon, were only thinking about today and how to get their golf balls around the course in the fewest number of strokes. The *really* smart ones were only thinking about the tee shot on the first hole.

I had a couple of hours to kill before our pre-show production meeting, which Oswald had scheduled today here at the inn, instead of down in the hubbub of Television City. I took a long shower and thought about the two murder cases. It seemed more than logical that they were connected, even though no one had yet developed the first indication that they were.

None of us had been able to figure out the link between Parker Long and Arnie Wasserman, except that they both worked for IBS. There was no apparent reason why someone would want *both* Parker and Arnie dead. Parker had been an experienced broadcaster in his last year of work and Arnie had been a hard-charging TV exec on the make. What was the connection?

I could make a case why Parker Long might have wanted to shoot Arnie Wasserman in the head—Arnie had talked about ending Parker's contract early and giving him the heave-ho. But of course, Parker was already dead when Arnie was shot.

Would Arnie have arranged to kill Parker, to get him off the payroll and out of IBS? That, too, was plausible, if more than a little far-fetched. But then who shot Arnie? And why? No good answer.

I shaved and dressed. I thought about the notebook belonging to Arnie that Jenny had kept. The New York cops would probably want to book that as evidence in their investigation, even though there was nothing in Arnie's organizer that I could see that led back to anyone. I should probably tell them about it, but Jenny seemed quite attached to it, and for understandable reasons, and I finally decided not to drop a dime on her.

I made another pod cup of coffee and while it sputtered and hissed in the machine, I thought about Bulldog O'Shaunnesey. He had been a homicide detective in Boston, way back in the day when I had left the PGA Tour and signed on as a cub reporter for the Boston *Journal*, covering the crime beat. Most of the time, that meant hanging around the old police HQ on Harrison Ave. waiting for someone to hand over the day's crime reports, then looking through them for something interesting. Like the wife who got tired of her husband's farting during the nightly news and hacked off his head with a machete. Or the guy suffering PTSD after two tours in Nam who started torching parked cars on St. Botolph Street with a stolen flamethrower. Napalm in the Back Bay. My editor loved stories like that.

I got to know most of the guys who worked in the cop shop along with Bulldog, suffering the usual amount of abuse for being both a civilian *and* a news reporter. Bulldog was one of the department's characters, a longtime homicide dick who could not more closely resemble the Irish cop stereotype: huge ruddy face, always wreathed in a wry grin, fast-talking smartass, big burly frame, red hair. And a heavy drinker.

Once he got to know you, Bulldog would occasionally invite you along on a squeal, letting you ride shotgun as he wheeled at high speed through Boston's narrow street grid, blue lights flashing. The car would pull up in front of a tenement somewhere—South End, Dorchester, Roxbury, Mattapan—and Bulldog, who moved with surprising ease and quickness for a large man, would dash into the building and up the stairs to wherever the dead person lay. He'd let me snap a few quick black-and-whites before shooing me back out the door to wait by the squad car while he did his cop thing.

Anyway, I learned a lot by watching Bulldog work, and asking him questions. And more than once I heard him say about a tough case, "Go back and start at the beginning. What happened? How did events unfold? Forget what you think you know. Go back over it and pretend you don't know anything. Ask some more questions. Something will pop up. Something you didn't think about the first time through. And there you are."

So, sipping my awful coffee, I went back to the beginning. Parker Long, sitting in his broadcast booth, commenting on a golf tournament. According to the cops, he was wearing headphones that were delivering an ear full of static, headphones that someone had apparently tampered with. I had been trying to figure out why someone would do that, tamper with the headphones.

But using Bulldog's start-over strategy, I should be thinking "What did Parker Long do?" He'd been a broadcaster for a couple of decades. That day, he had crappy headphones. He was getting static and white noise. He would have called someone for help. The IBS tech crew. "Hey," he would have said, "My headphones suck. Can't hear a thing. What's going on?"

They would have sent someone out to the tower on sixteen. Someone to fool around with the relay unit. If that unit had been in the booth overnight, it might have gotten wet somehow, screwed something up inside, which was causing the static. No? OK, check the headphone wires for frays. Maybe a wire was loose. Maybe the plug nose was broken. When nothing else worked to end the static noise, they would have swapped out the bad headphones for a new pair.

I sat up.

Parker Long had still been wearing the faulty headphones when I found him, dead. The ones I carefully removed from his body. The ones the Georgia cops had later examined and found to be tampered with. *They had still been on his head.*

Why?

I called Shooter Sciutto. He was in another room at the inn.

"Question," I said when I got him on the line. "If one of us in the booth had a pair of faulty headphones on during the broadcast, was getting lots of static and white noise, what would happen?"

"You'd call in on the intercom line, tell them you couldn't hear a goddam thing and have them send someone out to fix it," he said. "Happens a lot, actually. Our equipment gets more stressed than, say, the stuff they use in a studio downtown. We're out in the weather, getting rained on, moving from location to location. Stuff gets thrown around, banged up, and it breaks. A lot."

"So someone from tech would come out and fiddle around with stuff?"

"Yeah," he said. "They'd send Digby out, or someone else from that crew. Benny is good. Sheila knows her way around all the equipment."

"Would they bring a new pair of headphones?"

"Sure," Shooter said. "There's boxes of them in the trailer. New wires. Plugs. Cables. Probably back-up units for the audio relays. And our techies are good—they can rewire an entire camera in about three minutes flat if they have to. Unplug a circuit assembly and plug in a new one. I've seen 'em in action."

"Huh," I said.

"Why do you ask?" he said. "Did you have some problems yesterday?"

"No," I said. "Everything was cool. Does someone keep records on stuff like that? If they need to come out to the booth and change out a headphone unit. Who'd keep track of that?"

"I don't think there's a logbook or anything like that," he said. "As you've seen, things get pretty busy during the broadcast. You'd call in, say my headphones don't work, and Ben or the assistant director or whoever got your intercom call would call down to Tech and tell them to get out to your booth with some new headphones, stat."

"So the control room would contact Tech and whoever's on duty would grab some stuff and head down to my booth," I said.

"Yeah, that sounds about right," he said. "There a point to all these questions?"

"Contingency planning," I said. "Just in case."

"That's a little anal, Hack," Tony said. He hung up.

I smiled. I might have sounded anal, but I finally had the first glimmer of a clue. Or at least, a pathway to follow. If Parker Long's headphones had acted up, and the forensic boys in Georgia said they did, he would have called for help. Someone had taken that call and, in turn, called the Tech department to go fix it.

What had happened next? That I didn't know. But I could probably find out.

Our production meeting started at eleven. I showed up a few minutes early. I was looking for either Bill Stirling or Nancy Davis. Both were Ben Oswald's assistant directors, Bill handling the playback desk, Nancy in charge of graphics and Chyron, making sure the scoreboard screens and player IDs were ready when Ben put someone on the air.

Bill was sitting in the conference room when I walked in. He glanced up from the newspaper he was reading.

"Hey, Hacker," he said. "Ready for another five hours of fun today?"

"Ready as I'll ever be," I said. "Listen, do you remember getting a call from Parker Long that day down in Savannah? Something the matter with his headphones?"

Bill scratched his chin, thinking. "Nah," he said finally. "Doesn't ring a bell. Why?"

"I'm just pinning down some information," I said.

People began walking in. Van and Jimmy came in together, each carrying a cup of coffee. The Boz sauntered in, looking like he needed another couple hours of sleep. Some of the other control booth people came in. Kelsey walked in with Nancy Davis. They were laughing together about something.

I went over and greeted them. Asked Nancy if she remembered anything about Parker's headphones down in Savannah.

"Yeah," she said, nodding. "I told the cops down in Savannah when they asked that day. I got a message from Parker a little after five. Said he was getting static. He said it had been like that all afternoon and was getting worse. I called Tech and they said someone would get right on it."

"Do you remember who they sent?" I asked.

She shook her head. "No reason for me to know that," she said. "I just passed on Parker's complaint. I assume they went and fixed it, because Parker never called back."

"OK," I said. "Thanks."

Ben Oswald hadn't shown up yet, so I wandered over to the far wall where some coffee and tea service had been set up and poured myself a cup. This stuff came out of a big silver urn and tasted a lot better than the pod crap.

Kelsey Jenkins followed me and began getting her own coffee.

"What was that about, Hacker?" she asked.

"What?" I said.

"The questions about Parker's headphones," she said. "What have you found out?"

"Not sure," I told her. "But I'm pretty sure someone from Tech went down to Parker's booth in Savannah just before he died. He was having headphone problems."

"Yeah, well, that's their job, isn't it?" she said. "Fixing tech problems."

"True enough," I said. "But this someone may have fixed Parker's problems permanently."

"You mean?"

She looked at me aghast. I nodded.

Ben Oswald walked into the room.

"OK," he said, "Let's get this shit show on the road."

27

Oswald prattled on for about thirty minutes. He went over the tee sheets for the day, talking about the A-level groups that would be playing in the afternoon. The PGA of America sets its tournament pairings like any other professional golf tournament: the better players are placed in hierarchical groups and paired together. Former PGA Championship winners, other major tournament winners, multiple PGA Tour winners…all are tossed in the A-group. This puts the high achievers in the same groups, which the fans like, and the A-group players tend to get better tee times. Mid-to-late morning on Thursday, early afternoon times on Friday. Or vice versa. The others, the hopefuls and the also-rans, like the thirty or forty PGA of America club professionals in the field at this tournament, get assigned to early or late tee times. The dew sweepers, they call them.

So Ben went over the A-listers we would be covering that afternoon and tossed out some informational and biographical tidbits for the announcers to keep in mind. Most of which we all knew about, of course, but your executive producer's gotta produce, so we just sat there and listened.

Once that was done, there wasn't much left to say. It was day two of a golf tournament, no matter if it was the PGA or the East Jesus Open. The cameras were still the same, the audio was ready, the chyron was working, the ads were in place. All we needed were the golfers to go out and make their shots, and the early groups were already hard at it.

Oswald finally looked at his watch.

"OK, that's all I got," he said. "Get some lunch, be in place at one thirty. On air at two sharp. Questions?"

There were none. Ben nodded and we all got up.

Billy Joe Bosworth met me at the door. He looked like death warmed over: his eyes were bloodshot and his face drawn.

"You look like shit," I said. "Late night?"

"Oh yeah," he said, his voice phlegmy. "Very late."

"I didn't see you in the lounge," I said. "Where'd you go?"

He sighed. It was a deep, heartfelt sigh that I recognized as that which comes from a man deeply hung over.

"Went into the city," he said. "Hit a few clubs."

"A few?" I said, smiling.

"OK, I lost count after four," he said. "It's a big fuckin' town. Uptown, downtown, the Village. Lotta places."

"Meet anyone nice?" I asked.

"They're all nice after a few cocktails," he said. "But don't tell Sheila."

"Lips are sealed," I told him. "What time did you get back?"

"I dunno," he said. "What time is it now?"

I laughed.

"You need a long hot shower and about a gallon of coffee," I said.

"I need a head transplant," he said. "But I'll try the shower thing first."

He waved a weak hand at me and went off to find his room.

I caught the shuttle bus down to the Gold Club. The medieval jousting tournament was in full swing, pennants flapping in a nice breeze off the river, sunshine pounding down, crowds of people milling hither and yon. All that was missing was the sound of heavy hoof beats and the splintering of lances against armor.

I called Delbert Conner down in Savannah.

"Mister Hacker," he said when I got him on the line. "What a pleasant surprise. Who's winning the PGA?"

"Nobody yet," I said. "You'll have to watch IBS to find out."

"Which I intend to," he said. "After I take my boat out for a spin in the morning."

"Listen," I said. "Parker Long called in to the control booth when his headphones began to bother him, right?"

"He did," Conner agreed.

"And Tech sent someone out to help him," I said.

"They did," he said.

"Who'd they send out?"

"Ahh, let me see," he said. "I don't remember." I could hear him flipping through some pages, probably from his three-ring binder of a homicide book. "Yeah, here it is," he said. "Sheila Dunleavy. She told us she replaced some kind of fuse on his audio relay. Said she was up there with him for less than five minutes."

"And he was alive when she left?"

"Gee, Mister Hacker," Conner said, "I think she would have remembered and mentioned it if he was dead as a mackerel."

I was silent. Not what I was expecting to hear.

"Anything else I can do for you on this fine morning?" Conner said. "I mean, I got nothing else to do, no crimes what need solving, while I just sit here and listen to the sound of you breathing."

"So you think Sheila was the last person to see Parker alive?" I said.

"We have no record of anyone else going up to his booth until you did," he said. There was a slight pause. "But that doesn't mean that somebody didn't."

"I take it you checked out Sheila pretty good," I said.

"Oh, yes," Conner said with a soft chuckle. "Would you like a list of all her boyfriends since high school?"

"Not really," I said. "I take it you've found nothing that connects her to either Parker or Arnie Wasserman."

"Nothing that makes me think she's the one," he said.

"How come every time I talk to you I feel deeper in the dark?" I said.

"It's one of my many fine qualities," he said. "That, and my years of experience as a dedicated public servant."

"I knew it was something," I said, and rang off.

I set off in search of Sheila Dunleavy. I had seen her around, of course, had nodded at her pleasantly, but we had never spoken. I went down to Television City and entered the dark recesses of the Tech department's semi trailer. I made my way to the back, where the workbench stretched across the trailer's width. Benny Young, the third member of the Tech crew, was working on some piece of equipment with a screwdriver and pair of needle-nose pliers.

"I'm looking for Sheila," I said. "You seen her around?"

Benny nodded, not looking up from his project.

"She's up on eight tee," he said. "FlitePath camera was jostled by someone. Damn things are delicate as fuck. She went up to do a reset."

I nodded. I had learned from Shooter that the cameras they now use on almost every tee, the ones that track and show the path through the air of a tee shot, were fussy and delicate machines. Once you get them in place, aimed to show a lot of sky above the player's head so the path of the ball's flight will stand out, they have to be calibrated so the internal sensor can focus on the ball and the connected computer will calculate and display the ball's flight path once it is struck and sent down the fairway. And if a fan or an official or a caddie happens to brush up against the camera unit, the sensor and the high-speed computers that do all the millions of calculations won't work anymore. And then someone like like Sheila has to go manually recalibrate. The network tries to install the machines on poles or tripods that are protected and kept away from people, but at a golf tournament, anything can happen and often does.

"She coming back here when she's done?" I asked Benny.

He shrugged. "Dunno," he said. "Depends on what manner of shit happens next. She might come back here, or she might get a call to go over to twelve or down to fifteen. You want me to call her?"

"How does she get called?" I asked.

Benny reached up and pulled a small black pod out of his left ear. He showed it to me.

"Digital walkie-talkie," he said. "We got our own frequency. One of the directors in the control room calls…we go."

I looked at it. "You all got these?" I said. "You and Sheila?"

"And Digby," Benny said. He finished screwing in the last machine screw he was working on and flipped the black electronic box over, right side up. He plugged in a black cord to the back and flipped a switch on the side to the up position. Three green lights on the front of whatever the box was came on and began to blink. Benny made a satisfied sound.

"So anytime you get a call to go fix something, you all three hear the message?" I said.

Benny nodded. "Yup," he said. "Whichever one of us is free responds and off we go. Sometimes, we can go hours between trouble calls. Other times, it's like every ten minutes."

"Do you remember when Parker Long called in about his headphone problem down in Savannah?" I asked.

He nodded. "Sure," he said. "We all heard that. I was here in the truck. I think Digby was coming back from something he had been fixing out on ten. Sheila was closest and she took the call."

"They said she replaced a fuse or something," I said.

Benny shrugged. "I don't know what she did," he said. "I was in here, packing up for the day. It was late in the broadcast when Parker called in. Sheila came back about fifteen minutes later. Digby rolled in about ten minutes after that."

He looked at me.

"How come you're asking all this stuff?" he said. "The cops down in Savannah went over it all with us the next day. Told 'em the same thing I just told you."

"I'm just trying to figure out how Parker could have gotten electrocuted that afternoon," I said. "Nobody's been able to explain it."

"Explain what?"

The voice came from behind me. I turned around and saw Digby Allen standing there. He had a big black toolcase over one shoulder and was carrying a rolled length of black cable in one hand. He was staring at me with a kind of smirky look on his face.

"Oh, hi Digby," I said. "I was just asking Benny here about the afternoon when Parker Long was killed. Trying to put some of the pieces together."

"Why?" Digby asked. "You're not a cop. What do you care?"

"Geez, Digs," Benny Young spoke up. "Parker was one of us. We all want to know what the hell happened."

Digby shrugged, dumped his tool kit on the bench and turned away to stow the rolled up cable in a drawer behind him.

"I say let the cops try and figure it out," he said. "Not Hacker's job to solve the crime."

"You're not curious?" I said.

He shrugged again.

"I guess not," he said. "I mean, I'm sorry the guy's dead and all. But they'll figure it out sooner or later. I got work to do."

He turned on his heel and left. I heard his footfalls as he walked down the dark central aisle of the trailer and heard the door slam as he went out.

Benny looked at me and shrugged.

"That was the full Digby," he said. "It's why some people think he's cracked in the head."

"Do you?"

He laughed. "Naw," he said. "He can be a large dick, no question about it. But that's just Digby. Kinda weird, much of the time. You get used to it."

I looked at my watch. It was time to go. I had a golf tournament to broadcast.

28

Tell me, Boz, what do you know about Tommy Scannell?

The player in question had reached our tee on sixteen. It was late in the afternoon on Friday. Scannell, the first-round leader, was still leading as the second round was coming to a close. He was two under today, nine under for the tournament. He'd played the front nine in even par and dropped a couple of nice putts on the back nine to keep what was currently a two-shot lead over the rest of the field.

"Southern California kid," Boz said. "Played his college golf at Oklahoma State. I think he made it to the quarter-finals of the U.S. Amateur when he was a junior."

"So the kid's got game?" I said.

"Hacker, my man," Boz said reprovingly. "The kid is leading the PGA Championship. On Friday afternoon. Yeah, I think he's got game."

We watched as Scannell selected a fairway wood from his bag and prepared to hit his tee shot.

"Three wood," I said. "Smart play."

"He just has to find the fairway between the river on the left and the bunkers on the right," Boz said. "Straighter is better than longer. But the way these kids today hit the ball, there's not much difference on the longer part."

Scannell made a nice pass at the ball and the FlitePath camera behind him showed us the parabolic flight of the ball. It was right down the middle with a tiny draw on the end.

"That will play all day long," Bosworth said.

The camera followed the ball as it bounced on the fairway and rolled out another twenty yards or so.

"He'll have an easy nine-iron into this green," Boz said. "He looks relaxed and in control."

"It's good to be a twenty-something kid," I said. "They don't know what nerves are at that age."

"So true, pard," Boz said. "At that age, every shot is a green light."

Ben Oswald's voice buzzed in my ear and I and threw the live feed over to Van and Jimmy at eighteen, where Dustin Johnson and Patrick Reed were putting out. Both were within five shots of Scannell's lead.

Boz pulled his headphones off his ears and sighed.

"Man, what time is this thing over?" he said. "I need a drink."

"After last night?" I said. "You probably still have most of the alcohol you pounded floating around inside you."

"That's why I need a drink," he said. "It's starting to wear off."

"What'll you have?" came a voice behind us, We both jumped a little and spun around in our chairs. Digby Allen was standing there, smiling at us. "I can get you something from the hospitality tent down there," he said.

"Geez, Digby, don't sneak up on us like that," Boz said. "I almost crapped my pants."

"Oh, sorry," he said. "Guess you didn't hear me with your headphones on."

"What do you need, Digs?" I asked.

"Nothing," he said. "Bill Weaver's camera had an indicator light fail." He motioned upwards toward the camera platform on the top of our tower. "Had to replace the bulb. Just thought I'd stop in here for a sec and see how you guys were getting along."

"We're fine," Boz said. "Now that my heart rate has subsided to just under coronary level."

"Okey doke," Digby said. "Well, carry on."

He stepped back and ducked through the flap to climb down the scaffolding ladder. A second or two later, he poked his head back in.

"This belong to either of you guys?" he said. He held up a manila envelope. It was letter size, plain brown. There was nothing written on the outside. "It was taped to the scaffolding."

"Not that I know of," I said. I was keeping an eye on the live feed monitor. Johnson and Reed were still putting out on the last hole, but Tommy Scannell was getting ready to hit his approach to our green.

"OK," he said. He tossed the envelope down on the floor of the booth and ducked away again.

Ben Oswald's voice buzzed again and we were back on live.

"Scannell is looking at a nine iron for his approach," I said. "Trying not to look at the water behind and to the left of the green."

"But he knows it's there, Hack," Boz said. "He can focus on his target on the green all he wants, but he knows that any kind of a tug left means he's not in the lead any more."

Scannell made his swing. The timing at impact looked a little late to me.

"Fore right," I said.

The ball flew high into the air and hung there a long time before dropping down into the greenside bunker on the right. The crowd around the green groaned in unison.

"Rookie mistake," Boz said.

"Rookie guarding against a bigger mistake," I said. "But we've seen a dozen guys in that bunker today and I think only one hasn't managed to get up and down. It's a pretty routine shot for these guys. So he should be okay."

"Still, he missed the green with a nine iron," Boz said. "Back home, the guys would be all over me if I hit a shot like that."

"And deservedly so," I said. "Pro like you should hit the green with a nine iron from the fairway every time. Especially playing on the podunk muni where you spend all your time. But this is the PGA Championship, and Scannell knew that going left meant bogey or worse."

"Podunk muni?" Boz said, his voice sounding insulted. "I'll have you know that Goat Acres is a fine, fine golf course. Except for the occasional bad lies we get on the greens. Those armadillos can be pesky little bastards."

Ben Oswald buzzed at us again and I tossed the feed over to seventeen.

"Goat Acres?" I said.

"That's actually what we call it sometimes," he said with a smile. "But it's home."

I laughed. Looking around, I noticed the envelop Digby had dropped and bent over to pick it up. The flap was open, so I reached inside and pulled out a single piece of paper inside.

It was a white sheet of bond. Somebody had scribbled something on one side using a pencil.

NO MORE QUESTIONS ON SAVANNAH OR U DIE!!

I showed the paper to Bosworth. He read it and his eyebrows arched.

"Two exclamation points, Hack," he said. "I think they mean business."

"They?"

"Hell, it's obvious this is from the Mob," he said. "Didn't you watch *Goodfellas*? They were always sending out letters with multiple exclamation points. Just before they'd blow someone away and go bury them in some nearby forest."

"I must have missed that part," I said. I re-read the sentence, thinking about it. On the live feed monitor, one of the South Koreans was lining up a birdie putt. Twelve footer.

"Whaddya think, Hack," Boz whispered. "Fifty bucks ole Wan Hung Lo sinks it. You in?"

I smiled at his unpolitically correct reference. "Nah," I said, "I think he'll drain it too."

Lee Kyung-Ju rammed the putt home. It put him three shots behind the leader. The crowd went wild. Oswald tossed the feed back to us, where Tommy Scannell was shuffling his feet down into the sand at the bottom of the bunker, getting ready for his explosion shot.

He made a big, relaxed swing, thumped the sand at the bottom and watched as the ball floated up over the lip, landed ten feet from the hole, bounced once, checked, and rolled out to about a foot. The fans cheered, and Scannell waved his hand in acknowledgment as he smoothed the sand with his feet before jumping out the back of the bunker, slapping the soles of both shoes with his wedge and taking his putter from his caddie. He was smiling, mostly, it looked to me, with relief.

"Professional golf shot," I said. "Beautifully judged, perfectly executed. And Tommy Scannell remains in the lead with two tough holes left in today's second round."

"Yup," the Boz said. "Kid's got game."

Oswald sent the feed off to another hole. I looked at the letter that someone had delivered. It still said the same thing.

"You worried?" Boz said, watching me.

"What?" I said, "Worried? No, no. This is actually good news."

"How do you figure?"

"He's come out in the open," I said. "For the first time."

"Who has?" Boz said,

"The killer," I said. "He feels the heat. I've been asking questions of people here and there. What do they remember about what happened to Parker Long. It's gotten back to him. Or her. Heat is rising. Hence the warning. Stop or else."

"You gonna?"

"Gonna what?"

"Stop asking questions?" Boz said.

"Oh, hell, no," I said. "I'm finally getting close. I just wish I knew who I was getting close to."

"Yeah," Boz said. "That would help. So's you'd know when to duck."

29

After the round ended, the IBS crew got together in the trailer at Television City for a brief post-mortem. Ben Oswald was surprisingly calm.

"OK, people," he said. "Good work today. Let's all get some rest tonight. Whatta we got, fifteen golfers within six shots? Should be fun tomorrow. Let's be ready, OK?"

We all nodded, and he continued in his non-Ben way of being supportive and encouraging. That made most of us nervous—we were used to pencils being thrown, f-bombs being dropped and the back entrance to our colons being threatened with some kind of invasive force.

I rode back to the Cumberland Arms in a network van with Boz and some of the others on the crew. Everyone seemed wrung out. There wasn't much in the way of conversation. Of course, Boz was still hung over, so at least he had a good excuse for silence.

I waved to everyone in the lobby and went up to my room, thinking I'd have a quick shower, an early dinner and get myself into bed as soon as possible. I unlocked the door and walked in. Mary Jane was sitting on my bed, with DJ lying next to her, grinning madly and kicking his feet in the air.

"I'm sorry," I said. "Must be the wrong room. I thought I had a single."

MJ jumped up and gave me a big hug. And a kiss. Which I returned, with gusto. But it was hard to get anything romantic going, since we both kept one eye on DJ, who was watching us and trying to stuff some of his toes into his mouth.

"Well this is unexpected," I said. "But nice."

"I called in sick today," Mary Jane told me. "Just couldn't face the class today. It's been a long, long week. Victoria was invited to spend the weekend at Sally and Cindy's house—" She mentioned the O'Neal twins who were in Vickie's class—"And I finally decided I needed to get away for a while. So I packed up the boy and here we are!"

"Drive wasn't too hard?" I asked.

"Nah," she shook her head. "He slept the first hour or so, and then I played The Beatles CD, which he loved. And then we were here."

"Awesome," I said. "I'm glad you came. I missed you guys."

I laid down on the bed and DJ rolled over and crawled onto my chest. I planted a big raspberry on his stomach and held him up in the air. He squealed in delight.

"So who's winning?" Mary Jane asked.

"Kid named Tommy Scannell," I said. "But he's got a dozen or so battle-weary veterans breathing down his neck. Should make for a wild weekend."

"They have a spa in this place?" she asked. "Massages? Sauna? Hot tub?"

I reached over to my bedside table and handed her the inn's leatherbound volume of amenities. She flipped through the pages and found the inn's health and well being section.

"Ooo," she said. "Hot rocks therapy and reiki massage. "Should make for a wild weekend."

I laughed. "What are you gonna do with him?" I said, nodding at our son on the bed between us.

"Not my problem," she said. "But it says here they also have babysitting service."

"Yeah, but it's also PGA Championship weekend," I said. "Lotta people around. Might be tough to get one on short notice."

She looked at me. Didn't say anything.

"But I shall endeavor to find out," I said. "And leave no stone unturned in my quest."

She leaned over and kissed me softly. "And if you're successful, there's more where that came from," she said.

A COUPLE OF hours later, we went down to dinner, the wife and I. DJ had been fed, bathed, dressed in his PJ's and was being read a story from a book by Maria, a lovely forty-something local woman whom the inn had called in. Turns out that few of the people in the inn for the weekend, most of whom were employees of IBS, had much need of a babysitter, and Maria, who lived nearby, was happy for the work. When we left the room, DJ's eyes already looked half-closed, and we suspected he would be asleep in thirty minutes or less.

"She's not costing too much, is she?" Mary Jane whispered to me as we left the room.

I shook my head. "Naw," I said. "I'll just charge it to the room, which is being paid for by IBS. They don't give a crap. You wanna know how much the network is pulling in revenue-wise this weekend?"

"Not really, no," she said.

I laughed. "Well, it's plenty. So quit worrying."

She took my arm and smiled at me. "OK," she said, "I can do that."

We wandered over to the main dining room, checked in with the maitre'd and looked around. I saw Van and Jimmy dining at one table, and some of the camera guys, including Shooter, at another. And back in the corner, sitting alone at a table for four, was the gleaming bald-headed visage of Conrad Gold. He saw me from across the room and waved me to come over.

Mary Jane saw him at about the same time, and I heard her exhalation of recognition. "Isn't that...?" she said.

"Yup," I said. "C'mon."

We walked over and Gold stood up to greet us, smiling.

"Mister Gold," Mary Jane said, giving him a little peck on the cheek. "How nice to see you again."

"My dear Mrs. Hacker," He said. "Call me Conrad, please. After what we all went through in St. Andrews, I feel like we're almost family. Would you two care to join me? I haven't ordered yet."

"Delighted," Mary Jane said, and Gold held a chair for her. A waiter came over and we ordered some drinks and he gave us the menus to read.

"I didn't know your wife was coming this weekend," Gold said. "Or I would have arranged to eat down at my club."

"Her arrival was a last-minute deal," I said, "I was wondering why you were slumming in this dump when you have your very own palatial castle just down the road."

Gold laughed. "I'll have to tell my friend Benny Moskowitz that you called his inn a dump," he said. "Actually, I've been eating here for years and years. It's considered one of the best restaurants in Dutchess County. And sometimes, frankly, it's good to be a little anonymous for a change."

"I can imagine being a big famous celebrity like you could get old after a while," Mary Jane said.

"It does indeed, m'dear," he said. He paused. "But not enough that I wish to return to the state of being penniless."

"No," she said. "That wouldn't be much fun, either."

The waiter came back and we ordered.

"Didn't I hear that you two are parents now?" Conrad said when he left the table.

"We are indeed," Mary Jane said. "DJ is upstairs right now, hopefully sleeping and letting the babysitter watch TV."

"And you have a daughter, too, isn't that right?" he continued.

"Yes," Mary Jane said. "She's at home in Boston, partying like a sixth grader with her friends."

"Ah," Gold said. "Almost a teen ager." The waiter arrived with our drinks. "From what I hear from my friends with teenagers, you'll likely need lots of cocktails to get through those years."

"The Vickster is a pretty sharp and centered young woman," I said. "I'm pretty sure we'll be OK."

"Hope so," the two of them replied, in unison. Then laughed, together.

"How's the weekend going so far, from your perspective?" I asked Conrad.

He shrugged and sipped some of his cocktail, which looked like a vodka gimlet, with some fresh lime slices floating amidst the ice cubes.

"Business-wise, it's a total write-off," he said. "The members pretty much all stay away. Some of the local New York people will come up to watch the tournament, but they'll all go home at night. Our guest rooms have all been given to the PGA of America for their bigwigs and international friends. So except for the dining room, there's not much in the way of revenue coming in."

"And you're already in the hole for, what was it? Twenty-five million?" I said. "Paid for the rights to stage the tournament."

Gold grinned at me.

"You sound like my accountant," he said. "Always telling me what I can't do, what I shouldn't have done. I have no time for that."

"Will you make it back?" I asked.

"Easily," he said, nodding. "Look, thanks to this tournament, and your network by the way, the Gold Organization is getting massive amounts of national and international publicity this weekend. My marketing people tell me it's worth well north of a hundred million dollars in exposure. So the twenty-five mil I laid out is being paid back over and over. People all around the world, rich people especially, will see our brand. I may not get enough new members and property owners here in Cumberland, New York, to recoup the investment. But over the next two or three months, our projections are that we'll sign both membership and real estate contracts that will total maybe a quarter-billion. Company wide. Probably more."

"Sounds like a good investment," Mary Jane said.

"I thought so," Gold nodded. "That's why I did it."

The waiter arrived with our meals, and we waited while he passed around our food and wished us bon appetit. Then Mary Jane changed the subject.

"Do you have children, Conrad?" she asked sweetly.

He smiled, but it looked like with some degree of sadness.

"I do," he said, turning to Mary Jane. "My first wife and I had a son, out in Los Angeles. Thirty years ago. No, I think John is thirty-two now. Times does fly, doesn't it?"

"What does he do?"Mary Jane pressed on. She's always been good at getting people to talk about themselves. I must have cut that class at journalism school.

"He's a musician," Gold told us. "Plays several instruments and does a little conducting. He works mostly in the movie biz, playing in orchestras and bands for background music in films."

"That sounds interesting," MJ said.

"He enjoys it," Gold said. "And I like that it's at least steady work, which is unusual for a musician. On the side, he's had several rock bands over the years, and sometimes is invited to sit in with some of his friends at the jazz clubs."

"That's excellent," Mary Jane said. "An artist who can make a living doing what he loves."

"No interest in running an international real estate and resort chain?" I said. Unlike Mary Jane, I like to throw flaming Molotov cocktails into conversations. In journalism school, that class was called How to Piss Off Important People 101. I aced it.

"Not a scintilla of interest," Gold said. "And I'm glad. Because I'd never allow Johnny to work in my company."

"Really?" Mary Jane said. "Why is that?"

"Oh, hell," he said, waving his hands for emphasis. "Let me count the ways. First, I've never observed a family business which actually works as well as a non-family concern. Never. Second, he has no aptitude for the business world. He's immensely talented in so many other ways, but not in finance or commerce. So I think it's great he's found his own path through life. And finally, I'd never hire him because I wouldn't want to find out he might be better than me."

"Wow," I said. "Oedipus in reverse or something."

"I don't know about that," Gold said. "But this is my business. Nobody else's. I intend to keep it that way until I sell it. Or close it down. Whichever comes first."

I was about to ask him under what conditions he might consider doing either, when Stephanie Collier came striding into the dining room, looking around. She saw Gold sitting with us and came right over.

"Stephanie," Gold said when she arrived at our table, "You remember Hacker, here don't you? And this is his lovely wife, Mary Jane. Stephanie does the marketing for our organization."

Collier glanced at and ignored us.

"Problem at the club, Mr. Gold," she said. Her voice sounded a little strained. "Here, talk to security."

She handed him her phone. He held it up to his ear, identified himself and listened. I watched his face. It didn't change, but remained impassive.

"When," he said. He listened.

"Anyone injured?" He listened.

"OK, I'll be right over." He handed the phone back to Stephanie. Then he turned to us with an apologetic smile.

"I'm afraid I must run," he said. "Someone exploded a car bomb in the parking lot at the club. Nobody hurt, thank goodness. But I have to go meet with the police."

"Of course," I said. "Anything we can do?"

"No, no," he said, getting up and folding his napkin calmly. "But thank you for asking. Mary Jane? It was a delight to see you again. My apologies for this, but I have to go."

Mary Jane stood up and gave Conrad Gold a hug and another peck on his cheek. He walked out, followed by Collier.

30

I didn't learn the facts until the next morning. When Gold had left the table, my first instinct was to follow him, after making sure I had my reporter's notebook, a pen that worked and maybe a small camera at the ready. Car bomb? At the golf tournament site? Talk about catnip for a reporter!

But Mary Jane had stopped me. She saw the look in my eyes and had laid her hand, gently but firmly, on my arm.

"Sit down," she had said. "I'm not finished with my dinner, and I want dessert and a coffee, too."

"But—" I had started to protest. Then I looked in her eyes. And stopped. And sat.

"Not your business," she said. "Not in any way. Nobody was hurt. You heard him say that. Could have been something wrong with the car. Nobody knows. Let them sort it out. I want a quiet dinner with my man."

She was right, as she very often is. So I had sat back down, tucked in my napkin again and we finished our dinner. Conrad had ordered a very nice bottle of burgundy, so I refilled both our glasses, then raised mine towards my wife.

"You're right," I said. "*Slainte.*"

And we had quietly finished our meal, ordered one extra chocolatey sundae-and-brownie thing with two spoons, and enjoyed a nice cafe au lait. Then we made our way upstairs, bid Maria a pleasant evening, looked at our son sleeping on his stomach with his little butt in the air, comfy in his travel crib, and gone to bed.

The next morning, DJ was up and at 'em early, so we were among the first of the guests in the dining room for breakfast, a little before seven. But the place was abuzz.

Shooter was standing outside the dining room, scanning a newspaper.

"Hacker," he said when we walked up, "Did you hear about the bomb?"

"Yes I did," I said. I introduced my wife and son. "We were eating dinner with Conrad Gold when he got the call. What happened?"

Shooter shrugged. "Not much in the paper," he said. "But the grapevine says that a car in the employees' lot exploded, sometime around nine last night."

"Nobody was hurt, right?" Mary Jane asked anxiously.

"No," Shooter shook his head. "No one in the car, or standing nearby."

"They got any suspects?"

He shook his head.

"Cops have called in the bomb squad from the staties—they have a barracks not far from here. From what I've been able to learn, it sounds like it was mostly a dud."

"How so?" I asked.

"More noise than damage," Shooter said. "The car's hood was crumpled and there was a small fire that hotel security was able to put out with a fire extinguisher before the fire department arrived. But nobody thinks that Al Qaida or someone like that was involved. They're thinking more along the lines of a teenage prank."

"Well that's good news," Mary Jane said. "Be terrible if they had to cancel the tournament."

Shooter and I just looked at her. She saw the expression on our faces and laughed.

"Well, if it had been Al Qaida, they might have," she said.

I reached over and took DJ out of her arms.

"Why don't you go see the activities desk over there and get your spa activities arranged," I said. "Me and the boy will go find some bacon."

"Good idea," she said, turning away. "But he doesn't eat bacon yet."

"More for me," I called after her.

I turned to Tony.

"You had breakfast yet?" I asked. "Welcome to join us. Hope you don't mind a little spit-up."

He laughed. "I've eaten thanks," he said. "And I've got three of my own. Well versed in spit up."

He looked at his watch.

"Meeting today at eleven, right?" he asked. I nodded and he strolled off with a wave.

DJ and I went into the dining room, and I commandeered a table off in the corner, well away from anyone else. DJ was a pretty even-tempered baby for the most part, but he was capable, as all babies are, of quickly exploding with the force of a seven-megaton bomb. So we always tried to stay away from normal humans, just in case.

Today, he seemed happy and calm, smiling at everyone. Which was very effective in getting one of the morning waitresses to bring over a wooden high-chair without being asked. We went through the buffet line, and I selected a few pieces of fruit and some dry Cheerios for him, and some waffles, bacon, home fries and more fruit for me. The waitress, hovering, took my tray of food to our table, leaving me free hands with which I deposited DJ in his high chair and put some blueberries and Cheerios on the tray on front of him. He was only half-interested since it had not been all that long since his mother had fed him upstairs.

But he had a good time rolling the berries around and staring out at the bright sunshine of the day, and watching the other people come wandering in, so I had enough time to shovel down most of my breakfast. With the ever-changing moods of babies, one learns to eat fast when one has the chance.

The waitress had refilled my coffee cup and cooed over the boy when Kelsey Jenkins walked in, saw us and came over.

"Cute kid," she said, looking down at us. "Whose is it?"

"Funny," I said. "Go get some chow and join us. Kid seems to be in a good mood."

She went off to the buffet line, and arrived back at the table about the same time as Mary Jane, who was clutching some brochures and looked excited. I introduced her to Kelsey.

"I signed up for a Pilates class in about an hour," she said, looking down at her papers. "And after lunch, there's a meditation session followed by a massage and sauna. What are you guys doing today?"

"Nothing much," I said. "Heard there was a little golf tournament going on down the street. We might mosey over and see what's happening."

"The sauna and massage sounds better," Kelsey said. "Maybe I can get Ben to give me the afternoon off."

"Oh, that's right," Mary Jane said, "You guys have to work. What a shame."

DJ thought that was funny, because he screeched loudly and pushed a blueberry over the rim of his high chair tray. He thought that was funny, so he did it again. I took away the rest of his toys, and ate them.

"I take it you have someone lined up to keep an eye on this one," Kelsey said. She was watching the baby out of the corner of her eye while eating some granola and yogurt, the sight of which was causing my digestive track to get nervous.

"Maria is coming around ten-thirty," Mary Jane said. "There's a nature park just two blocks away, so I'll let her take him for a walk there while I exercise. Then we'll have lunch, and he'll probably go down for a nap for an hour or so. It might just work out perfectly."

"The best laid plans o' mice 'n' men," I said.

"Oh, shut up," she said. "What's your schedule?"

"We've got a production meeting at eleven," I said. "Kelsey…is that up here or down at the course?"

"Down there today," she said. "Ben wants us there at eleven."

I checked my watch. "OK, I have time for a shower. I want to get down there a little early and check out the scene of last night's crime."

"There was a crime?" Kelsey said. "What happened?"

"Somebody set off an incendiary device in the parking lot," I said. "Apparently it wounded an auto but nothing else."

"Geez," Kelsey said. "Terrorists?"

"Don't think so," I said. "If it was the real bad guys, they would have broken a few windows at the least. But I want to see for myself."

"You have an idea who it was, don't you?" Mary Jane said, looking at me sideways.

I laughed and held up my hands in surrender.

"Not really, no," I said. "But it could be our murderer. The walls are starting to close in and he … or she … might be getting antsy. This could have been a diversion of some kind."

"You mean he … or it … is planning something else?" Mary Jane said. She looked worried.

"Maybe," I said. "This weekend offers a big stage. If the killer is trying to make some kind of statement, this would be the perfect time and place to do so. Big sporting event. National television. Hundreds of media on hand. Yeah, it's a grand stage."

"All the more reason why DJ and I will stay here today, thank you," Mary Jane said. She stood up, picked DJ up out of his chair, nodded at Kelsey and headed upstairs.

"You really think something may go down this weekend, Hacker?" she asked me. "Do I need to be worried?"

I shrugged. "Worried? Probably not," I said. "Alert? Yeah, always a good idea. You're walking the fairways again today?"

"Yup," she said. "Ben wants me on Scannell's group. He's playing with Billy Calloway and that French guy, whassisname?"

"Henri Robitan," I said.

"Yeah, him," she said.

"I've been told that he has a certain Gallic charm that drives the femmes crazy," I said. "Is that true?"

"Dunno about the Gallic charm thing," she said. "I mostly notice his lack of deodorant. But I hear that's a French thing, too."

"Ah, yes," I said. "That stereotype goes all the way back to Pepe LePew."

She was still chuckling when I left.

WITH MY FAMILY all accounted for and spending IBS' money like it was fresh out of a Monopoly game box, I rode the van down to the golf course at about ten thirty and had the driver let me off up near the clubhouse. The crowds were noticeably larger and more enthusiastic now that it was the weekend. People were milling about everywhere and Conrad Gold's security people were busy keeping the great unwashed out of his multi-million dollar clubhouse.

My IBS credentials got me in anywhere I wanted to go. All hail the power of the press. I used them to make my way down into the basement of the clubhouse, where I found the security office. I was not surprised to find a number of police officers, both uniformed and wearing detective's street clothes, standing, sitting and talking on their cellphones.

I stood there for a minute or two and watched, and when I had determined which of the plainsclothes guys looked to be the man in charge, I went up to him.

"Hacker, IBS," I said, flashing my television credential badge at him. "What can you tell me about the incident last night?"

The head guy was a little bantam-weight, dressed in a coat and tie. He had a buzz cut on his head and a faint sheen of sweat on his face. He looked like the kind of cop who would pull out his Glock and shoot you in the head if you mouthed off to him, so I quickly decided to mind my manners.

He looked at me, looked at my badge and did a double-take.

"Hacker?" he read the name again. "Aren't you the guy who works with the Boz? Damn, you guys are hilarious. They never show us the inside of your booth, but my mental picture is you two guys slamming down fruity drinks and just making shit up as you go."

"Yeah," I said, "That pretty much sums it up. Who said drunk and stupid was no way to go through life? Now, what can you tell me about last night, officer…?"

"Detective," he snapped. Some cops are sensitive that way. "Detective Wally Howe. I can't tell you anything about last night. It's an ongoing investigation."

"What kind of bomb was used?" I pressed on. Because what else could I do?

"The kind that goes boom," Detective Howe said. "But this one just went pop, instead."

"I heard that the device was …" I deliberately left out the last word. Sometimes cops will play the word game with you when you do that.

"Mostly ineffective," Howe said. Not what I was going for, but I could work with it.

"Badly designed?" I said. "Or did it misfire?"

"I think it did exactly what the perp wanted it to," he said. "Make a noise, make some smoke. Scare some people. There was some oil leakage on the manifold of the engine, and that caught fire. The device itself had very little in the way of explosives."

"Not C4, then?"

He laughed. "More like a few cherry bombs attached to a heat source," he said.

I looked around at the police gathered in the security office and walking in and out of the small space.

"So why the show of force?" I said. "Doesn't sound like the general public is in any danger here today."

"Until we catch the guy, there's still a risk," Howe said, his eyes narrowing, "The device from last night was not a major threat to anyone, but the wiring on it was pretty sophisticated. Some of the connections were soldered. They did a nice neat job. Showed some good design and capability."

"Meaning?"

"Meaning, if this guy could build a small device like this, he definitely could build something bigger and more dangerous," Howe said. "So we're out there actively trying to find him."

I looked over at the wall of TV monitors that covered one wall. Conrad Gold spared no expense in security. It looked like he had cameras covering every square inch of the exterior of his buildings.

"Got him on video?" I asked.

"No comment," Howe said, with a little smirky smile. I took that to mean, yes, he did have him on video.

"What do we tell the viewers?" I said.

"You should be able to tell them that we have the perp in custody," he said. "You and the Boz should have some fun talking about it."

"I don't suppose you can give me a name?" I said.

He just looked at me, still smiling his evil little smile.

"No," he said. "But I'd love for you two to come to the press conference after."

"You sound pretty confident," I said.

He shrugged. "Matter of time," he said. "Just a matter of time."

31

Tommy Scannell began his third round as the leader by a couple of strokes. By the time he had played five holes, his lead was gone and there were twelve players bunched within four shots.

He bogied the first hole, never a good start. Saved par on two but only by getting up and down from the greenside bunker. Bogey on three. Par on four, bogey on five.

The New York gallery was ecstatic at this turn of events, notwithstanding Scannell's crestfallen look. Most of them, I hope, were just happy to be able to witness a close, hotly contested and bare-knuckled brawl between the dozen or so at the top of the leaderboard. A few of them, I think, were happy to witness another human's misfortune. New York sports fans can be tough like that.

Boz and I watched the early collapse from our booth on sixteen. Ben Oswald had told us to be ready to offer commentary for golfers when they played seven and eight. We were nowhere close to those two holes, but we had video screens, so we winged it.

When Scannell missed his par putt on five, and the feed went to a commercial, Boz shook his head sitting next to me.

"Could be curtains for the kid," he said alliteratively.

"Could," I said. "Or could not."

"What does that mean?"

"Could is one of those weasel words," I said. "Like when they say on the news, such-and-such *could* mean the end of the world. They don't say it *will* mean the end of the world, they say it *could* mean it. Of course, they don't say it also *could not* mean anything because then everyone will realize that they're just guessing. Or trying to blow smoke up your dress. But the implication is there—it could, or it could not. You choose."

"You make my head ache," he said. "And I didn't have anything to drink last night."

"Really?" I said.

"Well, I had a couple of beers with some of the caddies," Boz said with a smile. "But that doesn't count."

Scannell parred the sixth. Of the others in the field, the South Korean, Lee Kyung-Ju, was three-under for the day and right there near the lead. Enrico Paz, the Spanish Flash, had come out of nowhere, six under for the day, and was now just a stroke behind.

Ben Oswald buzzed in our headphones.

"Okay you morons," he said, "Our leader is playing seven. Call it straight, for Chrissakes. This is a major."

Van Collins tossed us the ball. "Tommy Scannell has moved to the seventh tee," he said. "Let's go to Boz and Hacker for the call."

"Tommy Scannell is leaking so much oil so far in this round that he's a one-man environmental disaster," I said. "Somebody should call the EPA and have him arrested. But the fat lady hasn't warmed up her pipes yet. Let's see what he can do on this hole, a long dogleg left."

"Worst feeling in the world, Hacks," the Boz said. "You're going backwards on a day when you need to put the hammer down. Scannell has made some bad swings so far today, and let a whole lot of people back into the contest. All the experts predicted that this young man would eventually fade away, and so far today, all the experts have been right."

"Ain't over yet," I said. "Let's see what he can do with this tee shot. You need a nice controlled draw around the corner, otherwise there are all kinds of problems to deal with."

We watched on the monitor as Scannell conferred with his caddie, pulled the driver and lined up his shot. He made a pretty nice swing at it and the FlitePath camera traced the ball's flight as it started just right of center and began bending back to the left.

"That's a beauty," I said. "He made a good swing on that one. No sign of the shakiness we've seen so far this round."

Oswald had us toss the feed up ahead, where Paz was chipping up onto the 12th green. He played that shot to about six feet for par, we broke for another commercial, and when it came back, Scannell was ready for his approach.

"Easy six-iron into this green," Boz said. "Pin is back left, which should work for Tommy's right-to-left ball path."

He made another nice pass at the ball, and his shot flew up onto the green, checked and rolled down to about ten feet below the hole.

"Man, if he can drain-o that one, he'll be right back in it," Boz said.

"Don't think he was ever out of it," I said.

"Leakin' lots of oil, tho, Hacks," Boz retorted. "Like you said."

"Or maybe getting used to the atmosphere," I said. "He's only played in two other majors, and never was on the leaderboard until this week. Rarified air up here. Now he's been through the worst of it, maybe he's about to turn it around, play some good golf again."

"You're such a glass-half-full kinda guy, Hack," Boz said.

"All-the-way full if it's a fine peaty Scotch," I said.

"I hear ya, my brother," Boz said. "Set 'em up, Joe."

"Geezus," Oswald said in our ears, "Are you guys drinking on the job out there?"

As IT TURNED out, Tommy Scannell did start playing better. He made that birdie putt on seven, made another on eight and once he made the turn, he relaxed and resumed playing beautiful golf. Some of the others did as well, so by the time the third round came to an end, Scannell was up by two shots again. Eight other players were within four shots. Sunday shaped up to be fun.

Once the last group had played our hole, we began collecting and stacking up our notebooks and other papers and got ready to head back to Television City. I still had my headphones on, so I heard the buzz when Bill Stirling, one of Oswald's assistant directors, called down from the control room.

"Hey Hacker," he said, "Can you see Kelsey anywhere? She's gone dark. Not answering."

I glanced out our small window overlooking the green. It was pretty empty around the green, as people began heading home once the last group has passed through. There were still crowds of people in the hospitality tents that ringed the green. But those places had air conditioning, soft seats and an endless river of booze for the guests to swill down. They'd still be serving people after the sun went down.

I looked around but didn't see Kelsey, one of the two fairway followers we had out with the last groups today. She wouldn't be hard to spot, with her fanny pack, microphone and a cameraman lugging around a portable camera who in turn was followed by the sound guy with his fuzzy microphone on an extended pole. But I didn't see any of them from my vantage point.

"No sign of her, Bill," I reported. "Where was she when you last talked to her?"

"Seventeen tee," he said. "If you guys are leaving the booth, would you mind going over there and see if you can find her? I'll bet her equipment crashed or something."

"Ten-four," I said.

I turned to Boz. "Kelsey is missing in action," I said. "We gotta go find her."

We climbed down from our booth and walked over to the tee of the par-three seventeenth. The semi-island green sat empty in the near-distance, with water on the left and those big glacial boulders protecting the front. More hospitality stands towered over the riverbank all the way down the right side from tee to green, and these, too, were filled with fans swilling down the free booze and food.

The Boz was staring up at the people partying in the stands. He looked at me. "Say, Hack-Man," he said, "I could use a wee bracer after all that hard work. You with me?"

"I thought we were looking for Kelsey," I said.

"We'll find her," he said. "After we fortify ourselves."

I sighed. "OK," I said. "One quick one."

"That's the Hack I know and love," he said, and he led me up the stairs and into the nearest hospitality stand.

There was a security type standing at the entrance, and he started to protest about our coming in. We apparently didn't have the proper badges or something. But one of the people inside—maybe it was the CEO of the energy company that had paid for the space—caught sight of the Boz and came running over.

"Billy Joe Bosworth!" he said excitedly. "Harwood Warwick. We met at a pro-am down in Houston a couple of years ago. I love your stuff on the golf broadcasts. Really great!"

"Well howdy, Harwood, good to see ya agin," Boz drawled in his best imitation of a Texas good ole boy. "Who do I have to pay off to get a cold beer around here?"

"Your damn money ain't no good here, my man," Harwood said, and he grabbed Boz's arm and led him off towards the nearest bar.

I felt slightly abandoned, but I didn't take offense. Instead, I glanced around the space. In the front, outside the windows overlooking the tee box, there were a few rows of stadium seats. They were mostly empty now, since play had ended for the day. Inside, there were two bars on either end, and a long table along the back which served as the buffet. I imagined during the long afternoon, the table had been filled with food and plates and utensils. Now, though, there were just some big bowls filled with popcorn, and some smaller dishes of peanuts, Goldfish and other snacks. They clearly were trying to gear it down for the day.

The middle of the space was filled with tables covered in tablecloths and ringed by white folding chairs. People milled about, some standing, cocktails in hand, others seated at one of the tables. It was noisy, it was happy, it was crowded madness.

I started to fight my way to one of the bars to grab something to drink when I noticed a table way on the other side of the room. Two people were sitting there, alone. I could only see the backs of their heads, since they were facing away, but one of the two was a woman who looked, from the back, a lot like Kelsey Jenkins. Sitting next to her was a slightly chubby, fuzzy headed man. From the back, he looked a lot like Digby Allen.

I changed direction, went over, saw that it was indeed Kelsey and Digby, so I pulled up a chair and plunked down across from them, facing back towards the crowded room.

"Hiya, kids," I said. "What's shakin'?"

I got no response. Kelsey sat stone-faced, staring out the Plexiglas window in the side of the canvas covering. Digby, who was sitting pretty close to Kelsey, shifted in his seat and glanced at me, frowning.

"We're having a private conversation, Hacker," he said finally. "Do you mind?"

"Not at all," I said. "Talk away. Pretend I'm not here. I'm just unwinding after a long day at the golf tournament. Can I get you a drink or something?"

Digby shifted again. "I said we're talking," he said. "Why don't you go away?"

"Well, gee, Digby," I said, feigning hurt feelings. "That's not very nice. Kels…you want me to go, too?"

She didn't say anything. She continued to stare out the window.

"Yes, she does," Digby said, his voice strained a little. "Now go away."

"Yeah, well, I can't do that, my friend," I said. "Until Kelsey here tells me what's going on. Because Ben Oswald has been trying to contact her and is worried. Hell, by now, I expect he's got the local cops fanning out across the golf course, looking for her. And after last night's bomb attack, everyone's on high alert. So maybe you'd better tell me what's going on?"

"He's got a gun, Hacker," Kelsey said, softly. She sounded scared out of her wits. "You'd better go. Before someone gets hurt."

"A gun?" I said. "Why in the hell do you need a gun to talk with Kelsey, Digs? You gonna hold her up or something? Hell, if it's money you need, I can lend you a few bucks."

He shifted his position again. When he did, I saw the revolver tucked in his waistband in front. Maybe that's why he kept shifting around…having the barrel of a pistol pointed down at your goolies would be enough to make any man nervous.

"Go away," he said again. He wouldn't look at me. "Just go. I don't want to hurt you."

"Fine, fine, I'm going," I said. I didn't move. "But before I go, tell me something Digby. I haven't been able to figure it out. Why in the hell did you kill Parker Long? I figured out *how* you did it. I just don't know *why*."

He shuffled around again, but he did look at me finally with something resembling pride.

"I did it for Arnie," he said.

"Wasserman ordered you to kill him?" I said. I hope I sounded as surprised as I was. "Man, that's ice cold."

Digby smiled at me, as if I was an idiot. "No, he didn't *order* me," he said. "Nobody orders me to do anything. I did it because he and Ben wanted Parker gone. Off the team. But they couldn't do it, because he had a contract through the end of this year, and he wasn't going to resign."

"How do you know all this stuff?" I asked. "That's all private personnel records and stuff like that. How do you know?"

"You people look at me and just think 'There's old Digby Allen, tech guy.' Everyone thinks I'm as dumb as a rock."

He straighted his shoulders. "Well, I'm not. I know how to access people's emails. I can bug a telephone. I know how to listen. I know things. I find out things. I'm not stupid."

He looked at me with a superior smirk. "I know what school your daughter goes to," he said. "Except she's not your daughter, is she? She's a step-daughter or something. Not really yours."

"Wow," I said. "You do know how to snoop around on people. That's pretty goddam impressive."

Kelsey looked at me sideways. I think—I hope—she understood I was just trying to keep him talking.

"So what do you mean you killed Parker for Arnie?" I continued.

"They wanted Parker gone," he said. "Him and Ben. I figured out the way to do it. I fixed up some earphones that would conduct an electrical charge directly from the router unit into the ear pieces."

He sat back in his chair and laughed.

"I gotta tell you, it was a bitch and a half testing those phones to make sure they worked," he said. "But I figured it out. Then I just had to wait my chance. I knew Parker would be calling for help after I screwed up his headphones so he got a lot of static. And sure enough, he did."

"But I thought Sheila answered the call that afternoon," I said. "She told the cops she'd changed a fuse or something in the desk unit."

Digby laughed again.

"And I was waiting until she left," he said with a grin. "Sure enough, ole Parker was sitting there, mad as a wet hen because he still couldn't hear a damn thing. So I just gave him my new earphone set and he plugged it in."

His eyes went a little unfocused for a moment. He was reliving the moment.

"Fuckers worked like a charm," he said. "Beautiful blue flash and zappo! That was the end of Parker Long. I unplugged the phones, plugged his old ones back in, put them on his head and got out of there. Pretty damn simple."

"And then you came back to New York and told Arnie what you did, right?" I pressed. "What…did you think he'd approve?"

"He'd know he would have to keep me around," Digby said, smirking again. "I had him. Him and Ben. They were the ones who wanted Parker gone. I just did what they wanted done."

"Well, Digs," I said, "The one small little hitch in your plan is that neither one of them wanted Parker Long dead, they just wanted him to retire."

"He's retired," Digby said. "Permanently."

"Yeah, but I imagine that Arnie was a little freaked out when you told him what you'd done," I said.

Digby frowned.

"Maybe he was so freaked out that he threatened to call the cops," I said. "Maybe he was so freaked out that he threatened to have you fired."

Digby Allen shrugged.

"Whatever he was going to do, he can't do it now," he said. "I followed him home that afternoon. Saw him go into that girl's apartment. I knew they were screwing. I monitored their emails. Saw him come out a bit later. Followed him to the grocery store. Knew he was going back for more."

"So you waited, just far enough away from the market to avoid the security cameras," I said. "And then, pop."

Digby giggled, "Pop is right," he said. "Pop goes the weasel."

Kelsey finally spoke.

"You're one sick fucker, Digby," she said.

Her comment landed like a slap across the face. Digby's face turned red and his eyes narrowed.

"Enough talking," he said. "It's time to go."

He rummaged around in his waistband and pulled the gun out. He kept it under the table so nobody standing nearby could see.

"Hacker, I want you out of here," he said. "I don't want to hurt you. You've been a good friend to me. So I want you to leave first. Once you're outside, Kelsey and I will leave. I've got a car stashed down by the trailers. As long as nobody tries to stop us, I'll let Kelsey live. If not…"

He let that idea drift in the air.

"Okey doke," I said. I stood up. "I'm outta here. Kels… I'd do what he says."

Digby looked scared. A little desperate. Perhaps at the end of his rope. Those were not good things for someone like Digby Allen to be thinking, with a loaded gun in his hand.

I glanced over at the bar. The Boz was standing there with his new best friend from Texas. He had a beer in one hand and some kind of munchies in the other. He saw me looking at him. I tried to send some mental warning messages, but I've never been very good at clairvoyance. And I couldn't really try to wave him over, without risking getting shot in the gut.

Kelsey shot a look at me, a look of desperation. I could imagine she was a bit stressed, having heard Digby's plan for her. I tried a short reassuring smile and hoped it registered.

"You guys take care," I said. I started walking away, but as I passed by Digby, I reached out, grabbed his shirt collar and yanked it hard, backwards and down. His folding chair tipped back and over, his feet coming up and kicking the big table hard and almost turning it over, too.

Kelsey screamed and leaped away. "He's got a gun," she yelled. "Gun!"

That was the magic word to create instant chaos. People in the hospitality space began to scatter. Women screamed. Men shouted. Chairs overturned. Doors slammed open as people began shoving each other out of the way in an attempt to escape.

I kept a tight hold on Digby's shirt collar, but he reacted quickly, turning and twisting to get free. I reached over and grabbed the gun from his hand, pointed the barrel straight up and put two shots through the roof of the place. I needed some police on the scene and that was the fastest way I could think of to get them.

The ear-splitting sound of the gun shots—after the cry of 'gun'—sent the panic level up a few more notches. More screaming, more shouting and people began leaping over tables, jumping over the front of the viewing area outside and otherwise scrambling away any way they could.

Digby gave a final hard twisting move—he was surprisingly strong—and I heard something tear. Then he was free and I was holding nothing but a piece of his collar which had ripped away at the seams. I was looking at the scrap of material stupidly when Digby picked up one of the white folding chairs and whacked me with it, across my back and shoulders. I went down in a heap.

"What the everloving fuck!" cried the Boz, as he picked me up a few seconds later. I looked around. Digby was gone. He had melted into the crowd of panicked people and skedaddled. Kelsey had disappeared as well, melting into the panicked crowd and hopefully getting outside and to safety.

I was still holding Digby's ripped shirt collar in one hand, and his gun in the other. The security guy from the door came up behind Boz and looked at me. He wasn't armed, of course, and he didn't know what the hell was going on.

"You'd better drop that," he said. "Cops will be here in a minute, if they see anyone holding a gun, it'll be shoot first and ask questions later."

I handed the security guy the pistol and grabbed Boz.

"We gotta go get Digby," I said. "Can't let him get away."

32

We dashed out the door to the hospitality space, ran down the stairs and headed out behind it. People were still fleeing the sounds of gunshots in various stages of panic, and I could hear the *whoop-whoop* of an approaching police car. There was a well-trodden swatch of grass where people walked going to and from the tee box to the green. Behind that was a long row of Port-A-Potties, probably twenty or more. The air was redolent with that delightful mixture of pine-scented disinfectant and ammonia seeping out from the collected gallons of urine in the tanks.

We did a quick scan up and down the length of the walkway. It was full of people, panicked and not so much. No sign of a fleeing Digby anywhere.

Behind the johnnies was a swath of woods: trees, underbrush, pine straw. I could see another fairway through the trees, about twenty yards away.

"C'mon," I called to Boz and he followed me as I dashed through the woods. Once past the trees, there was a short uphill bank covered in thick rough and then we reached the fairway. I think it was the eleventh hole, but I didn't stop to check. The tee box was about a hundred yards down to our left, and the fairway continued on to the right another hundred yards or so before turning left and heading up hill to the green, surrounded by bunkers and now in the shadows in the late afternoon.

And heading toward that hill, running in a kind of limping desperation, torn shirt flapping around as he moved, was Digby Allen. He was almost three hundred yards away, and getting further from us by the second.

I heard a motorized cart pull up with the squeaking of the brakes. I turned and looked and saw Willie McLeod, the Gold Club's Canada goose hunter. Sitting next to him on the bench seat was Bullet, his border collie. Bullet's head was cocked slightly and he looked at us with a *what the hell?* expression on his doggie face.

"Problem, gents?" Willie asked. "Heard on the squawk-box that there's been shots fired."

I pointed up the fairway at the figure of Digby Allen, who was struggling up the hill in front of the green.

"That's the bad guy," I said. "Can Bullet reel him in?"

"Ach, laddie, he was made for this," Willie said with a nod. "Would help if the yonder lad was a sheep, but not to worry."

He started to take off the dog's lead.

"Wait," I said. "This might help."

I was still holding the torn shred from Digby's shirt. I held it up to Bullet's nose, rubbed it around for a few seconds.

Willie snapped his fingers, twice. Bullet jumped down off the bench seat and went into full attention mode, eyes locked on Willie, body tensed, quivering, ready for action. Willie pushed his hand forward and gave a short, sharp whistle.

The dog took off as if the starter's pistol had fired for the 100 yard dash at the Olympics. We watched as Bullet tore up the fairway in a streak of black and white fur. It took him maybe ten seconds to cover the three hundred yards, and he caught Digby just as he reached the top of the slope at the front of the green.

Bullet nipped at Digby's feet, trying to gnaw at his Achilles tendon. He didn't succeed in actually biting him, but he did manage to trip him up, and Digby tumbled forward. The dog leaped on his back, barking and growling and jumping around in a frenzy. He had subdued his prey and he was not going to let it get away.

Digby seemed to give up. He curled himself into a fetal ball, covered his head with his hands and arms, and lay still.

We had jumped into Willie's flatbed cart and motored up the fairway after the dog. We arrived at the green at about the same time as three or four uniformed police officers, who converged from several different directions. Guns drawn, they approached Digby slowly and waited until Willie whistled his dog to heel. Bullet obeyed reluctantly and came trotting back to the cart, looking pleased with himself. The cops moved in, put Digby in handcuffs and led him off towards the clubhouse.

Willie gave his dog a couple of pats on the head, then reached into his jacket pocket and pulled out a dog bone. Bullet grabbed it in his teeth, jumped up onto the flatbed and, after three revolutions, lay down and began happily munching on it.

"You got a bottle of Scotch in that other pocket?" the Boz asked Willie. "Cause I'm thinking Hacker here could use a wee belt. Or three."

It was several hours later when the IBS crew gathered in one of Conrad Gold's meeting rooms in the big clubhouse on the hill. The sun had long since set, the people had finally been chased out of the hospitality tents and told to go home, the greenskeeper's crew had done their night-time duties closing down the course, and the cops had spent a lot of time huddled with Digby Allen, who was now in the back of a state police car on his way back to the city to await arraignment.

Mary Jane and DJ were there, having caught one of the courtesy buses from the Cumberland Arms to the Gold club. I had called her and told her to come down, knowing I'd be tied up for a while in the aftermath.

Kelsey Jenkins had refused all offers for a visit to the local hospital to get checked out. She swore she wasn't injured in any way, just freaked out when Digby had come up behind her and stuck a gun in her back. She had come up to Boz and me and gave each of us a big hug.

"You saved my life," she said.

Feeling my wife's eyes on me, I kept my hug short.

"For the love of God, Hacker," Ben Oswald said. "What in the hell happened here today?"

Oswald had lost his outward appearance of command and control. He looked shaken, shrunk, completely drained.

"Digby found out that you and Arnie had plans to let him go," I said. "He pretty much admitted that he's bugged and eavesdropped on everyone here and back at IBS head-quarters. That's the problem with really top-notch tech guys—they know how to access a lot of private conversations."

"How did killing Parker have anything to do with our plans for him?" Oswald said. He looked confused.

"I think it was a combination of audition and state-ment," I said. "He was showing Arnie—and, by extension, you—that he had the ability to do whatever you wanted. In his slightly addled mind, he thought he would gain points with you by eliminating another problem you had: what to do about Parker Long."

"Christ Almighty," Ben said, "We weren't trying to push Parker out the door. He and I had talked, and I knew he was ready to retire. Arnie and I had just talked about ways that would happen and what we'd do next. I liked Parker…hell, I even loved the guy in a way. How could that idiot Digby think we wanted Parker to be killed?"

"Well," I said, "We're talking about the mind of a psychopath, which is often very different than a normal mind. But I think Digby believed that after he'd told Arnie how he had solved his Parker problem that Arnie would be impressed, and maybe a little scared, and agree to keep Digby on. Digby was hoping Arnie would be appreciative, but if it turned out he wasn't, Digby figured at the least, Arnie would be scared. Either way, Digby would get what he wanted."

"Why didn't Arnie call the cops right away?" Van Collins asked. "Somebody came to me and said he just killed Parker Long, or anyone else, I'd have him in handcuffs in ten seconds flat."

"I don't know," I nodded at Van. "And we'll probably never know. Maybe he thought Digby was just kidding. Maybe he didn't believe Digby had it in him to kill somebody. Maybe he thought he could use this information *against* Digby somehow, use it to his, Arnie's, benefit. From the little I know about Arnie Wasserman, any of those alternatives are possible, even the last. Arnie could be, I'm told, a little manipulative."

"Yeah, that's true," Jimmy Williams said. "I don't think anybody here trusted Arnie a lot. You could never be sure about that guy."

There were several heads nodding around the table. Ben Oswald saw that and shook his own head.

"I can't believe you people thought that way," he said. "Arnie was good people. He was like a son to me."

"Sorry, Ben," Jimmy said. "From my point of view, he was the assistant to my boss. He was always writing shit down in his notebook. He also liked to crack the whip from time to time, remind us who was boss. Nope…I could work with the guy, but I never liked him all that much."

Ben put his head in his hands. "I must be getting old," he said. "Maybe it's time for me to go."

"Now Ben," Kelsey said. "Don't be maudlin. There's always a chain of command in any organization. We all understood who was who and what was what. Like Jimmy said, Arnie was an OK guy. You just had to remember who he worked for."

"Man, oh man," Ben said.

"How did you figure out it was Digby?" Mary Jane piped in, DJ squirming around on her lap.

I smiled at them. "It took a while," I admitted. "At first, it seemed obvious that someone, probably someone with a strong technological knowledge base, had electrocuted Parker with his own headphones. But then the forensic team down in Georgia reported that Parker's headphones were fine, except for the loose wires or whatever was causing the static interference. That wasn't what I expected. I was sure he had been fried with his own headphones. So it was back to square one."

"Then Arnie got shot," Mary Jane said. She knew how my brain worked.

"Yeah, that made me think entirely differently," I said. "If the two deaths were connected, and I thought they were, I had to figure out why. The strongest connection between the two was actually you, Ben."

"Me?" he sat upright, head thrown back in amazement. "You thought I killed them both?"

"No," I said quickly. "I didn't say you were the killer, I said you were the strongest connection between the two deaths. I knew you didn't kill Parker Long—he was in his booth and you were in the control room doing the broadcast. I was sitting there watching you operate. And I figured the New York cops checked out everyone's whereabouts on the night Arnie was killed, so I knew that they didn't like you for that murder."

"So?"

"So I started to think about other connections," I said. "Who would benefit from Action A and Action B. Nobody didn't like Parker Long, making the list of potential murder suspects very short. Everybody, as you heard here tonight, was a little suspicious of Arnie Wasserman. Maybe not enough to kill him, certainly, but at least there were possibilities."

"So how did you put it together?" Mary Jane asked.

"Well, Kelsey and I talked with Parker's widow," I said. "And we learned that Parker was planning to retire at the end of this year, but that Arnie had threatened to move on him sooner. Parker and his agent got hold of Ben and put a stop to that, but it got me wondering about who else knew about that. Information is power. And who controls the information?"

"The tech guys," Mary Jane said. "Tech guys is short-hand for information technology."

"Exactly," I said. "And that fit back into my original theory on Parker's murder being a tech event. The electrified headphones. So I began thinking of the techies on staff. Right away, I thought about Digby, because he's a little weird and because he was considered a genius with all the equipment you guys use. I mean, if you thought someone had jiggered around with a pair of headphones, figured out a way to turn them into a murder weapon…well, Digby Allen would be one of the first people you'd think had the smarts to do that. And, being Digby Allen, it wouldn't be a tough sell to think he might do something like that."

I paused, thinking.

"And I thought I had him," I continued. "When I figured out how he had done it…the static phones would lead to a call to the tech department, Digby would run out to the booth, give Parker a new set of lethal headphones and, once he had killed himself plugging them in, Digby would be right there to switch the headphones back again and take the killing pair away."

"But?"

"But then I found out that it wasn't Digby who'd answered Parker's call for help. It was Sheila," I said. "That also surprised me. But she had just changed a fuse out or something. Then I got the warning note. That's when I knew it was Digby."

"How?" Kelsey asked this time.

"Because Sheila wasn't there when I was asking about headphones and the service call in Savannah," I said. "It was just Benny and Digby I was talking to. So when I got warned off, I knew it was either one of them. And I always liked Digby more. He's got the outside-the-box brain that would come up with something elaborate and weird like this."

"And what about that car bomb?" Van Collins said. "Did Digby do that, too?"

"Yeah," I said. "That was a pure diversion, which is why it didn't do much damage. He wanted people around here nervous and thinking about bombers. Gave him the space to sneak away. But then Boz and I accidentally showed up and interfered with his plan to use Kelsey to help him sneak down to Television City. He figured if the cops were looking for lone wolf, they might not notice a man and a woman strolling together. Especially with millions of others milling around."

"So stopping in for a cold beer actually saved somebody's life?" the Boz said, and he began to grin.

"You could say that," I said.

"I think I just did," the Boz said. "And to tell you the truth, I'm beginning to feel the need to save a few more. Like right now. I'm buying. Who's in?"

33

Against all the odds, Tommy Scannell held on for the win. His first on Tour and, of course, his first major. With the victory, he got to heft the Wannamaker Trophy, bank a couple million bucks, pocket a Tour card for the next ten years, and punch his ticket for golf immortality. He would always be remembered, from this day forward. Of course, if he never won again, he would be remembered as the one-shot wonder. But if he did win again, which I suspected he probably would, he would be remembered as a better-than-most player, a winner of regular tournaments and a major winner. And there was always the chance that he would win lots more, both majors and not, lead the U.S. Ryder Cup team to glory and maybe invent the cure for cancer. Hey, it's possible.

The Boz and I had a good time on Sunday watching the field make a few runs at Tommy during the afternoon. We helped ratchet up the pressure when the lead was one stroke with five to play, and we expressed our admiration for the young pro's fortitude in fighting hard all the way in on the back nine, making great birdies on thirteen, sixteen and the final hole, where he drained a nice ten-foot birdie to accentuate the win and earn the ovation of the huge crowd gathered to watch.

Mary Jane hired Maria the babysitter for the early part of the day, and she came with me to sit in our airless booth and watch the fun. She went out and got us some sandwiches and drinks in the middle of the afternoon, and chuckled quietly at our patter.

When Scannell and the last group finished our hole and went over to seventeen, she gave the Boz a hug and me a kiss.

"I gotta get going," she said. "Got a three-hour drive back to Beantown and classes tomorrow. Back to the salt mines for me."

"I'll be home late tonight," I said. "Don't wait up. And I'll start loading boxes out to Milton tomorrow."

MJ looked at the Boz.

"Why don't you come back east to Boston and visit?" she said. "Aren't you guys doing the New Jersey Classic in a couple of weeks? Bring the wife and kids. We'll go eat fried clams and take in a game at Fenway."

"Little lady," he said, drawing himself up to his full height, "That sounds like an excellent plan. I'll have Sheila call you and get it going."

He turned to me.

"Hack-Man," he said, grinning at me. "This could be the beginning of a beautiful friendship."

"OK, Bogie," I said. "Just keep the Nazis away."

He saluted and disappeared.

I STOPPED IN to say good-bye to the rest of the crew after the tournament was over and the heartfelt speeches had been made on the eighteenth green. Ben Oswald was in his private office in his trailer, and I went and knocked on his door.

"Come," the raspy voice said. I went in.

He was sitting at his desk. His feet were up on the desktop. There were two glasses in front of him, each filled with a couple of inches of amber something. Neither glass had been touched. He was staring at them.

He looked up at me, and motioned me into a chair in front of his desk.

"Arnie and I would come back here after a tournament and have a little celebratory drink," he told me. His voice sounded a little husky. "We'd talk about what went right, what didn't, then one of us would say, 'awww, fuck it' and we'd slug 'em back. It was like our private ritual. That job's done. Next job's on the schedule, next week, two weeks, whatever. Draw a line under this one, get ready for the next. That's the business. Always the next job. Never stops." He stopped, looked at me with sad red eyes. "Until it does."

I reached over and picked up one of the glasses.

"Awww, fuck it, boss," I said.

He sat there a minute, staring at the glass on his desk. Then, with a little half smile, he picked it up. Held it over towards me. We clinked. Tipped them back. It was bourbon, and a good one.

"Draw the line," I said.

"Draw the line," he repeated.

ABOUT THE AUTHOR

James Y. Bartlett is one of the most-published golf writers of his generation. His work has appeared in golf and lifestyle publications around the world for more than thirty years. He was a staff editor with *Golfweek* and *Luxury Golf* magazines, and edited *Caribbean Travel & Life* magazine for several years during his "golf hiatus" period.

Bartlett was the golf columnist for *Forbes FYI* magazine for the first fifteen years of that publication's history and wrote a similar column on the golf lifestyle for *Hemispheres*, the in-flight magazine of United Airlines for nearly twenty years under the pseudonym of "A.G. Pollard, Jr."

His first Hacker Golf Mystery, *Death is a Two-Stroke Penalty*, was published by St. Martin's Press in 1991. *Death from the Ladies Tee* followed soon thereafter, and Yeoman House Books proudly continued the series with *Death at the Member-Guestt, Death in a Green Jacket, Death from the Claret Jug* and *An Open Case of Death.*

Bartlett is also the author of five nonfiction books. The latest include *Think Like A Caddie/Play Like A Pro: Golf's Top Caddies Reveal Their Winning Strategies*, and *Mastering Golf's Toughest Shots: The World's Best Caddies Share Their Secrets of Success*, both published by Sellers Publishing in cooperation with the Professional Caddies Association of America.

For more information about the author, the books in the
Hacker Golf Mystery series, and his other fiction and nonfiction work, please visit his website at

http://www.jamesybartlett.com

The Hacker Golf Mystery series

DEATH IS A TWO-STROKE PENALTY
DEATH FROM THE LADIES TEE
DEATH AT THE MEMBER-GUEST
DEATH IN A GREEN JACKET
DEATH FROM THE CLARET JUG
AN OPEN CASE OF DEATH
P.G.A. SPELLS DEATH

Other titles by the author:

CADDIEWAMPUS: LOOPING FOR GOLF'S GREATS
SERPENT POINT: A POLITICAL THRILLER[*]

* written under the pseudonym Caleb Clarke

www.ingramcontent.com/pod-product-compliance
Lightning Source LLC
Chambersburg PA
CBHW070241140726
47909CB00018B/1792